TERI WOODS PUBLISHING
PR

THE ADVENTURES OF GHETTO SAM

AND

THE GLORY OF MY DEMISE

BY KWAME TEAGUE

For information on how individual consumers can place orders, please write to Teri Woods Publishing, P.O. Box 20069, New York, NY 10001-0005.

For orders other than individual consumers, Teri Woods Publishing grants a discount on the purchase of 10 or more copies of a single title order for special markets or premium use.

For orders purchased through P.O. Box only, Teri Woods Publishing offers a 25% discount off the sale price for orders being shipped to prisons including but not limited to federal, state and county.

Published by Teri Woods Publishing

TERI WOODS PUBLISHING
PRESENTS

THE ADVENTURES OF GHETTO SAM

AND

THE GLORY OF MY DEMISE

BY KWAME TEAGUE

The Adventures of Ghetto Sam and *The Glory of My Demise*

This novel is a work of fiction. Any resemblance to real people, living or dead, actual events, establishments, organizations, and/or locales are intended to give the fiction a sense of reality and authenticity. Other names, characters, places and incidents are either products of the author's imagination or are used fictitiously.

Published by:
TERI WOODS PUBLISHING
P.O. Box 20069
New York, NY 10001-0005
www.teriwoods.com

Library of Congress Catalog Card No: 2003100730
ISBN: 0-9672249-2-6
The Adventures of Ghetto Sam Copyright: Txu-957-027
The Glory of My Demise Copyright: Txu-957-087

Novel Credits
Story by Kwame Teague
Edited by Shira Szego
Cover concept by Teri Woods
Cover graphics by Mike Alvarez of Uniquest Designs
Printed by Malloy Lithographing

Printed in the USA.

ABOUT THE AUTHOR

Kwame Teague is a Newark, New Jersey native. Following the successes of his premier novel, a compilation of *The Adventures of Ghetto Sam* and *The Glory of My Demise*, Teague has recently completed his second novel entitled *Dutch*. He is currently working on *The Adventures of Ghetto Sam, Part II.*

Because he is presently serving a life sentence, proceeds from the sale of this book will be contributed to the Kwame Teague Relief Fund.

To donate and/or write to Teague, please use the following address:

> Kwame Teague Fan Club
> P.O. Box 201
> Dudley, NC 28333

The Adventures of Ghetto Sam and *The Glory of My Demise*

ACKNOWLEDGEMENTS

All praises are due to Allah (SWT), first and foremost...

Then:
My lil' sister Babygrrrrl (Boogas!), my wife Lashonda (a.k.a. Chocolate), my seeds Ali and Nesha, Nina (Thank you for my moon), Cawania (Thank you for my sun), Tanya (a.k.a. KoKo (siempre)), my shahada brother Sugar Sha (fatboy!), my lil' brother and akhii B.U.C.C. a.k.a. Tracy Coad, my cereal partner B.A. Brent Robinson, Abdul Jabbar (Shaykh West Virgini), Kabir (unk from B-More), Muhammad a.k.a. Lou the Butcher, Bino, all the Rasheeds, can't forget Harlem World, Terry West a.k.a. Shyheed Shagoor, TAHA Jabbar, and of course my man akhii Shannon Holmes (Bulletproof from B-More to the Bricks), Frog (Platinum toothpick? Playa Playa), Freddie Gunz, Frankie Knuckles, Pharoah, One Eye, Jamal Myers (my literary critic), Taqwa, Big Wop, Crime, I-Shine, Big Trusell...

My family:
My Mama, my Abu, beggin'-ass Keisha, RonRon, GiGi, Derrick, Cooter Cat, Shawn Shawnette Shawnette Shawnette!, Robin, Chris, Mallory, Sharon, Mike, Isaiah...

The Empyre:
Malik McNish and everyone at 97.5 in Raleigh, NC, Val the Super Producer, Kelly the dressmaker, Rak Vigor, Shabazz and Millennium Mogulz, Chryst, RaRa, Ski and Spot Rushaz, Meka Swain, Big Daddy Kane, my man my man Boogie Blutcher, Y.O. Rogers, Sharlease "Cookie" Collier, Sharon "off tha" Hooks, can't forget PR Reppin', Tashia Turner and Trina, where my peoples?!, Fathead and Mi-Mi (ghetto love) D-Will and the Federal Reserve, Qlwest (my sister my sister), Twip and Campus Hill representing Dirtie Nation, Flam (444) Dirty Smurf Jazz, Black Ass Nate, Cool-ass Ty, Kwame Brown, T.O. Holmes, Fleetwood and the Foundation, K-Nice, Mick Benzo and the whole Zulu Nation, Mos Def...
To all the Muslims worldwide (As Salaamu Alaikum).

To all black women writers, from Zora to Toni. Thank you for showing me that language can dance, but especially to Teri Woods, thought I forgot? Thank you for your love and support, for being at my Nikah and for giving the caged bird a chance to be heard... Love you madly.

THE ADVENTURES OF GHETTO SAM

CHAPTER ONE: GOT A LIGHT?

Yo... I'm waitin' on the subway. Three o'clock in the mornin'.

Three o'clock in the mornin'. I'm smokin' a cigarette—well, actually, I *got* a cigarette but I ain't got no light...

It's three o'clock in the mornin'...

I holler down the platform to my man, who getting brained by a prostitute. "Yo, sun, you got a light? Some fire?" ...Nigga's eyes roll up in the back of his head.

Fuck it. Take a piss.

Where the hell is this train? is what I'm thinkin'. Shit, it's three in the mornin' and I'm tired as hell; head aches, feet hurt, no match, I'm fucked up... Shoulda stopped at the bodega like I started to.

So while I'm thinkin' all this, some nondescript character fall up on me. "Yo, my man"—this the cat speakin'—"you got a light?"

What the fuck?! Is it a world shortage on sulfur?! I'm in the middle of so-called civilization, Zoo York, three in the mornin' in the Rotten Apple, waitin' on the A Midtown, and *this* cat ask *me* for a match?!

Picture dat...

Shit been like this ever since Disney colonized Times Square, for what, go figure, yo, Mickey the pimp, what is the world comin' to? That's what I'm thinkin', but I translate the shit and say, "Naw, man, get the fuck out my face," real calm-like, but dude get the point and peel out.

1

Probably think I'm a Yankee fan... Yeah, 'cause, yo, I got the fat leather custom joint. Butter. Shit got the hood wit' the Yankee emblem on the left breast and another big as hell on the back. 'Member them Carhart joints? Yeah, like that, 'cept it's leather... Plus rockin' the crazy hard Levi's wit' the original flava Tims and the plaid scully... I'm dipped, but I ain't no Yankee fan. I like 'em, you know, they i-ight, but pompoms is for cheerleaders...

Anyway, all of a sudden, like seven hooligan-ass kids roll down the stairs, wildin'. I could tell these some Bronx heads 'cause word, them BX cats is some real troublemakers. I got mad fam in the BX, so I know how they rotate. My man Mick Benzo, E.T., Fathead and Lil' Short and all them, so I know these kids comin' wit' they scope on vic. But yo, I'm warm enough, you know, plenty of heat, feel me? Plus, my ox... So I'm like, whatever.

Where were we? Oh yeah... So the cats lookin' to form Voltron, two of 'em see my man getting brained and run him up the stairs wit' his pants around his ankles.

Funny sight...

Remember the dude ask me for a light? Yeah well, I don't, 'cause money vaporized as soon as the cavalry came. So it's only me and them, three in the mornin'...

So I step to the tall cat. "Yo, sun, let me get a light?" Guess what he say?

"I am the light; what you seek is fire."

Yeah i-ight, Mr. Philosopher, give a nigga a rope... But fuck it. Besides, by the look in his eyes, he ain't got one anyway 'cause whatever he smokin' is gone. Then the short cat... I'm sayin', why it always gotta be the littlest muhfucka tryin' to be the tough guy? Go figure... Anyway, this lil' muhfucka roll up like, "Salute the flag!"

The fuck is he talkin'?! "Fuck, is you the general now? Uncle fuckin' Sam? Well fuck it, you got your army, be all you can be." Whole time, I got my hand in my pants, shit 'pon cock. Cat don't even know he marked for death. Red dot on the cat forehead got me thinkin' 'bout Hindus...

But his man say, "Naw, chill, Gut. I recognize sun. You Money's people, right?"

I just look at the cat like, whatever, but lil' man, he committed to a certain course of action that he ain't ready to let go of yet. He like, "Who the fuck is Money?! Fuck Money, I told this nigga, salute the flag!" But he see his peoples don't wanna bring it, so he grillin' me hard... So hard he must want me to sizzle. We eye boxin' and shit for a minute, but since looks can't kill, I'm like, whatever.

I pull my cigarette from behind my ear like, "Yo, shortie, let that go and let a nigga get a light, you know, civilize. I'm sayin', I pledge allegiance, cross my heart hope to die, what else you want?" That cracked them cats up... Broke the ice.

Situation defused.

"Yo, sun, you get charmed?" I hear the peace offering vociferate from the rear of the mob.

"No doubt," is my emphatic reply. I put my cigarette, unlit, back behind my ear and light the el... I hear the A comin'...

Life is good...

CHAPTER TWO: SHE

So, yo, I emerged on Forty Deuce, three feet high and risin'. I big my mens and them up for De La'n' my soul and mercked, feelin' lifted like a crane, say word... Floatin'... Not even thinkin' about the fact that I still ain't get a light for my cigarette when I had a chance. I'm nice though, yo, feelin' like Sade whisperin' in my left ear and Erykah Badu echoin' in my right and I'm listenin' to 'em build on universal matrix-type harmonies and shit...like...like, two sirens wit' golden harps just serenadin' a nigga:

OOH LA LA LAAAA...

I swear I hear music in the air, but it turned out to be a cat in a black six pumpin' Quest's first album. So, yo, path of rhythm? No doubt, let's travel... So I'm walkin' and the sights, the lights, the people, the noise... Shit go vertigo on me and start swirlin' like them kaleidoscopes little kids be playin' wit'. Everything lookin' psychedelic and I'm like, word, the Deuce... Just the Deuce ain't the Deuce no more, you know? Like '88-'89, now *that* was the Forty Dime, all heads that know, say word... When Brooklyn used to come through like thirty thousand deep, terrorizin' crabs and Jersey City and Newark was beefin' Journal Square-style... When you could always catch "Penitentiary III" wit' that lil' black-ass midget! What was his name? ...Um... Umm... Sweets, yeah that's it, Sweets.

When cats used to flick it up wit' they honeys and the streets be packed wit' the illest whips, yo! Dapper Dan was the man, sun had ere'body Gucci or MCM'ed out...

4

Strictly phatness, yo, strictly.

Yeah, but dig, while I'm nostalgically savorin' this, I ain't watchin' where I'm goin' and by the time I realize it, I'm in the middle of the damn street. That's when I hear this loud-ass, irratatin'-ass car horn. I'm 'bout to flip! That is, until I turn around and see I'm directly in front of this white Q4, and drivin'...

Damnnnn...

Yo... Aw, man, I thought. It was, like, fuckin' Sanaa Latham exotic Tahitian treat; my shit was mesmerized. But yo, never let 'em see you sweat...

I say, "I mean, what? You gonna run me over?"

That's when I see her lips... Her succulent, no-lipsticked lips silently say, "If you don't move." Then she let out play wit' a smile. I'm junglistically attentive at this point.

And her eyes...

Ay, yo... Where was I, or where *am* I 'cause Ma got me discombobulated. I'm holdin' up traffic, cats behind her is layin' on they horns, cuttin' the lane, cussin' me out, but I ain't even hearin' 'em.

I'm like, "Yo, Ma, throw on your blinkers! Throw on your blinkers!" Then I holler at the cats behind her, "Go around, go around! She broke down, car won't crank! Yo, Ma, throw on your blinkers!"

She find the shit amusin' and shake her head no, smilin', just enticin' a brother. So I attempted to appeal to her sympathies...

"Yo, Ma, I'm all alone in this cold city, lost and lonely, and you gonna deny me the only friendly face I've seen since triple heart bypass brain surgery on my appendix?" Then I cough for effect and grab my heart like Fred Sanford and shit.

At least I got her laughin' but she say, "I don't think so."

But I'm persistent.

"Come on, Ma, at least tell me how to get uptown," then I give her the puppy dog look. That usually works.

She sigh like, "Okay, if I do, can I go then?"

"If you still want to," then I flash her the Colgates and she throw on her blinkers.

Now mind you, the whole time we done created a traffic jam and cats is cussin' me out in several languages, but fuck it, this New York. So I approach the window and she hit the button to let the window slide away, removin' the barrier between me and Paradise... It's a November-type nip in the air, but when she lowered the window, I feel a rush of warm air and I'm wonderin' if it's the heat or Ma. Is it live or Memorex, ya'm sayin'?

But just when I'm about to throw rhythm, I hear *WHOOP! WHOOP!* And that's the sound of the police. But I'm thinkin', where the hell was y'all a minute ago when I was about to get bagged by them Bronx Zoo escapees?

So the Officer O'Malley-lookin', freckle-faced, Opie-ass white boy put down his window and say, "Miss, is your vehicle inoperable?"

But before she could answer, I turn to Officer Dickhead like, "Naw, man, she ain't from around here and she was lookin' for uptown, so I was just doin' my civic duty, officer." I started to salute the cat, but he might be gung-ho.

He says, "Well, you can't tell her in the middle of—"

I cut him off. "I know, I know, I was just about to get in and show her myself," and wit' that I'm around to the passenger side but the door is locked. She look at me, I smile.

"Please? That bad ol' cop gonna get me if you don't..." then I puppy dog her again. I hear the lock clunk her reply...

Psss, I'm in.

I slid into the plush, milk-beige leather interior like a slipper and closed the door.

She speaks. "I'm only takin' you around the corner, and drop you in front of the A Uptown. Just go down—" but I cut her off and say, "You smell nice." Plus she got an accent I can't place. Somewhere between Queensbridge and

Swahili...

"Excuse me? I smell what? Surely you can think of something better than that," was her reply.

"I bet your name is Jazmine. It fits you 'cause it's Arabic for flower."

She sucks her teeth like, "Please," as she throws on her left turn signal, waitin' on the light to change. "You saw that on the license plate. Two strikes."

I laugh, you know, 'cause I did peep the plate.

"Oh, you saw that?"

"Yeah, I saw that."

"But if you wouldn't have seen me see that, I woulda got that off, huh?"

Light turn green as she cracked a dimpled smile. The digital quartz clock on the dial says 4:12. I recline my seat, 'cause word, sun, I'm snuzzled in this piece. She pulls over in front of the subway entrance and says, "You comfortable?"

"Why? You puttin' me out?"

"Didn't I say around the corner?"

"Yeah."

"And aren't you headed uptown?"

"Not anymore," I say, then push in the lighter 'cause I can finally light my shit. I'm diggin' the ambiance while she size me up, throw me a dimple and then say some shit like, "I don't think you know what you're getting into," accent sharp like Bayou-lian Creole from the Mississippi, not the Queensbridged Swahili from earlier.

I replied, "Yo, long as it don't involve blood sacrifices or midgets wit' whips, I'm probably already into it."

Shortie expression seemed to say, you just don't know, but her words were, "I'll tell you what. How about I take you where you need to go, conduct my affairs, and later..." She let a smile lay across her face and let her words drift off, givin' me the impression of endless possibilities. I'm thinkin', whatever her native tongue, shortie speak seduction fluently, and I put two and two together and came up wit' twenty-two. Foreign accent, nice whip, affairs

7

that can't wait... Ma must be fuckin' wit' some cats in high places—or low places, dependin' upon your perspective.

So I say, "Whatever, yo, I feel like I'm in good hands," then I light my shit and blow out a smoke ring, crackin' the window for the fumes.

She pulls off.

"Uptown, right?"

I say, "Naw, that was just a stunt. I was headin' for the Path back to Newark."

She say, "Newark?! Newark, New Jersey?!" then she glance at the clock. 4:21. She sigh like she aggravated, but I know she ain't 'cause, yo, on presence alone, I'm a dime-ass nigga. Not that I'm conceited, just let the record reflect.

So I say, just to test the depth, "I'm sayin', if it's stress, you know, I don't wanna get you in no trouble wit' your man or nothing," just throwin' words at her, but it don't register no reaction, no front of pseudo-feminism, just a matter-of-fact, "I'm my own man."

Damn... Never heard it put like that before. Not that Ma exhumed any dyke properties or nothin'. Naw, far from it. 'Cause dig, wit' the sensuality she radiated, she could bring them faggot niggas back to reality or bring the bitch outta thugs. I was neither and her image was so vivid, giving me visions of spoken word poetry and Nas-like ghetto mantras at the same time. Everything about her demeanor said she let her woman be woman and her man be man, but in the absence of such, she'd take up the slack.

I checked the ashtray for history, you know, cigarette butts on the right side of the tray wit' candy lipstick rings or masculine crushes. I found neither; the ashtray was showroom clean, except for a pair of diamond earrings and a jeweled bracelet wit' gems I couldn't identify. And I consider myself a jewel connoisseur. Besides, my ashes were getting long, long like them old men when they fall asleep wit' it lit, but the ashes never fall. I used to watch my grandfather do that shit for hours, fuckin' amazed me. I ain't got Gramp's confidence, so I'm holdin' the cigarette erect, and say, "Yo, Jaz. This ain't no ashtray, it's a jewelry box."

She say, "I know. I don't allow cigarettes in my car."

"Why you ain't say nothin'?"

"You didn't ask."

I shrugged it off and flicked the ashes out the cracked window, watched 'em blow in the breeze. Just then, the phone rings. She flips open the armrest and inside was a zip-lock baggie three fingers full of that red hair sticky, which she handed to me. Surprise, surprise, look what's behind door number two. Jewels in the ashtray, la in the phone box, shit, I wonder what's in the trunk?

She answered the phone, "Yeah," then dialogued in a tongue so rare even the lingual linguist would be like, "Huh?"

I'm like, whatever, I ain't the nosy type; besides, the way her words flowed and mixed wit' the acoustics of Dr. Spot... Life is good. Not to mention the baggie on my lap. I hit up my inside pocket for a Phillie, never leave home wit'out one for occasions such as this. Damn, where I'ma dump this? is what I'm thinkin'.

I guess besides bein' fork-tongued Jaz read minds, too, as she hands me a Sak's Fifth Avenue shopping bag. Small. Just the size for a perfume purchase or very revealin' lingerie. I dump, but I see it been dumped before because it's mad tobacco in the bag, but the bag ain't old... So I'm rollin'. Roll and lick it. Lighter pops out on cue, I'm blazin'...

She hang up the phone and let it drop to her lap as I hand her the charm.

"I thought I knew all of Victoria's secrets, but yours eludes me."

She inhaled the earth as she entered the Holland Tunnel, and said, "Shhh," real soft-like, then, "Don't speak... I can hear you."

Now the way she worded that, a weaker head in my position woulda probably curled up and put his thumb in his mouth. But I know every story has its villain and every beautiful princess got issues, 'cause if Dorothy could sup wit' munchkins and Goldilocks could do a B&E, imagine if

Rapunzel let down her hair and it turn out to be a weave? And yo, I ain't been played by a shortie since Now and Laters went from a nickel to a dime and Lisa Richardson had a thing for pineapple flavor... I found myself suckin' Lemonheads for a week. But that was then and this is now...

Or so I thought...

But right now, I ain't thinkin' about nothin', I'm just focused on the tail lights of the Mazda in front of me, 'cause this herb got me zonin'. I'm feelin' like Poseidon in a sea chariot in pursuit of mermaids through this underwater tunnel that leads to hidden aquatic societies, where sharks is soldiers and I'm crowned king wit' coral reefs.

I'm buggin', right? Yeah, and I knew it, too, when we exited the tunnel—not in Atlantis but Jersey City 'cause I could tell by the smell.

Jaz passed me the el, and said, "You hungry as I am?"

I said, "I thought you said you was listenin'," just to let her know that I was.

Dunkin' Donuts lit up the horizon like a bazaar in the Sahara and I could tell Ma was nice, wit' her eyelids at half-staff as she navigated right to left lane, headin' for Dunks. She ain't get all corny, though, like a lotta mommies who charm, so I knew right then I was fuckin' wit' a veteran. But let record reflect, though, I got All Pro my rookie year in this game, ya'm sayin, I *do* this. But ahhh...

She turned into Dunkin' Donuts parkin' lot and slid the whip between a Caddy and a Porsche. If cars had attitude, the Caddy and the Q exchanged pleasantries, while the Porsche just nutted up.

So Jazmine hops out like, "Donuts on you."

I say, "Yeah, but not the glaze." Her glance told me, message received.

Now yo, remember I said Ma looked like Sanaa Latham? Naw, 'cause first impressions can be deceivin', especially when you tryin' to leave one. I was mistaken. Jazmine had a look all her own, distinct yet hauntingly familiar. So familiar, she was makin' my dream girl jealous.

(*We still here, though, Ms. Badu)*

The autumn night air was crisp and Jaz was prepared in riding boots, black, knee-cut fashion, and stirrup tights. Not too tight, just molded enough to show off her equestrian-trained thighs. Her quarter-length suede and leather belted jacket kept wanderin' eyes from advancin' too far, too fast, and her hair... Black and silky in a ponytail that probably reached the small of her back, but no perm, no weave. This here was her birthright. Reminded me of *Coming to America*... Berries and juices.

So we slide up on the spot and she holdin' the door for me 'cause I lost a step watchin' her and peepin' the Caddy... '85 model, spinners and a rag... I know this jawn from somewhere.

We get inside and it's a few heads. There was a truck driver looking like a disgruntled postal worker, and an insomniac from the suburbs, middle-aged white cat...probably a writer. There was also a jeweled-out cat that I recognized as the owner of the Caddy. Kid named Murph from Communipaw in J.C., we bumped heads a while back, but that's a whole *'nother* story. Remind me later, I'll tell you about it...

Anyway, we inside and Ma choose the booth directly in front of the Q4 parked outside and take off her coat to reveal a cardigan sweater, woven brown and black, oversized enough to pick up where her coat left off. Yeah, shortie definitely keep her garden a secret and I dig that. She sit facin' the door, my usual spot, but I defer and recline opposite, take off my coat, my four pound playin' hide and seek. So I adjust my hoody to conceal and sat down just as the waitress comes up, popping gum... That shit is *sooo* irritatin', say word. To all y'all waitresses, yo, that shit ain't cute, so she just lost ten percent on her tip for faulty approach.

"What can I get y'all?" She lookin' at me like, it's late and a donut is a donut, so get on wit' it... I dig the fact she ain't offer a menu, 'cause word, a donut *is* a donut, fuck

11

you need a menu for, anyway? She just got back five on that ten.

"Ask her," I say, "I'm here for the elevator music." Bing Crosby playin' in the background. I thought that cat was dead?

Jazmine come straight outta Brooklyn, no Swahili-ting, no Bayou drawl and say, "Yo, we charmed and got the munchies, what would you do?" No sarcasm, just matter-of-factly and I guess the waitress do her thing too, 'cause she wink and go, "I got you," then bungeed.

I'm like, where's the accent?

That's when she turned to me and say, "I apologize if my phone conversation offended you. I wasn't trying to hide any—"

I stopped her. "Naw, don't sweat that. I could say some things you couldn't understand, too." She smiled.

The waitress came back with a box of Munchkins and two glasses of Swiss chocolate, warmed. She and Jaz exchanged sisternesses and then she vaped out. Now, weed don't make me hungry, so I stick my straw in my milk and blow bubbles while Jaz is diggin' in the box. First chocolate then powdered, no nibbles. I like a shortie that ain't scared to eat, but you couldn't tell by her figure.

I speak. "I ain't think the supermodel type cared for caloric indulgences, 'specially after midnight."

"I don't like to take pictures," she says, and keeps eating.

Okay, I see information isn't volunteered 'round these parts, guess I'll just be frank.

"So what do you like, na'm mean? I'm sayin', what makes Jazmine Jazmine?"

I bit off more that I could chew wit' that one, 'cause shortie started runnin' off shit like Mona Lisa did to Slick Rick: *Well I got courage but I don't like porridge,* shit like that, when she said, "I was born and raised just off the coast of West Africa, on a small island called Amantu. I'm the daughter of the king, which makes me a queen and I received my tutelage in Westminster. England, that is. I speak eight different languages but I only dream in full color French. For my fifth birthday, Michael Jackson sang at the festivities. I have jewels so rare, they aren't even commodities yet. And here I am, a guest of your country. So now, who are you and why are you even worth my time?" Then she sipped her cocoa, leavin' a hint of dark brown remaining on the pink of her inner lip.

Now, some cats woulda taken that last line offensive, but I can tell she ain't throw it to be... I mean, if she was big on herself, that's to say, siddity, why even scoop a cat in the middle of the night, New York-style, three in the mornin'?

So it wasn't arrogance, she was just testin' my character; but old school-new school, rules is the same and I'm well versed in the curriculum. Besides, she already said I had two strikes, so I shot back nonchalantly...

"Well, I've never been to France, so I only dream in Newark, and if you speak so many languages, which one do you think in? 'Cause me, mine be in English and I always speak my mind." I took a sip of cocoa. Since I had her attention, I let it dangle momentarily then continued...

"And as for Mike, when I take my cornrows out, I always thought I was nicer in the mirror wit' a broomstick. So at five, I entertained myself. And yeah, I noticed the jewels, but a diamond just ain't a diamond no more once everybody got 'em. So rare is good, but the most precious jewels are the ones that can't be bought."

"Everything has a price. You just have to be able to pay it."

"Or willing," I say, and she nodded me touché as another munchkin disappeared from the box. So I sit back a sec to dig on Ma profile 'cause it's somethin' about this chick I just can't put my finger on...yet. So I continued.

"You know, you remind me of those caramel apples at the carnival. Taste like chocolate but underneath is the forbidden fruit."

She laughs and say, "I like that. Forbidden fruit. But to whom is it forbidden?"

13

I ain't say nothin' 'cause I'm dead-ass and I can't figure Ma out. But um, when it comes to women, if they equal energy, then I'm mass-times-light-squared; I always got the formula. Just gotta find it, which is usually in their eyes. 'Cause if you follow a person's eyes you can see beneath the mask, 'specially females. Just gotta throw male figures at her...a significant other, a child, a father, et cetera and so on. Then watch and see what registers, but you gotta be sharp 'cause it's quick... Like a blink. Pupils dilate like a flash of light hit 'em or a subtle movement, a shifting of weight. But you gotta know what to look for... Wit' this chick, it wasn't a man and I could see she wasn't the motherly type, so I throw one mo'...

"Yeah, you definitely got it together. The total package, and I don't say that often 'cause pussy and pumpkin pie only two things the same everywhere. But uh, yeah, I know your father must be proud."

There it is—the look. For a split second it was as obvious as snatchin' the covers off your naked wife to find she in bed wit' a midget. Truth leave you naked like that until you find the linen of a lie. She regained her composure as if she never lost it, and to the naked eye, she didn't.

"Wouldn't you be?"

Typical. Whenever at a loss, answer a question with a question. Yeah, I found the chink in her veneer.

"Proud?" I ask. "Well, that depends if I knew my baby girl was ridin' around wit' strangers, steamin' trees and sharin' donuts at sunrise."

She wiped the corner of her mouth and said, "Daddy's little girl grew up a long time ago."

But she wasn't really talkin' to me, you know? Like that was for her, past and present, ya feel me?

So Jaz come again. "I like you," lookin' at me as if she been psychoanalyzin' me from jump, surmising my aptitude.

"But?" I say, 'cause I can hear it in her tone.

"But...it's my situation, I'm..."

"I thought you were your own man?"

14

"It's not a man... I mean... It's the timing."

So I shot back, "Well, unless you're psychic, I'm sure you ain't plan on meetin' the man of your dreams holdin' up traffic. So expect the unexpected."

Jazmine snizzled a smile, like she bit the proverbial apple and was offering me some, when she said, "Expect the unexpected? Then what should the unexpected expect?" then sipped on her cocoa for a taste.

Ma got kinda deep wit' that, but before I could begin exploring that, the earth disemboweled some shit I was totally unprepared for.

"What if I told you that I had a body in the trunk and a million in government bonds under my seat?"

Yo! I almost choked on my milk bubbles I was blowin' until I realized she said *if*, so I figured she was just checkin' to see if I'm ticklish, so I signify, "What if I told you I was totin' a whistle?"

She like, "If you mean by whistle the forty-five caliber Desert Eagle in your pants, I already know. Besides, how do you think the body got in the trunk?" Then she smile like, checkmate.

"Touché, touché, you got that," I conceded. "Is it anybody I know?"

"Probably not."

"Cheatin' boyfriend, or should I say, very *ex* boyfriend?"

"No."

"His mistress?"

"No."

Then I thought...HOLD UP! "He ain't somebody you picked up off the street, is he?" Word up, tell me now.

But she don't answer that, she just giggle like a nigga jokin' and say, "Now you know what the unexpected expects, huh?" Then she looked out the window at her $40,000 coffin.

So I finish my cocoa and I see the sun yawnin' in the east, and although I like a challenge, Ma a little more complicated than I'd like to indulge. I'm ghost.

15

"You ready?" I ask. She answers by standin' up, throwin' on her coat and I'm right there. I hit the waitress wit' a dime, but I'm too tired to wait on my change. She look at me like, 'preciate that, as me and Ma slide out.

"You know how to drive?" she asks me, then, "I'm crazy tired," for good measure.

I don't answer, I just head around to the driver's side and she tossed me the keys. Caddy gone. Porsche still holdin' its breath. We hop in. I adjust the seat, thinkin' 'bout reachin' underneath to see what's what, but when I glance to see if she lookin', she peelin' off her boots to reveal her stockinged feet. Nails pedicured to perfection and I forgot all about whatever was supposed to be underneath the seat. All I'm thinkin' is, aww, man. Damn, my foot fetish.

But, yo, never let 'em see you sweat.

She curled up her legs in the seat and the radio was on some jazz station playin' that joint called "Harlem Blues" and Ma knew it word for word. So as I whip out on the highway, sun over my shoulder, pound in my pants, supposedly a slab in the trunk, a brick in bonds under the seat, la in the armrest and an African Queen lullabyin' me, I'm thinkin', if 5-0 do pull me I'll just tell 'em I'm from Newark. They'll understand.

"You know," Jaz started after the song went off, "what I told you could cause a lot of people a lot of problems. Maybe I should kill you, too?"

I glance over to catch a mischievous smile, but really I'm lookin' for malicious intent. The sparkle in her eye gave her away, so I shrug and say, "I hope not. I ain't got nothin' to wear to the funeral. Besides, I specialize in keepin' women's secrets," or keepin' women *a* secret, dependin' on the circumstances.

So I'm on Pulaski Skyway, eighty plus, lane to lane, tryin' to avoid Ma little side glances and... Well, Ma, she was a tough nut to crack but I could make Monica fuck on the first night although I seldom go there like that. 'Cause I like to know what I'm getting into so I know what to do

16

when I get there, you know?

No?

Okay, put it like this. If women were states, my name would ring bells all over Virginia. Now we on the same page?

All right, then. Not to mention the fact Ms. Thang might be into some ol' freakiness and I ain't the only sun she slum on any given night... Humblin' thought. But if so, what up wit' this body shit? Not hers, which is immaculate, the one in the trunk. Why even tell me—a total stranger— incriminatory shit of that nature? Shit don't add up and I'm too tired to play calculator. I hit the off-ramp and enter the city, just as Newark was puttin' on its boots.

But back to Ma...

A woman is real subtle wit' her shit, right, 'cause she throw out signals, once received and acted upon, that make it look like you initiated the shit, but in actuality it's all a part of the cat-and-mouse. But see, we ain't the cat, 'cause if you notice, that's why they compare pussy to cats and men to mice. But I'm telling Ma in so many words, go 'head wit' dat, 'cause she fightin' a Parsons' Cause to build a Virginia fence and that there ain't good for the effeminate type of ego. Besides, race fans, when you fuckin' wit' a thoroughbred like this, it's good to know what your pony can do before the derby...

All y'all players build on that.

Anyway, Jazmine takin' it all in stride, a sign of player breedin'. By the time we get to my spot on the bully, Brick Towers Apartments, she hit me wit' some shit that let me know it ain't over. I'm writin' down my beeper number, one foot out the car door, and I'm like, "You know, after all this, you still don't know my name."

She responded, "I haven't thought of one for you yet."

Her look says, go marinate on that for a while...

THE END????

17

Now I know y'all probably wonderin' about shortie lunch bucket in the milk-white Q4, but before I get into that, let me tell you where I'm at now...

I'm on the coast of Africa, thirty paces from The Door of No Return. For all you cats not hip to your history, you need to get on it. But for now, just know that that's the spot where slaves were taken through onto boats bound for bondage, so those left behind called it The Door of No Return.

Yeah, but I'm loungin', snuzzled under a date palm feastin' on dates and mangoes, watchin' the brothers net fishin'. Yo, I wish you could see this, 'cause the view is lovely.

The crystallized sea...

I once heard a cat call it the cradle endlessly rockin'... Say word. This the type of shit make Stella get her groove back and the natives still talk about the day the sky rained gold. Matter of fact, I caught a bucket for myself, so I guess you could say I'm at the other end of the rainbow. 'Cept ain't no little white cats in green suits. Just me, a bucket of gold bullions and the story of a lifetime.

So sit back and snuzzle wit' me and all your questions will be answered...

Hold up, let me get my cigarette... Anybody got a light? I guess some things never change, huh?

CHAPTER THREE: JAZMINE...WHO?

I-ight, back to the story at hand, like Dre say. I woke up the next mornin', well, not really mornin' 'cause two in the afternoon ain't really mornin'. But to me it's early. So like I was sayin', I resurrected. Hungry. I'm headin' for the kitchen and my mind alludes back to the night before, and I'm wonderin' if I dreamed up all of what I'm tellin' you. I check the inside pocket of my coat and find the earth I excavated from Jaz's baggie. Not that I'm no squirrel-ass character, but yo, this what I call my opportunity costs. 'Cause I figure like this: if it's real and I see Ma again then the steam on me and she none the wiser, but if it was just the passin' of two ships then, like I said, opportunity costs. 'Cause, yo, a cat of my caliber, my time is valuable and ain't no tellin' what I mighta fell up on had I not spent the night chess boxin' wit' an alleged serial killer.

Typical day for me is, I stroll to the store for a Snapple and a bag of chips and I end up in Michigan... Now *that* was some shit—remind me, I'll tell you about it later. For now, go figure, 'cause word, life is good, right? Yeah, that's what I been tryin' to tell you.

So anyway, I hit the kitchen and grab the usual suspects: bowl, spoon, Raisin Bran, sugar... Plenty of sugar. Milk... No milk... Fuck it, put the bowl under the faucet and water it down. Don't front like you never did it, and if you ain't, get the stick outta *your* ass.

Anyway, I flips on the TV to CNN 'cause I like to stay informed, you know, make sure none of me or mine on

"America's Most Wanted" or nothin'. Then I turn on the stereo 'cause to digest the images of worldwide famine, international war, sex, murder, mayhem and what-have-you, I need the rhythm of the boom-bap, ya feel me? Yeah, I'm an avid hip-hop head. Official. 'Didas only if they leather and so forth...

Yeah, so, I'm about to eat breakfast, right, when I hear a knock-knock-knock at the door.

"Sam? Ay Sam, open the door," sound like a pint-sized thug.

I open the door and standin' there is my next door neighbor's bad-ass son, Tyrone.

"Yo, I got somethin' to tell you," he say, rubbin' his chin.

I look at him. "What is it?"

He hold out his grubby lil' hand, talkin' 'bout, "Gimme ten dollars and I will."

Ain't this some shit? Here I am, not even all the way woke and I'm being extorted by a miniature gangster.

"Keep it to yourself then," I say, and then try and close the door.

He lean against it like, "Yo, I'm tellin' you, it's *important.*"

"Nigga, if you don't—"

"I-ight, i-ight. Five."

I stop shovin' the door, 'cause I'm about to spill my cereal. "I'ma give you five, i-ight, you don't get yo' lil' ass outta here."

So he look at my bowl and ask, "What's that?" And me, like a dummy, lower it to his eye level and say, "Raisin Br—" but before I could get it all out, he done took it out my hand.

"Thanks," then brushed his lil' mannish ass past me and walked in my livin' room, eatin' my shit!

Didn't I tell you he was bad as hell?

Man, I remember I came home one mornin' after stayin' out all night. I walk in and this cat got a bunch of lil' niggas and lil' girls dancin' in my livin' room, shootin' craps

20

in my bathroom and flippin' burgers in my kitchen! And if you think that's some shit, you shoulda seen the time he kidnapped the lady's cat in 8C and, peep this, made *me* the pickup man!

The lil' muhfucka had wrote a ransom note for twenty dollars and told her I'd pick it up, then he tell me the lady in 8C lookin' for me. She cryin' and shit when I got there, but I finally got it out of her what happened.

You still say violence on TV don't affect kids? Nigga ain't no older than 11.

But anyway, that's Ty for you. So I go in my living room and he kick back, eatin', remote in hand, and say, "So you gonna gimme the nickel or what? I'm tellin' you, you better hurry up, too."

I sit on the couch, snatch the remote and answer, "You need to have your nickel-ass in school." I started to say somethin' about, when I was your age, but damn, I was doin' the same thing...

So I'm channel surfing, tryin' to kill time 'til cartoons come on, when guess who I see?

Her. Jazmine on CNN!

While I'm sittin' there smokin' my cigarette, I see my loveliness at some African inauguration-type ball or somethin'. Shortie lookin' regal. Headdress like Erykah Badu and a long, flowing purple and gold silk dress, barefoot and an entourage of little girls all dressed like her in various flavas and shades.

I turn down the radio just Tyrone say, "Man, turn this shit. Go to BET, see some as—"

"Shut up," I say, 'cause the reporter was about to talk. I turned up the set as they was showin' a picture of the Q somewhere near some docks, mad cops around and all the doors *and* the trunk opened.

I slide to the edge of the couch as the reporter said, "The car, which belongs to Princess Fulani, heiress to the Amantu throne, was found early this morning in Jersey City, New Jersey."

I'm thinkin', so she was headin' my way the whole

time, huh? Not necessarily a good sign, from the looks of things.

The reporter continued.

"In the trunk was found the body of one of her bodyguards, badly beaten with a single gunshot wound to the temple that proved fatal."

Damn, she wasn't frontin'.

"The Princess herself was not found, but drops of blood and several unidentified fingerprints were. This is a crucial time in the affairs of Amantu, as the rebels and the Amantu government wage a bloody battle between dictatorial rule and democracy. King Mofusu, who was in Washington, D.C. during the week, flew into New York immediately upon receiving the news."

Yo, I'm buggin'! I done fucked wit' shorties whose pops had weight—hustlers and preachers—but never a muhfucka that commanded a whole army! Well, then again, that depends on whether or not you can count Big Ben and his three hundred goons as an army... Long story...

They showed her father. Cool-lookin' cat, not too old, but then again, that African air ain't got all the side effects our shit over here carry. Ya'm sayin', Egyptians still look good after five millenniums, so on a scale, he could be sixty-plus or a hundred and sixty-plus.

The reporter asked him, "Do you think your daughter's disappearance is in any way connected to the rebel influences she has been linked to?"

Rebel influences?!

Tyrone point to the king and say, "Yo, he look like all them black cats down—"

But I cut him off, like, "Ty, you wanna spend another afternoon tied up in my closet?"

He get the point and shut up.

The king speak through an interpreter.

"My daughter has always been very liberal in her thinking and very lax in the respect of tradition and custom. This I attribute to her tutelage abroad, and her naïve worldly view has influenced her choice of associates.

Unfortunately, it has opened her up to the danger of the dissenters in my country present."

He spoke mad cool—kinda laid back, takin' it all in stride—and it reaffirmed that the apple don't fall far from the tree in Ma case.

The reporter went on.

"But what do you say to the reports that she is working directly with the American government as a liaison between them and the rebels?"

Pop just smiled and his interpreter said he said, "Where in the world is there civil unrest and the American hand is not covertly or overtly present?"

The reporter couldn't answer that one, so he cleared his throat and threw the anchorman a weak-ass, "Back to you, Bob," type of line.

But yo, pops had a point. And Jazmine—or Fulani—did say she was sittin' on chrome. Bonds that is. But Ma an African Pocahontas? Naw... Hell, no. But you never know, even roses got thorns, huh? The news went to sports... Giants lost.

Oh shit!

"Unidentified fingerprints?!"

I was so caught up in this African espionage, it totally missed me that my prints is all over that whip!

Tyrone say, "Damn, I knew I shoulda asked for twenty!"

But I still ain't caught on. Later for Ty—this shit is gettin' deep! I grab my four pound. Then I think, no, then I think, yeah... Shit, motherfuckas is dyin' in this shit. Then I think, no, again, 'cause if I do get bagged and I got my joint, they'll probably run the serial and I got this shit from Bino and ain't no tellin' where he got it from. Not to mention the body in the trunk.

The knock-knock-knock at my door deaded my dilemma.

"Who is it?" Like I ain't know.

"Newark police. Open up."

Picture that... Ay, yo, you know that old "Saturday

23

Night Live" skit wit' Eddie Murphy playin' Mr. Rogers? When he go out the window when he hear his landlord coming? I-ight, then you know what *I'm* 'bout to do. I grab the four pound and dash for the living room window.

"Nope. Can't go that way," Ty say, bobbin' his head to Eve on BET.

I hit the fire escape, but when I look down there's two black sedans parked directly below and three cats in sunglasses lookin' like they from *The Matrix*. They all look up in deadpan unison. Can't go down.

The knock at the door getting more persistent.

"Mr. Black? This is the police. Open the door."

I get ready to head up on the roof, but when I look up, it's a muhfucka perched on the roof wit' a really really big gun. Can't go up. Just then I hear the crashin' of wood as them muhfuckas kick my door in! Newark po-po don't even get down like that, so you know what I'm dealin' wit' now!

So I try to dip back through the window, just as the cat that musta kicked in my door come in the room wit' five more suits behind him. Cat kick in my door make Andre the Giant look bitch! And guess what this cat do?

Smile.

A big cheese-eatin' grin and say some shit in a language I don't know, but I pretty much understand the gist. Translated... Nigga, you short, in so many words. Somewhere in my head KRS-ONE say: *Now tell me what the fuck am I supposed to do...*

Love got me.

So as they draggin' me out Tyrone, who been sittin' on my couch, remote in hand, swingin' his little short-ass legs, he say, "Shoulda just gave me the five dollars and I woulda been told you."

"Just lock the door when you leave," I hiss back.

CHAPTER FOUR: USE THE FORCE, LUKE!

Now, Rodney King I'm not, but I do think the way this cat yoked me off the fire escape and half dragged, half threw me down the steps could qualify as police brutality. Thing is, though, I ain't even sure these cats is cops. Only one speak English, he 'round my age and he speak it wit' the same vernacular peculiarities as Jazmine—I mean, Fulani—I mean, *whoever* she is.

And another thing, they didn't even show me a badge. Not that they really needed one, you understand; the Mac 11 currently at my neck will do. And plus, I know damn near ere' Newark detective, but none of these dudes is even remotely familiar. *And* we in a black Lincoln Navigator wit' two black Continentals escortin' us, front and rear.

I'm in the backseat between Mighty Joe Young—you know, the cat that yoked me up—and the English-speakin' kid, and all these dudes is *jet* black. Blue black. *Black as hell.*

Is this a kidnappin' or an arrest? is what I'm thinkin'... I need a cigarette. So I try to reach for my inside pocket, but Gorilla Man jab the Mac in my neck like he checkin' my tonsils.

"Calm down, brother, I'm just getting my cigarettes."

Gorilla Man didn't say shit but the English cat say, "Smoking is bad for your health."

Oh, like a gun to your throat isn't?

I guess my man realize his contradiction so he try to assuage me by sayin', "I understand that this is an...inconvenience, but it's only for our safety—and yours."

"Safety? How 'bout you just gimme a seatbelt?"

He just smile and say, "We'll be there soon."

Be where? That's what I'm thinkin'. Surely they don't think I kidnapped a princess, iced the body in the trunk, then went home and ate cereal? This is *definitely* no arrest, so Central Booking is out...

Shit, I hope we ain't goin' to no Africa. What if they locked me in Mandela's old cell? Or worse, maybe they plannin' to torture me wit' no sleep, playin' classical and opera music over and over and over...

Or...or sew my asshole closed and keep feedin' me and feedin' me and... Damn, I been listenin' to too much *36 Chambers*. Word.

Now I'm thinkin' like Bogart. Of all the cities in the world and streets in New York, I had to cross *hers*.

We pass the same Dunkin' Donuts as we hit the Lincoln Tunnel, and I'm thinkin', I'ma blow that muhfucka up if I get outta this. The Dunkin' Donuts, I'm talkin' about...

To my relief, we ain't head to the airport; instead, we ended up in Midtown Manhattan. The African Consulate.

Before we get out, my man English turn to me and say, "You know, foreign dignitaries such as my colleagues and I are granted immunity from all sorts of crimes. Including murder. So please, don't make a scene."

Then he smiles and I turn to Gorilla Monsoon and he smilin' too and I'm wonderin' what the hell is so amusin' to these African-ass gangsters! But bein' he had possession of Belinda (Translation: my four pound), I thought maybe the advice was kinda helpful, 'cause the thought of getting out and screamin' like a bitch did cross my mind. But New Yorkers? Psss. Yeah, right.

26

No scene. We go inside.

On the inside of the Consulate, shit is plush. A lot of cats in African garb and some Armani. Kinda ironic, 'specially when a cat got the African garb and Armani shoes.

I saw a couple of secretaries that were truly delectable, but shit, *that's* the kind of shit that got me himmed up in the first place, so I avoided all eye contact. A dude in Armani approached me wit' a metal detector and scanned me like one of those cans at a supermarket checkout counter. I'm thinkin', I ain't the one totin' missiles, but I guess in here they 'posed to tote missiles. Besides, these cats didn't exactly frisk me at my crib. They saw Belinda and confiscated that and then Mighty Joe sorta turned me upside down and shook me to see what fell out, but other than that, no frisk. I guess they ain't up on the razor in my mouth, huh? They could learn a thing or two on Riker's.

Anyway, the English-speakin' cat say somethin' to my man in they tongue, and he and Gorilla Man step off as the metal detector dude sorta extend the detector in a gesture to a door off stage right. Never spoke. We head for the door, and he open it for me but don't go in. I look in, peep on the floor lookin' for plastic laid out like my man from *Lethal Weapon*. No plastic.

Good sign.

Rug thick, plush like everything else, so I step in and Metal Detector close the door behind me. Then I hear it lock...

Not a good sign.

So I'm lookin' around. The place is laced. Heavy wood paneling, two leather armchairs, a glass table and two flags, one American and the other I guess African. A fish tank built in the wall wit' some real fly fish. Not *flyin'* fish—I said fly fish. Yeah, so I sit down in one of the armchairs, just as the door unlocks and the English speaker come in followed by two military-lookin' dudes—I guess guards—and the King, shortie father. Cat real short but he walk tall. Kinda give you the impression, if stature was height he'd have to duck for the clouds.

The English speaker say, "Rise for the king."

I'm thinkin', fuck is this, court? Then again, in a way it is, so I obliged the dude. The king come over, half nod to me, then sit down wit' a guard on both sides of him. The English cat nod and I guess he mean, lounge, so I sit. Now, yo, remember the dude—I mean the king, was speakin' on TV through an interpreter? Yeah, I'm expectin' the English cat to do the same here, so I turn to him and say, "Ay, yo, man, tell the king—"

The king cut me off.

"No need, young man. I can understand your every word." He real polite, but I can tell he ain't here for no bullshit. He cut right to the chase. "Where is the princess?"

I'm thinkin', what the hell, what I know? I just met the broad outta the blue. So I tell him, "Well, Your Honor"—force of habit, too many pending charges—"I mean, um, King... Well, see..."

I'm tryin to figure out a way to say this. I mean, how do you tell a girl father, who also happens to run a small country, that you and his seed spent the night blazin' and engagin' in intellectual sex? So you can understand why I proceed wit' caution.

He, the king, smile like the wise old man I figure he is and say, "There's no need to be alarmed, my son. I realize you are only a pawn in a very dangerous game my daughter is a part of."

Pawn? Hold up pop, gotta stop you there. Sam never been the pawn, so I figure my character in question.

"Excuse me?"

The king waves off the English dude and the two guards. They turn to go but as they leavin', one of the guards look at me as he close the door as if to say, i-ight, don't get fucked up.

After they go, the king say, "Do you drink, my son? Would you like one?"

Rule #1: Never drink what you leave at the bar.

28

International rule #1: Never drink the offerings of foreign inquisitors.

"Naw, I'm okay." I don't drink anyway.

"Tell me. How long have you known my daughter?"

"Well, sir, really I don't *know* your daughter. I mean, see, last night I'm on my way home from a party, three in the mornin'. So I'm crossin' the street and I was really—" I almost said twisted, but instead I said, "tired, when I was almost hit by a car your daughter just *happened* to be drivin'." I emphasized "happened" so he know, yo, this just some freak occurrence and not planned.

"Well, I guess she saw how, uh, tired I looked and offered me a ride home, which is way in Jersey. We stopped at a diner to grab a bite to eat and then she took me home." Which was the truth, except the lil' part about the slab in the trunk.

The king was takin' it all in. He stood up, went over to the fish tank, looked at 'em swim for a minute, then he turned to me and said, "I'm sure the two of you talked along the way."

Yeah, she told me she laced a cat and she dream in French.

"Well, yes, I mean, of course, but it wasn't really of any importance. Like I said, she was very gracious in takin' me home and I thanked her. I realized we had a common interest in music and our conversation sorta stayed on those kind of topics."

He said, "She never mentioned who she was? Even when she introduced herself?"

"Well, sir, besides her name"—which, by the way, she lied about—"besides her name, I really tried not to get too personal because I, myself, don't like to divulge personal information."

The king smiled as he caught the implications of my last statement. He slowly returned to his seat as if to say, let me come at you from another angle.

"I am the ruler of a small African country, Amantu. My father fought off British hegemony for our independence

29

and I have desperately tried to maintain that same independence for the last thirty-six years. I have six children, but only one female child. Our tradition states that rule must pass through the maternal lineage and so, in keeping with tradition, I sought a wife, and twenty-two years ago she gave birth to Fulani after five other children. All males. She was to reinstate the maternal rule and marry, and her husband would be king. I loved Fulani... I love Fulani. As a child, I took her everywhere I would go. France. Europe. Egypt. America. All in hopes she would learn the ways of the world. I even enrolled her in school abroad so she could understand the evils of the Western world. But evil is alluring and Fulani was allured. I thought I had sufficiently rooted her in our ancestry's principles and traditions. Her schooling abroad educated her but she did not learn. She acquired their doctrines and ideologies and brought them back to Amantu. This subsequently helped to exacerbate the already seething dichotomy of unrest, and now, civil war. But this was not the end. I soon found out, not only had she aligned herself with outside influences ideally, but financially. When I found out she was having opium processed in Amantu and exchanged for arms and money, I confronted her. She denied it, until I showed her pictures of herself and certain rebel leaders and American intelligence officers. I was to have her arrested, but she fled the country."

He dropped his head and pinched in his eyes, then continued.

"You must understand that I do love my daughter and I only wished to bring her back to reality—to see reason—but she has decided to lead the rebels, whom I know are backed by the Americans, to overthrow me and rule like...like a puppet for Western interest. I have said too much but...I am desperate. You see, I am a family man. A humble man. But I am also a just man and I cannot allow thousands or even hundreds of my people to suffer for one. Even if that one is flesh of my flesh and blood of my blood."

Damn, I feel you, pops. Maybe Ma is a Pocahontas to

her country—not to mention, a female Sosa and a murderer. And to think I was type big on her... Well...not *that* big.

The king came back to his seat and sat down.

"I realize you may be puzzled as to why I would tell you all I have, but it's not like my daughter to...fraternize with no less than royalty and circles of that ilk. No offense, as you appear to be a very honorable and intelligent young man, but street corners are not my daughter's frequents so it is not like her to solicit the streets. Not to say you have been less than truthful but there must be more to it because I feel she will contact you, and—" he smiled and said, "I know that she is very beautiful...and has been...deflowered." Then he looked me in the eyes like any father would, tryin' to see if I "deflowered" his little girl. Nothin' to hide there; so satisfied, he continued.

"She is very intelligent. She knows herself well and can allure men into things. Things they shouldn't be allured into, very dangerous things. I hope I am making myself clear?"

"Very."

"Because I realize you do not want to become involved, which is the best thing, but you are...already involved, to an extent. I feel that you are not telling me everything, nor did I expect you to, but there were things in her car and you were in her car, and..."

He left the sentence hangin' in hopes that I'd complete it.

"Look, uh, King, whatever you and Jaz—I mean, Fulani, got goin' on is on y'all, you know? You right, I am involved and I don't wanna be involved, so as soon as that door opens, I'm washin' that girl right outta my hair. So the only thing that'll be between me and her is distance." I looked him in the eye, square, 'cause I wasn't lyin'...exactly.

He said, "I believe you, I truly believe you, because like I said, you look like a very intelligent man. My daughter is obviously a little confused and whatever happened to Jaffe must have her groping for solace. For some reason,

31

she saw something in you and I'm sure the feeling is at least mutual. So when she contacts you, as I know she will, it would be best if you contacted me immediately. Not only for your safety, but I would also be *very* grateful. Very."

Ooohhh, this dude on some international crime stoppers-type shit, huh?

(Your call will be confidential...)

I stood up then, 'cause fuck if I offend him, I'm offended. "I don't know how y'all do it in Amantu or whatever, but where I'm from, that's called snitchin'. So like I said, *distance*. Between me and her, me and you, *y'all* and *me*. The whole situation. So unless you gonna keep holdin' me against my will, I think we've said all it is to be said."

He stood slowly and extended his hand, and I hesitantly grasped it. Not that he seemed like a bad guy, but I guess he ain't hip to the code of the street and how questions of honor ruffle feathers.

"Yes, I think so, too."

"Likewise," is all I say, though, and head for the door.

But yo, as I open it he say, as if to himself, but obviously to me, "I wonder how long a million dollars would last the average man in this country."

So there it is: WANTED: DEAD OR ALIVE. Old West-style or *Star Wars*, but I ain't no Boba Fett so Chewbacca on that.

I closed the door behind me...

CHAPTER FIVE: JUST CALL ME STONE

Now I *know* I ain't gotta tell you who been wit' me since I left the Consulate, do I? Come on, did you really think they'd let me out of their sight? The only link to Princess Leia and the Force wouldn't be with me? It's two of them, a man and a lady, tryin' to front like tourists... Yeah, right. I been hip to the chase from jump but since nothin' about my next move was even clear to me, I figured, why not let 'em tag along?

Besides, it's too nice a day to be cooped up in the Consulate. So I stop and buy a hot dog, but I pay for three and three iced teas.

I tell the vendor, "See those two over there? Actin' conspicuously inconspicuous? When they walk by tell 'em lunch is on me." When I look back, I see them lookin' kinda confused, but the Africans just like black folk over here... They didn't turn down a free meal. They took the hot dogs and nodded me a subtle appreciation.

Well, since they dressed for the occasion, complete with camera, I guess I'll take 'em on a little tour of the city. Besides, wouldn't wanna lose 'em too quick, might get in trouble wit' the king.

So I'm takin' 'em up the block, down the block, around the block, across 7th, through 8th and everywhere in-between. As I pass tourist vendors, I'm coppin' 'em souvenirs; you know, Statue of Liberty crown for the sister 'cause you know Ms. Liberty really 'posed to be black, and coffee mugs for my man. It got so that all I had to do was hold up a t-shirt or somethin' and they'd shake their heads yes or no. No, I'd put it back, yes, I'd cop it, leave it at the stand and they'd pick it up as they passed...

But yo, I'm tired of goin' in circles, plus these souvenirs is breakin' a brother. So I walk up to my pursuers and say, "Dig, here's two tokens. We on our way to Harlem."

They look at each other, hands full of trinkets, and reach for the tokens.

I hit the first subway entrance I see, span the stairs, hop the turnstile... What? Surely you don't expect me to pay... Then I hit the platform for the A Uptown. My pursuers sit on the bench, exhausted, 'cause I been walkin' they dogs off.

Five minutes and I feel the rumble, then the A appeared. The door bonged open and split, releasing a flood of people. So I get on...dipped...dodged...ducked...and then got back off a second before the door closed, leaving my pursuers on the train. The brother looked surprised, like I was Merlin or somethin', but the sister dug my acrobatics and smirked. Both of 'em looked relieved, though, and sat down as the train pulled off.

I'm on the platform, waving. "Buh-bye! Buh-bye! You'll love it in Harlem! Don't forget to write!"

That was fun, but now it's time to catch the opposite A to Crooklyn 'cause I need to see my man. So I backtrack and I'm Crooklyn bound...

So I hit the A. People get off, me and some more people get on, including a cat wit' a change cup. I slide a five in his cup. His eyes say, "preciate that"; mine say, "don't sweat it," and he move on.

I see this shifty-eyed-ass crackhead motherfucka eyein' this old lady wit' a purse and a shopping bag. Yo, if it's anything I *despise*, it's a weak muhfucka preyin' on the weaker. So I get up and go over to the lady's seat and ask her, "Is this seat taken?"

She begrudgingly move her shopping bag and hug her purse to her bosom. That's what I wanted her to do. Then I look at the crackhead and give him my Professor X leer...

This is protected by the red, the black and the Sam... Sissy!!

He shuffle off to the next car. Whole time, the lady don't even know what's goin' on, probably think I'm the crackhead, the way she huggin' her purse. No problem, long as she i-ight.

I get to my stop, but before I go, I turn to her and say, "Be safe."

First she look surprised then thankful... Anytime. Remind me of my grandmother.

God bless the dead.

I-ight, I know y'all dogs got a partna, and ladies, y'all got girlfriends, that as soon as somethin' happens, they the first person you tell. Mine is Fathead. Some people call him Bobcat, but those who can get away wit' it call him Fathead. He work the underground—subways, that is.

Remember Lenny from "Good Times"? He like, Lenny nephew or Lenny 2G, 'cept for the coat wit' all the shit and the rhymes. Naw, he got a different sales pitch...

Extortion.

See, he sell everything: oils, mix tapes, newspapers, magazines and what have you, but have you ever heard of a hard sell? You ain't seen nothing 'til you've met Fathead. I can think of several occasions, but once, I seen him wit' this black, yuppity-lookin' dude—you know, the upwardly mobile and not-lookin'-back type? Well, he had already purchased a *Wall Street Journal*, but it happened to be his luck, or lack of, that his train pulled up to the platform Fathead was working that day.

35

Fathead say, "Yo, you need a *Wall Street Journal.*"

The guy, in his best white stick-up-your-ass-type voice say, "Thanks, but I've already got one," then he held up his copy.

Fats get in his path and say, "Naw. I *said* you *need* a *Wall Street Journal.*"

The guy still don't recognize, so he like, "No thanks, guy. I've already purchased the latest edition."

So Fathead—I be buggin' when I think about it—say, "But what if you lose it?! Huh?! What if you lose it?! I'm lookin' out for your best interest!" Then, in the calmest voice, Fathead end it like, "That'll be three-fifty, please," and extend his hand, palm up, with a crooked-ass Crooklyn grin.

Now, it musta been the combination of Fathead's tone plus his dreads and heavyweight boxer frame, 'cause the guy buys another *Wall Street Journal*—and a *New York Post* just 'cause Fats said it's an article in it he want him to read. The guy actually say, "Which page?" after he buy it.

Fathead like, "I forgot. Now beat it," and he now five dollars richer.

Fats swing in the Bronx, and I told you, them BX cats is troublemakers. Funny guy as long as you ain't on the wrong end of the joke, as you can see.

Yeah, so anyway, me and Fats go way back. Funny story how we met... Tell you sometime. But for as long as I can remember, Fats always be readin' Westerns. You know that Wyatt Erp-type novel? Yeah, he read them shits. Probably only kid in the projects know how the West was won... Or give a fuck. He been a ghetto cowboy long before them Bone cats. So yeah, Fats my confidante 'cause he got this crazy-type logic. He usually tell you a dumb-ass story outta one of them Westerns and then give you his own interpretation of the moral. Shit be so stupid it be makin' sense. So here I am, lookin' for him to tell him what been goin' down since last night, three in the mornin'...

I find him and he wit' some middle-aged Woody Allen-lookin' dude, and get this, he tryin' to sell him *The*

Source magazine.

I hear the dude say, "But I don't listen to raps!"

Fat say, "Ohhh, don't listen to rap, huh? What's the matter? You don't like *black* music? It ain't good enough for you, or something?! Y'all hear that?! My man say he don't like *black* music! Howard Beach, Howard Beach!"

He got people lookin' and it's a lot of black people wit' good memories, so my man break down and buy *The Source* and then haul ass, fast as he could.

I walk up to Fats. "Yo, somebody gonna stop you one day."

He say, "I ain't met a motherfucka who could do that in this lifetime," then smile that Fathead smile. I give him a pound and a brotherly hug.

He ask me, "Yo, where you been? You ain't been duckin' dominatrix again, have you?" Long story....

"Naw, but I shoulda ducked, just the same," I say, then I tell him the whole story 'bout Fulani, the Q4, the body, the brick in bonds, the king and, of course, the weed, of which I'm currently in the process of rolling.

He like, "Yeah, I saw that shit on the front page of *The Post* and *The Times*. Shortie a dime, too. You ain't hit dat?"

"Naw I ain't *hit* dat, she doin' too many hits as it is. Here, light the blunt."

He light it.

"Her pops even offered me a million dollars if I find her."

He damn near choke. "A million?! Dollars?! Aw, man!"

I say, "Yeah, but I gotta tell him where she at."

"Damn. That's snitchin'."

Like that never crossed my mind.

Then he say, "But yo, it *is* his daughter, not like a cop or somethin'. I mean, I done told your mother plenty of times where you was."

I shoot back, "Yeah, and most of the time she was lookin' for my ass just to whoop it. Pass the blunt, man."

Fat's a fuckin' blunt hog. So then he say, real philosophical-like, "Yeah, I can dig it. Sound like you got a real dilemma. Almost like my man Stone in this Western I just read."

Oh shit, here we go.

"Ay, yo, Fats, why you always readin' them shits, and on top of that, turn around and tell me about it?" I say, in between hits of the el.

"'Cause, pilgrim, horse thieving a serious crime in these parts."

Whatever the fuck *that* suppose to mean.

"What you talkin' 'bout?"

"Sounds to me, you plannin' on ridin' that lil' filly off into the sunset."

Told you that stupid shit be makin' sense. He go on.

"Now let me tell you 'bout Stone. Stone is Stone, rough muhfucka. He got a dog wit' three legs, blind in one eye *and* got the mange, but he call the dog Lucky. Go figure. Anyway, Stone hate women. Ain't always hate 'em but he hate 'em now, let me tell you why."

I stop him 'cause I could tell this gonna take a minute and he got the blunt.

"Pass the el."

"Huh?"

"The el, Fats, pass the damn el."

Fats start talkin' and do that shit all the time. "Oh, oh, here," he exhales, "hold up. One mo' hit... I-ight. Now, where was I?"

"Stone hate women."

"Yeah, yeah, Stone hate women and got a fucked-up dog named Lucky. But the reason he hate women is 'cause one winter he shacked up wit' this Mexican chick. Hot chick but the winter colder than a muhfucka and they stuck in a cabin. Now Stone may hate women, but he love coffee, but ain't no water in the house. He send mamasita out to get some ice to melt for water. She go, gone damn near all night. So he go out and find Ma frozen in the snow. That's why he hate women."

I pass him the blunt, but I had to ask. "Why he hate women if she froze to death, Fathead?"

"'Cause she had his only coffee pot in her hand and it took all winter to thaw her ass out! Told you muhfucka love coffee."

He laugh and I laugh 'cause the kid shot out, plus I'm buzzin'. But still, what that got to do wit' me?

"'Cause women might be cold, but they always got somethin' we want."

I ain't say nothing, just nod my head and hit the blunt. All of a sudden I hear, "There he is, officer!"

I look around 'cause whenever somebody say "he" and "officer" in the same sentence and it's a black man around, 'specially if *you* the black man, it pays to be alert.

But it turns out it wasn't me, it was Fathead, and the voice is the little white cat wit' *The Source* and a Transit cop.

Fathead say, "Oops. Well, boys and girls, gotta go now, but remember the word for the day. Fuck her. Can you say fuck her? Say it with me, fuck her."

"Fuck her."

He say, "I-ight, One," then he gimme dap and dip, minglin' in the crowd. Plus he took the blunt... But he right, as usual, wit' that dumb shit.

Yeah, I think, fuck her, as I light my cigarette, fuck her. Then, right on cue, I feel my beeper vibrate. I don't even look and I *know* I ain't gotta tell y'all who it is, do I?

TIMEOUT

I-ight, second quarter, down by six baskets and the other squad on the run. Only advantage is the possession arrow my way...

Time for a sixty second timeout.

I can almost hear Spike Lee yellin', "Defense, you pansy! De-fense!!"

First off, this...*girl* just smiled and finagled me into her car, *knowin'* she had luggage in the trunk. Of all the dirty, underhanded...

Hold up. She did say somethin' about not knowing what I was gettin' into. I always was hardheaded... Okay, okay, but she lied. Yeah, she lied about her name and if it's anything I hate it's a liar. *Definite* foul call!

Then again... Not exactly. I just saw "Jazmine" on the vanity plate and assumed it was her and she just let me have my assumptions. Instead of a foul, that was a charge on my part...

Damn.

Okay, sports fans, time in and I'm at the Nynex checkin' my pager and dialin' the math...

She answers. "Didn't I tell you—"

I finish her sentence. "Yeah, yeah, I didn't know what I was getting into. Like, for instance, the newspapers, "Live at Five," the Most Wanted list."

"At least there's no midgets with whips."

"Pardon 'self?"

"Midgets with whips. Remember? You said—"

I cut her off 'cause she's takin' this extremely too calm. "I remember, *Fulani.*"

She let out a muffled giggle. "I never say that was my name, did I?"

I already thought of that, smart ass. "I already thought of that," I say, leavin' off the smart ass. "So, who's Jazmine?"

"The car."

"The what?"

She like, "The car. You know, like you name a horse. I named my car."

Rich chicks.

"Naw, I never had a horse, and usually, all I name my cars is stolen, but later for that. I finally got the answer to an earlier question."

"How so?"

"I don't think your father is very proud of you after all."

Silence... Then, "You've met?"

"Yeah, we *met* and it seems you got quite a history behind you. But silly me, I mistook it for a fat ass."

Silence again, then she say, "We need to talk."

"We talkin' now."

"Yes, but I wasn't prepared for... I'll call you back in an hour," then she hang up.

Oh, okay, so this how it's goin' down, huh? A few cryptic words like a box that say: Don't open, Pandora, and inside... International intrigue, civil war, veiled threats, million dollar bounties and she keep me open wit' some ol' cliché shit like, "We have to talk."

Why y'all ladies always say that? I mean, really. A friend you been platonic wit', one night up and say, "We need to talk," and the next thing you know, you washin' honey and whipped cream out of your only good sheets in the house.

Or your girl of the past six months say, "We need to talk," and the next thing you know you hopin' the baby got her eyes but your smarts 'cause shortie dumber than a muhhh...

So here I am, in the middle of some ol' ghetto James Bond shit, and she drop the oldest line in the book. We need to talk. But that ain't the dumb part, the dumb part is I'm actually *goin' for it*. Yeah, shorties is cold, but I love coffee, too—'specially black.

Just call me Stone.

CHAPTER SIX: CHINATOWN

I'm thinkin', I'm gonna need a quick brush-up on my current affairs, 'cause they say it's three sides to every story and I could tell the king was bein' selective with his explanation of the situation. So I need to know what side of the fence he really on. I mean, he could be the Willie in this web and throwin' shade just to get me to cop out to his sob story. 'Cause, yo, let's keep it gulley; men always blamin' women for they woes. Look at Adam and how he put the apple on Eve, we all know it ain't really go down like that, but ahhh, that's another story...

Anyway, I slid up on Utica to a little record store that shall remain nameless because of its basement activities, lookin' for my peeps.

I walk in the spot to the sounds of Ninja Man blarin' out the speakers, and head over to the Dread behind the counter.

"Where gwan, my yout'?" he ask when I approached.

"I need to see M."

He eye me for a minute, runnin' his fingers through his Rasta beard.

"M?"

"Tell him it's Sam. He'll know what's up."

Dread walk away from the counter and say somethin' to some dreaded sister sitttin' on a stool, then he disappear around the corner. In a few minutes, my man M-1 come from the back, followed by the dread.

"Sam! Whut up, sun?" He step up and gimme a

brotherly hug, "Where you been, yo? I ain't seen you in a minute."

"You know how I do," I say, keepin' my answer vague.

He look at me like, "You i-ight?"

"I need to holler at you."

M nodded his head for me to follow him into the back. We went down some stairs to a little storage room that served as The Black Uhuru Movement's Brooklyn headquarters. It was dark and dank, but the walls were covered in colorful red, black and green-based murals, a Malcolm X poster and a few full-body target posters riddled in the heart and head areas.

Stic-Man was sittin' behind the makeshift desk in the corner readin' a newspaper as I walked in.

"Ahhhh, my mannn! How you, baby? How you?" He gave me the same type hug M gave me.

"Loungin', duke," was my answer.

"So whut, you back to reenlist? The Revolution needs brothers like you, sun, you know that."

I light my cigarette and say, "Not right now, Stic. I had to hang up my beret for a minute. But yo, I need some information."

M like, "Whut up?"

So I take a seat and run the whole situation down to 'em. I start by tellin' 'em about them BX cats on the train.

M-1 like, "You talkin' about little Gut from Co-op? Yeah, my uncle used to fuck wit' his cousin."

Didn't I tell you about them ghetto connects?

Anyway, I explain about the body in the trunk, the king and the gorilla and about the Q4 and the fingerprints.

Stic-Man say, "So *you* the unidentified fingerprints in the whip, huh?" Then he chuckle like, "Man, how you be getting in shit like this?"

I shrug my shoulders like, "I ain't have no light," then I blow out a puff of smoke.

So M-1 like, "So what is it you need to know?"

"What's the science on this king and Amantu? He

one of them Crazy King cats or what?"

M-1 stand up and walk over to a rolled-up world map, like be in school. He pull it down wit' a yank, then say, "As far as the day-to-day, I ain't up on Amantu like that, but I do know a little about the history. Peep it, this is Amantu." He point to a tiny dot right off the coast of Cameroon, right below Nigeria.

"That's it? That lil' joint is what all the fuss is about?"

M-1 continue like, "It may be small, but it plays an important but very little-known part in our history. Back during the early days of the slave trade, one of the first big rebellions took place at a nearby slave port. Members of several tribes defeated their captors and fled to the island."

"Sorta like Amistad?" I ask.

He nod, then say, "It became a guerilla island of sorts because they would launch night raids from Amantu, sabotaging slave ships, freeing potential slaves and getting more guns. Britain couldn't have it, so they tried to subdue the island. The Amantians fought hard, so in the end the British realized it wasn't worth the effort. It was one of the reasons that this particular slave port was closed down, which subsequently led to the British attitude of abolishing slavery.

"Years later, Britain, being one of the first to outlaw slavery, sent ambassadors to Amantu and slowly but surely won their trust."

"Tricknology. Kill 'em wit' kindness."

"Exactly. Unfortunately, the Amantians didn't see it until too late. They began to rely too heavily on the British administration and pounds, so in the early 1900's, they took control of the island and backed a half-bred puppet ruler. Then about forty years ago, along comes Mofusu."

"Shortie father, the king?"

M-1 say, "Yeah. His father started the fight for independence and Mofusu finished it. He tossed out the entire administration and attempted to return to pure Amantian tradition, which is really a hybrid of the traditions of the original tribes who first fled to the island. But Amantu fell on bad times—that is, until they found oil in a remote part of the island."

"Black gold," I say, 'cause everything startin' to come together now.

"Black gold. Now, since Mofusu had had his fill of dealing with Europeans of any kind, he refused to fall into the Western web of the United States. Iran, seeing Mofusu's stance, thought they had a prime candidate for OPEC, but Mofusu declined but said he'd be a supporter. Smart move, if you ask me, not to commit to someone until they commit to you." I nod in agreement. He continued.

"Then, Mofusu step to Libya and Nigeria and try to get them to join an all-African type OPEC, but including all the natural resources of the continent. He wanted to unite all of Africa. Now just *think* what kind of power would be created in the Motherland if *all* of Africa united? Half the world's resources are right there."

"Say word."

"Word," M repeat, givin' me dap. "So needless to say, America asshole get tight. They tried the diplomatic approach at first, but word now is that they're behind the civil war in Amantu. And if what the king say about his daughter is true, then it ain't hard to tell they planning to install—"

I complete the sentence. "Fulani."

He nod... Damn. She *is* an African Pocahontas.

"Her father said the same thing."

Stic-Man can tell by the look on my grill, this shit a little too much to swallow, so he say, "Yeah, sun, shortie might be a dime, but shit, black widow spiders probably look good to the male, too... Before they kill 'em."

So I'm like, "I feel you, but yo..." my voice trail 'cause I'm at a loss for words.

M-1 cut in. "Peep show, just the fact that when the heat was on Ma came to America, that says a lot. Why here? Why not...London or France or wherever? I'll tell you, because this her comfort zone. She down wit' America."

45

I can't front—the shit make sense—but how could Ma be so fuckin' naïve? I'm in the midst of marinatin' on all this when I catch a sensation on my hip... My beeper. I check the number and it's different than the first time so I figure this is it.

"Yo Stic, lemme see your celly." He hands me the cell phone and I dial the math.

"It's me," she say.

"I know," I monotone my reply.

"You okay? You sound, I don't know..."

I answer for her. "Confused?"

"Somewhat."

"And I shouldn't be?"

No response, so I reiterate. "Well?"

"You hungry?" she ask.

Ay, yo, what is up wit' this girl and food? Now what would Freud say? Hmm...

"Naw, not really."

She like, "Well, too bad. Meet me in Chinatown at Fong's and order shrimp fried rice for two. No shrimp. Just like that, you got it?"

"Yeah, I got it, shrimp fried rice."

"With no shrimp," she adds.

"Yeah, yeah, I got you, but yo, Ful—"

She had already hung up. I close the celly, take a deep breath then look at M-1 and Stic-Man.

"Chinatown."

Stic just shook his head wit' a slight smirk as he handed me the keys to the whip.

I'm like, "What?" 'cause of how they lookin' at me.

Stic like, "I'm tellin' you sun, you in over your head with this one."

"Yeah well... I guess I'll just hafta tighten up on my backstroke, huh?" I said, takin' the keys... Then I dipped.

So I'm drivin' outta BK, smokin' a Newport, thoughts

swirlin' over this shit. I'm sayin', what do *you* think I should do—or better yet, what would *you* do?

You ladies probably wanna see a brother throw on the shining armor, mount up my steed and hold Ma down. And you fellas probably like, "Man, shortie got mo' issues than *The Source*! She done killed one nigga for God knows what *and* she an international snake. Never get involved wit' somethin' you can't leave in thirty seconds. Fuck how fly she is—bounce!"

I hear all y'all, but yo, I'm a strong believer that everything happens for a reason, you know? So I'm sayin', meetin' Ma like I did... It's more to this shit than just oil and pretty eyes, say word.

So yo, ladies, I'ma hafta go wit' y'all on this one. But know this, I ain't goin' in wit' no "S" on my chest. And fellas, Sam ain't sold out the code, but I gotta at least find out what my prints is tied up in 'cause they'll be comin' for me anyway, ya'm mean?

So basically, I'm headin' to Chinatown for answers— no expectations, you feel me? She owe me at least that much, then I'm out, no long kiss goodnight...

Did somebody say, "Yeah, right?" Maybe it's just me.

I-ight, next page...

Ahh, Chinatown. The ghetto emporium of my youth. Who could forget the Cazal stolen right off of Canal and all the ten-carat door knocker earrings your girl used to sweat you to cop her? Don't front; Canal had you open, sellin' fireworks and shit. So you know the spot, but for those who don't, just take a chunk of China's metropolis and put it in New York, you wit' me?

Okay, if you are, you realize every other corner got a Chinese restaurant and it seem like they all named Fong's, Wong's, Chong's... Yo, I wonder what "ong" mean in Chinese 'cause it seem to be interchangeable.

Anyway, I find the spot and go in. Regular-looking

joint. I'm lookin' around. Couple of Chinese cats in the back, sound like they arguin' or just talkin' fast and a middle-aged Chinese lady behind the bulletproof glass.

I approach the window.

"Yeah, um. Let me get shrimp fried rice for two..." Then I remember, "Oh yeah, no shrimp."

She look at me like I'm crazy. *Shrimp* fried rice wit' no *shrimp*?

So I'm wonderin' if this is the right Fong's, or maybe she said Wong's... But just as my memory start boxin' wit' my thoughts, she say, "Hold on," then she pick up a phone and say some shit in Chinese.

I realize, yo, I remember the language. This the language shortie was speakin' in the car the night she scooped me...

Make a mental note of that.

So boom, conversation take, like, thirty seconds, then she hang up and say, "Follow me," then she open the little side door into the kitchen.

As we walk through the kitchen, I'm lookin' for signs of cats—fur, tails, muffled meows, anythin'—but I find nothin'. No offense to my Asian cats, but you know the ghetto rumor.

We go out through a door in the back of the kitchen that leads to a set of ascendin' steps. We go up, get to a door down the hallway. She knock, then open the door, but she don't go in so neither do I. I'm like, you first, but I don't say it; I just stand there. She wave her hand towards the door then go back downstairs, and on her way, she say somethin' in her language I swear sounded like, "dumb motherfucker"—but maybe it was just me.

So I peep in. First thing I see is one of those Chinese screens, you know, type shit people get dressed behind wit' them fly little dragons painted all over it? Yeah, like that. I see Fulani's silhouette behind it.

She say, "Well, are you coming in or not?"

I enter, shuttin' the door behind me. Besides the screen there's a bed wit' red satin sheets pushed back like she just got up, a TV in the corner and a small patio-type table and chairs over by the window.

Fulani come out in a kimono-type robe, all purple wit' little red and yellow flowers on it. She got her hair in a bun and it look like she just got out of the shower, skin tone glowin' and glistenin'. I'm standin' there, fuckin' mesmerized, yo, and I don't even see the black cat she bend down and pick up as she sit down at the table.

Ohhh, so this is where they be hidin' 'em, huh? Cat purrin' on her lap, she strokin' it...

I wish I was a cat.

She say, "Have a seat. I had Ching Lee bring up some tea—Jasmine."

She smiled, and her smile brought me back to reality. I shake off her beauty and sit down, ready to get down to business.

"Ay, yo, now what up? I'm here."

Fulani like, "Oh, you're going to just waste my tea?"

"You gonna just waste my time?" I shoot back, 'cause I'm getting a little vexed wit' the persona, ya feel me?

"What did my father say to you?" she say, then sip her tea as she rubbed the cat; cat purrs...

...and for my next wish...

"What he said, what he didn't say."

She found that interestin'. "Oh? And what *didn't* he say?"

"I'll get to that. First, what he *did* was send a team of gorillas to my spot, kicked in my door and yoked me up like egg whites. He basically had me kidnapped and took me to the Consulate, then shit got really deep. To hear your father tell it, you a conniving little wench with your hand in a dirty, little cookie jar."

I pause for effect but her composure remained steady... Too steady. She put the cat down and repeated, "Conniving little wench?"

"Well, not in those exact words. It was more to the effect of you got American bed partners wit' a whole lot of money and guns and you got a whole lot of drugs and land

and everybody gettin' along just fine."

"Is that all?"

"Is that all?! Damn, he put your name in everythin' but the Kennedy assassination! What else is there?"

Yo, Ma is too calm. I thought, naw, I hoped she'd be like, oh, the news, my father, it's all lies, boo hoo. Even if she *was* lyin' it would be better than this complacent shit.

She light an incense and say, "Do you believe him?"

"Should I?"

She offered me the cup of tea again but I shook it off. "Does it matter? I'm sure we all have a few bones in our closet," she said, eyeing me slyly.

"*Bones*, not *bodies*." Yo, I'm startin' to feel like a dog chasin' his tail, goin' in circles.

Fulani stirred her tea, still eyeing me, then asked, "What do you want out of life?"

"What?" I'm not wit' this parable shit.

"Just what I said—what do you want out of life? Don't you have dreams? Goals? Everybody does—I do. I want to be queen of my country and own parts of the world explorers didn't know existed. Don't you ever think about stuff like that?"

I say, "Yo, what I'm thinkin' 'bout now is what the hell is you talkin' about? What I want? I'll tell you what I want—a fuckin' straight answer, Madame Butterfly! Fuck the metaphors! You got my name mixed up in some bullshit concernin' a body—that alone got me thinkin' not only about life, but *twenty* to life!"

I'm heated now; dime or no dime, shortie gonna make *me* get ugly.

She say, "So, you want the truth?"

"Please." I almost expected her to say, "You can't handle the truth," but I guess she ain't see the movie. Instead she said, "Everything my father says is true," then kinda shrug her shoulders, like, fuck it, I'm an African Pocahontas, then she sip her tea.

I'm dumbfounded.

"Everything?"

She slowly nod her head while she eye my reaction. So I'm like, "Hold up, let me get this straight. You *are* sellin' drugs to America?"

"Yes."

"In New York?"

"Mmmhmm."

"To *my* people?" Ay, yo, I hate drugs, word up. And I know some of y'all sayin', but you smoke weeeed. Shut the fuck up. I'm talking about sell-your-soul, kill-your-baby-type drugs, i-ight?

After a moment of silence Fulani stand up, float over to the window wit' a giggle, and say, "Oh, come, come. Don't get all self-righteous on me now. Not the pistol-packing, weed-smoking roughneck I picked up last night," all facetious-like.

So I stand up. "Whatever, i-ight, I'm talkin' about that shit killin' my people, *your* people, in the streets... And not only that, you got the fuckin' American government fightin' your wars against your own?! Killin' *your* people in *your* country! What—" then she cut me off and blazed me.

"I'll tell you what's killing my people! You want to know?! It's backwards-ass traditions! Outdated, archaic... governments! Not enterin' the twenty-first century with an eye on expansion, technology, strategic global partners! That's what kills more than any drug I can manufacture.

"With America behind me, I can fortify a strong position. Sure, Amantu may be small, just an island, but once I'm in the door, once the groundwork is laid... Today, Amantu; tomorrow, all of Africa!"

In my mind she sound like Pinky and the Brain, but wit' the physique of Cleopatra.

She went on as if tryin' to convince herself. "...And so what if I ship in a few pounds or tons or whatever? If I stop, will Columbia? Bolivia? Indonesia? As long as there's demand, there'll be supply."

As she turned to look out the window, I think her argument sound a whole lot like the one that goes, "they gonna get it from somewhere, might as well be from me," I

51

just ain't know that lame-ass excuse was international.

"Look Jaz—I mean, Fulani. You probably got good intentions for what you doin', but like they say, the road to hell is paved wit' 'em."

"My people are living in hell now, as we speak. I didn't start this war, I merely gave vent to the seethe already there. Why should my people live like peasants, depending upon the whims of nature to subsist, while the rest of the world so lavishly laps away at our resources? I refuse to sit idly by, doing nothing. I am to be a queen, responsible for countless lives, and—"

But I cut her off, like, "And what about the ones that's been lost? 'Cause you damn sure responsible for that."

She shrug it off and answered, "They were fools to attempt to fight the inevitability of change."

"And you really think a few extra dollars and American guns can undo what your pops done did for the last thirty-somethin' years?"

"My father...was a different man then. He has changed," she responded, as she looked out the window over Chinatown.

"Naw. Maybe it's you that changed."

"Maybe."

Now I see where all this is comin' from, so it's my turn to dig deep. "This ain't about the money, though, is it 'Lani?"

She turn and look at me like I'm crazy. "Not about the money?" Then she throw her head back and laugh, but she just like a book to me and I still remember her Chapter One: Daddy's little girl.

"What's the matter? Daddy forget too many birthdays?"

She still chuckles, but subtly the giggles subside. Just like I thought.

"I mean, come on now, you already got mo' cheese than you could ever spend, right?"

"You mean, my family—"

"No, I mean your *father*."

She turns back to the window, but I can tell she's still all ears. "Naw, this ain't what you really want. Power. Money. You—" Now *she* cut *me* off.

"How in the *hell* could you possibly fathom what *I* want? I can't even tell you my dreams, because you can't speak the language! ...All the money you've ever had in your life was probably less than my weekly shopping sprees abroad," she said, as she flipped me off with her wrist and said somethin' foul in French. But I disregarded the insult and continued.

"I can see you now. Your own horse, probably your own horse ranch...diamonds to your elbows, up to your ears in fly whips. Personal yachts. Everything a girl could ever want... That is, until you said, Daddy, can you play with me? See what I made, Daddy, I drew it just for you."

She said it low, in a whisper, but I heard her. "Shut up."

But I wouldn't. "Look Daddy, I can spell my name. But he still wouldn't look, would he?"

She gets louder, "*Shut...up.*"

"Or, when you fell off your million dollar horse and scraped your million dollar knee, I bet you said, look, Daddy, I'm hurt. I'm hurting, Daddy, will you look now? Will you kiss it? But he didn't kiss—"

That was as far as I got.

"*Shut up!*" she screamed as she lunged at me, swinging wildly, but I just sidestepped and grabbed her, pulling her to my chest. She pushed away with tears streaming down her cheeks. "Get out!"

She scared the shit outta the cat but not me. I didn't budge.

"Get out!" Now she really cryin'. Maybe I did go a little too deep too fast, so I turn for the door, hatin' that it had to end like this. But as I reach for the doorknob, Fulani come from behind me and slam shut the half-cracked door I just opened... In or out, damn, make up your mind, but then I see in her eyes...

THE LOOK...

She grab my head and pull me damn near down her throat. I had to wrestle to get my lips out her mouth and I'm on fire instantly. Tongue taste like strawberries and shit, so I...

Hold up... Naw, this ain't right. I'd pushed her buttons, caught her off-guard, uncovered wounds that never really healed... So I push away.

"Naw, 'Lani, you upset, just—"

That's when she let down her hair, shit hang down damn near to her ass, and then... She slowly undid her kimono belt and let it hang open. Nothin' underneath but yellow satin panties.

Aw, daamnnn!! I try and speak, "Um, y-yo, I-I—"

She let the robe drop...

Ay, yo, my whole body achin', sun, no doubt, and I'm thinkin', Yo, Ms. Badu, I'm sorry but just this once...

Naw. Fuck am I thinkin'? I can't do Ma like this. It ain't right. That ain't lust in her eyes, it's confusion. A scared little girl playin' a dangerous game... But if you look in most women eyes who easy wit' they sex, you see the same thing.

So I say, "Fulani, maybe I said too much. No, I did say too much, but whatever you feelin' you can't get love like this."

"Did I say love? I wanna fuck." She step closer to me.

Yo, it's takin' everything I *got* not to push up on Ma. I'm thinkin' of fat white men in thongs tryin' to keep my soldier from salutin', and I'm like, "Them just words, Ma, them just—" then she hug me real hard, and I realize it ain't a sex hug. Yo, it's like somebody hold on to a rope when they drownin'... Holdin' on for dear life. Her whole body tremblin' like she don't never wanna let go. Ay, yo, sun, I almost cried, but don't go tellin' ere'body 'cause I ain't no sentimental motherfucka.

I picked up her robe and draped it over her shoulders and then I laid down wit' her. So I just hold shortie 'til she fall asleep. After a while, I'm layin' there

thinkin', yeah this is i-ight, but I swear I gotta piss...
Fade to black.

Now, hold up! Another timeout, 'cause I can hear y'all out there now. "That's it?! A hug?!

Y'all shorties was probably expectin' some shit involving the words "slow...long...and deep" and you dudes probably was wonderin' why I ain't got Ma climbin' the walls and waking the neighborhood, huh?

Well, I'll tell you why. 'Cause Sam ain't no trick wit' an easy dick, that's *why*. I don't take no charity pussy, and I don't give no charity dick. You get this, it's 'cause you earn it, not 'cause you beg for it.

So all y'all ladies out there, next time you just want your man to hold you close and he can't wit'out wantin' to fuck, drop his trick ass. He probably fuckin' your cousin, too. And you cats who can't say no to some quick ass, that's the difference between me and you. I probably turnin' down mo' pussy than you pay for. Trick-ass muhfuckas...

Okay, time in. I had to get that off my chest...

Now, where was I? Oh yeah. Yeah, we fell asleep.

Strange dream. Tell you 'bout it sometime... But ahh, somewhere between Lalaland and reality, I heard a voice—better yet, a melody—hummin' in my ears. I open my eyes to see it was Fulani sittin' in the open window, half on the fire escape, smokin' a el and singing a song in her native tongue. I see the sun has gone down and I start to get up but refrain, scared I might stop her song that was serenadin' me like a summer breeze. I lay there and listened.

When she finished, I let silence have its way wit' the tempo and then I said, "Your father wants to see you."

She didn't respond. Just took another toke of the el,

so I sit up.

"You know, he offered me a million dollars for your safe return."

"You mean my capture, don't you?" This time I ain't respond, so she continued. "Why didn't you take it?"

"How you know I didn't?"

"Well, here I am," she said, and mockingly extended her wrists, palms up, like I was gonna cuff her or somethin'.

"I been called a lot of things, most of which was spelled right, but s-n-i-t-c-h just don't fit my character." She hand me the el. I decline, don't ask me why.

She repositioned herself on the windowsill to face me and said, "It wouldn't have mattered anyway. I would've seen them coming a mile away, and then *poof*, I would've, how do you say, vaporized?"

I figured as much. You don't travel in the circles Ma in and not recognize the double cross.

"So then," I say, "what you gonna do?"

She walks over to the bed and sit on the edge. "What do you mean, what am I going to do? What I've been doing, that's what. Nothing's changed."

"But I'm sayin', your father's onto you and any minute he can blow the cover—"

She cut me off wit' a defiant chuckle.

"My father is in no position to meddle in my affairs. He's finished, I assure you of that. In seventy-two hours, it is the beginning of the end. The Amantu apocalypse."

Apocalypse?

But before I could quip I hear the TV, which been on a "Martin" rerun the whole time, make that ol' irritatin'-ass buzzin' noise, then the announcer break in like, "We interrupt this program for a special announcement."

I turn my attention to the TV; it's a repeat of the earlier scene wit' the Q4 at the docks, but this time they got a composite sketch...of ME!

What the fuck?! I knew it was just a matter of time before them prints came back. Damn!

I turn up the TV just as the announcer say, "The fingerprints found in the car of Princess Fulani have been identified to be those of one Samuel Black. This is his composite. He is now *the* prime suspect in the murder earlier in Jersey City and the possible kidnapping of Princess Fulani, heiress to the Amantu throne. If you see this man..."

I didn't hear nothin' else 'cause I went blank until I hear Martin sayin', "Daaaamn!" Damn, Damn, *Damn!* Murder? Kidnapping? Aw, man! I look at shortie and she lookin' at me in amazement. Well, now it's definitely too late to wash this girl outta my hair. I'm in the game 'til the final score. "Damn," is all I can say.

"Sam..."

"What?"

"Don't be upset with me."

Don't be upset?! Don't be upset?! Just because of my charming personality, I'm now implicated in a fuckin' murder *and* potential kidnappin'...and she say, don't be upset—like she made a mistake and I got pickles wit' dat instead of tomatoes!

I guess she saw all this in my eyes for the second or so before I responded, so she say, "Listen, I know everything looks bad now, but in seventy-two hours everything will be fine. I can't tell you why, not now, but please trust me. I have friends..."

But I'm like, "Seventy-two hours?! Friends?! Look, I don't know what you got up your sleeves, but from what I could see of your hands, I don't *wanna* know! All I want is out, ya'm sayin'? O-u-t!"

"But what about the police?"

"Fuck the police," I say, sounded like Eazy-E, "them I can handle. You, I'm not so sure."

"So what are you gonna do? Just run out in the streets?" she say, flarin' her arms like a hit pigeon.

"You got a better idea?" is what I wanna know.

"Look, you don't know what's going on."

So I shoot back, "So why don't you tell me?"

57

"I will, but for now, you have to trust me."

"Trust you?! I—" but I was cut off by a knock on the door.

"Who is it?" Fulani asks.

"It's us."

I guess she know the voice 'cause she start to answer the door, but I grab her arm. "Yo, don't Ching-a-Ling or Ching Chong always call 'fore she send somebody up?"

'Lani answer, "Yeah, but these the friends I to—" That's all she got out before a shotgun blast blew a hole in the middle of the door...

Time to go!

I grab Ma hand and instinctively reach for my... Damn. They got my Boom Boom Belinda, so I grab my coat and we do a catwalk to the fire escape just as a barrage of bullets lit up the apartment. On her way out, Ma reached behind the screen and snatch up a Mac 11. Surprise, surprise—say hello to my lil' friend!

"Go 'head up, I'm right behind you," I tell Fulani as I return fire on these crabs who I can't see 'cause I'm on the fire escape shootin' back down into the apartment. I run and catch up wit' Fulani and when we hit the roof, I say, "You got a helluva idea of a friend!"

But before she could respond, two thug-lookin' cats come out on the roof and open up wit' what seems to be the biggest gun in the world. The Mac 11 just bitched up and jammed.

Damn!

So me and Ma runnin', duckin', dodgin' and leapin' roof to roof, tryin' to get away from these motherfuckas. Nothin' major about roof jumpin', like cracks in the sidewalk...until we come to the Grand fuckin' Canyon!

"We can't leap that!" Ma holler hysterically.

I look back and I see the cavalry closin' in. "You know a better way?" I shout as I'm duckin' slugs at the same time.

"But, but—" she stammers, so I grab her hand, "Yo, I got you, i-ight?"

Corny, I know, but effective. So we back up ten paces and sprint. The Lone Ranger and Tonto musta thought we couldn't make it, either, until we landed safe on the other side...barely. They start back a-cappin', but we protected by the extended lip of the building's masonry.

"What are we gonna do?" she ask me, like I'm *Nas*tradamus or somebody, but I holler back, "We gonna live, fuck you think?"

And in between automatic bursts of artillery, we take off for the roof door, just barely makin' it, shit is ricochetin' everywhere. But we ain't out of the woods yet... Naw, not by a long shot, 'cause we still gotta go down eight flights of stairs and I don't know *what's* waitin' for us in the streets. Ay, yo, ain't no use to me lyin', I was scared than a muhfucka!

We hit the street, I hear mad sirens and for the first time in my life, I'm *glad* to hear 'em. We see an officer on horseback.

"There! It's a policeman!" I hear 'Lani yell, and we run over to him. I say, "Excuse me officer," I'm outta breath, "we're being chased—" I couldn't even finish before this motherfucka blow his whistle and he start reachin' for his joint!

I don't know where Ma got it from, but she grabbed this nigga waist-high and flipped him off the horse! Ay, yo, I know y'all think I'm lyin', but word, sun, Ma went *Shaolin Temple*-style on this cat. He col' sleep.

She hop on the horse and lean down, extendin' her hand to me... Hell, no! But then I glance back...

I see a cop car comin' hot and heavy, I'm like, damn, I *am* a fugitive. But hol' up, it's dark, how the fuck the cop recognize me? Then I think, Ching Lee, maybe she dimed me out. But didn't 'Lani say she knew these cats? Yo, man, will somebody tell me what the *fuck* is goin' on?!

This is what I'm thinkin' on my way up the side of this horse. Damn, I hope Ma did have a horse ranch, 'cause if not...

She break out like the wind and this lazy-ass glue

59

factory reject of a horse take off like, ohhh, you wanna get own like *that*! I ain't know them New York horses had it in 'em. Anyway...

We gallopin' towards the intersection when two cop cars skid up and block the street. Ohhhh, shit! Then I saw how close Ma was gallopin' towards the cops and I'm like, what she gonna do, ride through 'em? But when them hooves hit the hood of the car, I knew, nooo, we gonna ride *over* 'em! I heard somebody scream like a girl and I started to tell Ma to hold it down—that is, 'til I realized it was me.

I look back and cops is everywhere, but they can't shoot 'cause so many people around.

Round One to Ma Duke! I knew she had equestrian thighs for somethin'. But... I knew it was too good to be true. I'm sayin', that ol' horse was doin' okay, gallopin' along, had my nuts vibratin' and everything, until...

He saw *her.*

Her, as in the all-white mare pullin' the carriage up Delancey Street. Just our luck, or lack of it, that in the middle of a heated police chase, the damn horse gonna wanna get some pussy! Now *that's* somethin' you'll never see in a Western, huh?

Damn.

Soon as he saw her, he slowed up, ears perked erect and I swear the motherfucker started grinnin'. So there we are, these two horses nose to nose in the middle of the street, and we got half the fuckin' NYPD in hot pursuit!

Fulani try one more time to get the nigga back on track, but he just looked back at her like, shiiittt, and continued wit' his date.

"Later for him, Ma, we got to go!" I holler, grabbin' Fulani hand and slidin' off the horse. So boom, we hop off and run straight across the street, damn near gettin' hit twice and 5-0 closin' in. Ain't no way we gonna beat 'em on foot.

Thank God for red lights.

'Cause, yo, I caught some kid on a CBR 1200. *Now* we talkin' 'cause Ghetto Sam *do* the bikes, say word. And to my man on the CBR, sorry 'bout that devastatin' right hook I had to splash you wit', I was in a hurry, but hit me on the hip (www.ghettosam.com) and I'll straighten you for the bike.

Where was I? Oh yeah, so when my man hit the pavement, me and 'Lani was 0-60 in two blinks, puttin' distance between us and po-po. But since I ain't fluent wit' the ins and outs of Chinatown, 5-0 still keepin' pace. So I'm lookin' for a way to lose these muhfuckas... That's when I see the crowd of people in front of some warehouse-turned-rave-club. Perfect opportunity, so I head straight at the club, full speed, 'cause I don't plan on stoppin'.

Fulani yell, "What are you doing?!"

"I hate waitin' on line!" I'm sayin', don't you?

The bouncer a big dude, but not big enough to stop a 1200, so he wise up and dive aside as I drive straight through the front door to the amazed applaud of the crowd.

Now to all y'all gate crashers, don't try this at home, because I had to do it... I wasn't on the guest list.

Once we get inside, I drop the bike and half the club turn around and look at me. Now you know what they say'll happen if you shout, "Fire!" in a crowded theatre? Imagine what happened when I shouted, "Raid!" in that crowded club... Muhfuckas snatchin' off wigs and other muhfuckas grabbin' 'em and puttin' 'em on as they bumrush the door, just as 5-0 was on the way in...

I love it when a plan comes together, 'cause now all me and Fulani had to do was follow the frenzy out into the street and scatter. Wit' a couple hundred people runnin' in every direction, who 5-0 supposed to chase?

We sprinted another three blocks until we reached a dark alley and all I could hear was sirens everywhere. Out of breath, she look at me and say, "Are you crazy?! Riding up in a club like that! You're going to get us killed!!"

I just look at her like, *I'm* gonna get us killed? "I-ight, what the fuck is goin' on?"

"I-I-I don't—" she stammer, and I can tell shortie totally discombobulated. "I recognized the voice but..." her voice drowned in a flood of confusion.

"Well, for whatever reason, your friends have switched allegiances," I say, but I'm still thinkin' about the cop on the horse.

"I need... I need to make a phone call," Fulani say, then she starts walkin' toward the nearest phone booth, but I grab her arm.

"And call who, more friends?" She marinated on that, so I added, "Look, the way I see it, whatever was, ain't no more. This mighta been your game but you ain't holdin' the ball no more."

She look at me in an irritated fashion, like, "What are you talking about?! Speak *English!*"

So I throw it back at her. "You gotta trust *me* now. That proper grammar enough for ya?"

"Trust you?" she say, wit' her arms folded across her breast, lookin' me up and down.

"Yeah. Now let's go."

The Adventures of Ghetto Sam

CHAPTER SEVEN: HOMELESS ROYALTY

Okay, for all y'all keepin' stats, let's recap, shall we?

Cat meets girl, girl has body—well *a* body and a *dead* body—cat gets kidnapped by girl's father, girl's father tells cat that girl is the embodiment of Lillith, cat still sees girl, girl gets naked, girl needs love, cat feel sorry for girl, cat catches murder rap, cat *and* girl get shot at by girl's friends, cop chase cat and girl through New York on horseback...

All caught up?

I could tell you who's winnin' *if* I could figure out who's on first and what's on second, ya feel me? So that's what me and shortie Costello gonna vociferate on now... Here... Where else? Under the subway, in a cut wit' a few of my friends—homeless, that is—Minnie Pearl and Waterboy.

Shortie was buggin' when I told her where we were headed; she thought we were getting on the subway.

She sounded like Rae Dawn Chong in *Beat Street*. "Down there? I'm not going down there."

But I was like, "Oh, yes you are, 'cause we ain't safe nowhere until you tell me what's goin' on... Oh yeah, watch the third rail."

So here we is, where rats the size of small dogs sexually assault felines that stray from the pack. When we get to the spot, Minnie Pearl and Waterboy done made a pot of beef stew as the subway rumbles in the distance. I could tell Ma ain't too comfortable around my less-than-

63

enthusiastic-to-shower friends, but fuck it; she got a smell that's startin' to make the rats smell sweet. So if anybody, it's time *she* come clean.

When Minnie Pearl see me, she holler, "Binkie!"

That's her name for me. Only family call me that so watch your mouth. Minnie Pearl good peeps, yo. I don't know how she ended up like this, 'cause she ain't never tell me and I ain't never ask.

But Waterboy... His mother was a dope fiend, and he was born some say retarded but I say pure 'cause he ain't gotta deal wit' the day-to-day bullshit come wit' bein' so-called normal; I'm sayin', what's normal anyway? His mama see his condition when he was an infant and she left him in a dumpster...

Bitch.

Minnie Pearl come along and find him. Raise him up. He like twelve now and big as hell. Pearl say his first word was "Wata."

Minnie Pearl say, "What?"

He repeat. "Wata?" and point to the faucet. Cat love water, so ever since, Minnie Pearl call him Waterboy.

They like family to me. Matter of fact, they *is* family to me. Whenever I need a spot to lounge or get away, you can find me in the heart of the urban catacombs. Either that or when I'm in trouble, as usual...as in now.

So yeah, Pearl say, "Binkie, you just in time for dinner, as always." Then she see Fulani. "And who is this pretty young thang here?"

Waterboy point at Fulani's robe and say, "She naked," then he cover his mouth and giggle. Fulani pull her robe tighter.

"Hush, Water," Pearl tell 'im, then she say, "Why is this child naked in the middle of November, Binkie? What you done got into now?"

"Ask her!" I say, 'cause I'm vexed. "Ask Shortie Shootout what I'm into now!"

Fulani like, "Look, I don't know what's going on now, *either*, all right?!" Then she start shakin' like she cold. Yo, it is pretty breezy down here, so I throw Ma my coat—hard. She look at it like she gonna throw it down, but a sharp gust of air made her think otherwise. She put it on, then she say, "What do you want me to say? I already said I was sorry, okay?!"

"Sorry? Sorry?! You got me a murder rap, damn near get a motherfucka killed and—"

"Binkie," Minnie Pearl say, cuttin' me off.

"Ma'am?"

"Watch yo' mouth."

"Yes, ma'am." I'm pacin' back and forth, boilin'. I catch my breath and look at shortie and she look like she about to cry. Why I always gotta be a sucker for tears? "Look, sh—I mean, stuff might not be all that clear right now, but dig, we *both* wanted and I need to know why. Who was that back there?" I'm tryin' to be calm.

'Lani tell me, "Some friends of Phil." Just like that, like I kick it wit' "Phil" all the time.

"Phil who?"

Phil Donahue? Phillip Banks from "The Fresh Prince of Bel Air"? Phil—

"Chambers," she say, like it's the most natural thing in the world to be talkin' about Phil Chambers, owner of Banktel, the biggest bank in the fuckin' world. Cat got so much cream, in *Fortune 500*, his picture ain't got no figures next to it, it just say, this motherfucka got dough, ya feel me?

"Phil Chambers? As in Banktel Phil Chambers?" Shit is getting deep *fo' real.*

"What other Phil Chambers is there?" she quip, real sarcastic-like.

"You tellin' me Mr. Monetary was the cat payin' them slugs back there?"

I'm tryin' to imagine this geeked-out, four-eyed dude holdin' a cannon, talkin' 'bout, "Bitch, better have my money." It would be comical if the cannon wasn't pointed at me.

"No, of course not. People in his charge that I've dealt

with before." She lookin' for a place to sit, but everything is, uh, either wet, stank or dirty, so she just kinda lean on the wall.

"Yo, 'Lani, I think we better take this from the top."

Man, listen. The story Ma lay on me is straight outta some espionage spy book. Shit that'll make James Bond be like, yo, I can't fuck wit' that. She start off by tellin' me the war in her country ain't about rulers and democracy, but about land and untapped oil reserves her father just came across in Amantu, which I already knew. But her pops, smart man, ain't fuckin' wit' the U.S. on the crude like that, confirmin' M-1's earlier theory. So Ma met Phil Chambers in Hawaii three summers ago. The way she said it, I *knew* it was more to it, but later for that right now.

Anyway, Banktel is like the liaison between the American government and Fulani and her rebels. This way America can keep its hands clean. Since Chambers got carte blanche around the world, his trips to third world countries seem benevolent when in actuality they're malevolent—feel me?

Okay, now evidently, America sent in some provocateurs to stir up the natives in Amantu and promise Fulani support in a militarized democracy, *if she accepted their terms on the oil.* She agreed and the CIA sent in mercenaries to raise the natives. Some rolled wit' it while others got murdered or died fightin' for not rollin' wit'.

God bless the dead.

Now, the drug smugglin' was a term of Fulani's and the dead cat, Jaffe, who had been dippin' and dabblin' for a minute anyway, but we'll get back to him. America agreed to turn a blind eye to a deal Phil Chambers worked out personally with, get this, Mayor Tucci of New York! He guaranteed a harbor, Pier 57, and a monthly shipment of the uncut been floodin' New York ever since...

Oh yeah, Jaffe, the dead cat. Jaffe was 'Lani partna. He from Amantu, too. He was the one turn Ma out on this opium shit in the first place 'cause he was growin' the shit in the mountains of Amantu. But her father, a strict traditionalist, abhors drugs and drug dealers, and get this, feed drug dealers to the sharks. Smart man. So no need to tell you, drug dealin' in Amantu is at an all-time low—zero percent.

So Jaffe blow Ma head up; bein' she the king's daughter, who better to smuggle than Daddy's little girl? But shit got deeper when I asked, "What about the seventy-two hours you told me about?"

That's when she tell me the American government is goin' before the Security Council of the UN to request peacekeepers be sent to Amantu—who, like always, go under the assumption of peace but really bringin' war by takin' more arms and support to overthrow the king. Because the King's army is a little too much for the few mercenaries the U.S. initially sent in, so they sendin' in the heavy shit now for some final push-type shit. Then they install Fulani as puppet queen. This is why Jaffe got rocked to sleep. He found out why New York was so open to his wares. He figured out the whole shit was a front for the political upheaval back home. He knew Ma was about to blow up, so he wanted to be the man—but to be the man, the next king of Amantu, he had to marry Fulani, and Ma wasn't wit' it. He threatened to expose the whole shit. Ma got scared and whip out, but she ain't plannin' on wettin' him, just stoppin' him. But Jaffe don't see it like that so he tried to take the gun, they tussle and remember Ma got some Jet Li in her so boom...one to the dome, no more Jaffe.

Enter naïve ghetto cat. Me.

Needless to say, my head is doin' cartwheels! Banktel? New York City? The fuckin' government? And all 'cause Ma was neglected as a child. Damn, I wonder if Hitler's mother loved him? So I ask her, "If everybody so cozy, why is Mr. Monetary tryin' to play casino?"

"I-I don't know."

Play wit' fire... I gotta figure this shit out and wit' all this mixed up, it's gonna take a minute.

"I-ight look, I don't know, either, but whatever is

goin' on, we gonna chill here until—" Ma cut me off wit' that ol' conceited shit again.

"Here?! With these...these *people*?! Do you really expect for a princess to be accommodated here?!" Then she laugh that ol' frivolous, fake-ass rich people laugh.

So I say, "Look, I don't care nothin' about *status*, i-ight, only *survival*! I don't know, maybe all this is some game to you 'cause all you gotta do is boo hoo and immunity step in, but me, I ain't immune to shit! So I don't give a fuck—"

"Binkie!" Minnie Pearl scream on me.

"Ma'am?" I say, but I know what it is.

"Now, I done told you about yo' mouth 'round Waterboy! You know how he pick up words." And then, as if on cue, Water say, "I don't...fuck!" Then he giggle, pointin' at me.

"See?" Minnie Pearl say, then she turned to him. "Water, don't say that no more." He nod.

"Now, you mind yourself and remember, ain't nothin' you got to curse at the Lord can't fix, you hear?"

She got me like a choirboy now, 'cause I'm scared to even think-cuss. "Yes, ma'am."

Then Pearl turn to Fulani. "And as for you, young lady, I don't know exactly where it is you come from or who you is or what you got, but 'round here folks ain't as blessed, but we make do, you hear me?" Fulani don't say nothin'. She fuc—I mean, messin' wit' the right one now.

"I say, you hear me, child?"

Fulani say, "Yes."

"Now, from what I hear, you young folks done bit off more than you can chew and got a whole lot of big people angry wit' y'all. Well, now, I don't know how you do in your country and I don't know about government folk, but I do know if you got the New York City police lookin' for y'all, it ain't safe to be runnin' 'round up in them streets.

"This here the safest place for you 'til you can figure out what it is y'all gonna do. When it comes to trouble, if Binkie can't get out of it, it ain't to be got out of. Lord knows he been in enough to know. Now, we got plenty of food and love 'cause that's all you really need. 'Sides, I do believe Binkie smitten wit' ya 'cause he ain't never brought no girl here to meet Minnie Pearl." Then Pearl smile that ol' snaggletooth smile of hers so big, even Fulani had to giggle.

Yeah, Minnie Pearl definitely right... Not about the smitten part... Okay, maybe *half* right, but I'm still fumin'. But she all right about trouble. I been in my share to know how to maneuver, but how the hel—I mean, heck I 'posed to sidestep some shit like *this*?

So, yo, after Pearl finish eatin', I guess Pearl see we need some time alone, so she stand up and say, "Well, I told Waterboy I'd take him to play some video games after we 'et, so y'all excuse us. But Binkie..."

"Ma'am?"

"Don't eat all Pearl stew."

"Yes ma'am. Ay, Pearl, bring an apple pie back, okay?" She nod as I add, "Oh yeah, and a gun."

I know I'm about to hear it now.

"What happened to Belinda? Boy, I *know* you ain't lost my Boom Boom." She put her hands on her hips and I knew I done fuc—I mean, messed up.

"Come on, Auntie Pearl"—I call her that when I'm in a bind—"you heard the kind of day I been havin'. I just missed losin' my head!"

"Yeah, I guess you right. I'll see what I can turn up." She and Waterboy start to walk off. I shout, "Bring two." 'Cause I look over at 'Lani and at first I was like, should I trust her wit' a gun? But considerin' the fact she done smashed two cats twice my size, I figure she woulda been kicked my ass if she wanted to.

So now Minnie Pearl and Waterboy gone, and it's only me, Ma and a pot of beef stew I'm about to fuc—I mean, oh yeah Pearl gone... Yeah, I'm about to fuck shit up 'cause, yo, Raisin Bran and hot dogs ain't shit for a brother like me. And when Pearl cook... Yo, she do wonders wit' an open fire, my word. The beef be in big chunks and the vegetables and potatoes be street corner fresh. Word up.

So I look at Ma as I slide up to the pot and sit on an ol' milk crate. "You gonna eat or what?" I ask her. She still leanin' on the wall lookin' cute wit' her arms folded like she ain't really hungry, so I say, "Fuck it, then. Starve." Shit, more for me. No spoons, no bowls, just gotta dig right in.

"How can you eat that...mess? You don't even know what's in it," she huffs, but she done inched closer to the pot.

"Yeah, and you don't know what be in them Chinese dishes. Meow."

"Please," she say as she pull up a crate, "Chinese food is a delicacy, not like this peasant shit."

There *she* go.

"Dig, Ma, what the hell is your problem? Yeah, granted, you rub elbows wit' a few high and mighties, got cream comin' out of your pretty little ears, but yo, what you think, your shit don't stink?" She really startin' to get on my nerves now. I'm tryin' to help this ol' dizzy chick 'cause she seem i-ight, even though she almost got me killed. I mean, it ain't the first time a shortie almost got me laced, but all this beatin' me in the head wit' this ol' fly shit is a bit much, so I ask her, "Yo, if you so above motherfuckas, why the hell did you scoop me up?" Even though I already know I'm a dime-ass cat in any language, but... Ahh, I've digressed.

Fulani shrug, like, "You looked like a nice diversion."

Diversion? I been called a lot of things, most of which I can be at times, but a diversion? "Oh, so you was like, well, I just murdered a muhfucka, fuck it, I'll smoke an el or two wit' a total stranger and then casually, over donuts, inform him of the contents of the trunk?"

She dart a sly glance at me, then stick her index finger in the pot to taste Minnie's stew, but she don't answer. Dig, remind me and Stone we gotta cut back on our coffee. She stick another finger in the pot. "Ay, ay, ay, don't be fuckin' pokin' in the pot. If you gonna eat, eat," I say, wit' a mouth full of stew and white bread.

"How else am I supposed to eat without utensils?"

70

she asks.

"Like this. Take the bread and use it like a scoop. And the beef chunks big enough to scoop with, too." So I show her and some of the shit drip on my hoody. She giggle. "You need a bib."

"Yeah, and you need a spankin'."

"So why didn't you give it to me when you had the chance?"

"'Cause I ain't your fuckin' *father.*" Low blow. She instantly lose her smile. "Dig... I ain't mean it, but I'm sayin'..." I just shrug it off 'cause I did mean it, I just ain't mean it to come out like that.

We silent for a few minutes, I'm eatin', she pickin'.

"I'm serious. Why didn't you? Men all over the world have offered me everything just for the chance you had and all you do is hug me. What's wrong? Are you gay?"

"*Gay?!* Damn, Ma, don't flatter yourself, i-ight. Why women think 'cause a brother don't push, he gotta be gay? I'm sayin', pussy and pumpkin pie," I tell her.

"What?"

"Nothin'. But to be honest wit' you, I don't know why. I know I wanted to like a muh... It's a long story. And stop pickin' in the damn stew."

"What else am I to do? Where can I wipe my hands?" she quip.

"Look around. Where *can't* you wipe your hands?"

So we sittin' there eatin' and she start hummin' that tune she was singin' back at the Chinese spot. "Ay, yo," I say, "what's that song you keepin' singin'?"

"Just a song my mother used to sing to me. I think about her a lot lately, especially now, you know, how we're eating. It reminds me of home, eating out of one bowl. The whole family. Yam foo foo and bitter leaf soup, that was my favorite. I used to help Mama prepare it and then we'd all sit down to eat. My mother and my brothers and I... Sometimes Father, too. I used to love that, you know?" She diggin' right in now, so I could tell she a little more relaxed.

"Ay, yo, 'Lani, don't let this go to your already swoll-

71

ass head, but uh...you real cool peeps, you know? Once you get past the international attitude, that is; but word, you a Class-A dime on the inside. So I'm sayin', how in the *hell* did you get mixed up in all this nonsense?"

She look at me and wipe her hands on a paper bag and kinda look off, like, "I don't know, you know. One day I'm breeding horses, going to boarding school, and then... I guess it started with Jaffe."

"The dead cat Jaffe?"

She nod. "He was from one of the smaller villages in the province. His father was a respected elder. He had high hopes for Jaffe because he was smart. Astute. But Jaffe...he had other plans for his life. I saw him one day at one of the yearly festivals my country loves so much. I think it was The Feast of the New Yam. He didn't have much, but he had this air, you know—proud, but not arrogant. Like you." She smiled like it was a compliment, but shit, she *killed* Jaffe. But I don't say nothin' and she continued.

"And I was young. He taught me so much. Any time I wasn't away, I would sneak away to our rendezvous and we would run in the mountains and down to the lagoons. I loved Jaffe, but not like a lover, for we never touched. Nor as a friend because I was too guarded to confide. No, I loved Jaffe just simply as one would love a life they never had. Freedom... Jaffe was my freedom. He started telling me how people in Europe and America go crazy for the opium that grew like weeds around us. How they paid money for, what for us, grew so freely.

"Now, I was not so guarded as to not have been exposed to drugs, although I never indulged in anything except marijuana."

"Noooo, get outta here," I said sarcastically, which made her smile. She replied, "I'm not *that* bourgeois, but I just never realized where the stuff came from, you know? That's when he told me that he and a few others had been processing it. But he was scared my father had gotten wind of it and would have him fed to the sharks, so he needed somehow to get it to the people. Some people he knew in

London. Well, I was going to school in London so I agreed. Just small quantities at first, but the demand grew and so did my involvement. It wasn't the money... I don't know...maybe it was the thrill of getting away with the forbidden."

So I'm thinkin', yeah, I feel you. We always want what we ain't 'posed to have.

"Well, at the time, I'm learning things on my own, about life and the world, how it runs. Socialism, communism, totalitarianism, all sorts of 'isms,' and I'm thinking how simple and backwards my country was in comparison. Yes, we had peace, but that was all we had. We didn't have technology or the industrialization other countries had—things that so-called civilized nations had—and I was ashamed.

"I told Father of my discoveries, my studies, facts and figures, but he just said that 'isms' lead to schisms and we had no need for schisms because we have tradition. I mean, I love our traditions—at least, some of the traditions—because some of them were inherited from mainland Africa and come from hundreds of years of foreign influence. But I longed to have both worlds.

"We had the chance when Father discovered the oil sites but he would not agree to American terms and they wouldn't agree to his. He called them heathens, savages, devils, but when I looked around it was the savages with all of the wonderful things my people had never seen! Never dreamed of... That's when I met Phil."

She stood up then and wandered to the edge of the alcove Minnie Pearl called home and just looked at the track. A train rumbled by and I watched the breeze blow up her robe enough to expose her chocolate thighs and I'm like, damn, I shoulda...

Naw, fuck dat.

I stood up as the train passed, tryin' to evade my thoughts as she turned to me to finish her story.

"It was in Hawaii, as I told you, three years ago. It was my eighteenth birthday present, a Hawaiian vacation.

Phil was there, at a conference, or so he said... I see now it must've been planned. He was so charming, so intellectual, so sophisticated. I-I was enraptured." She turned away and I'm like, awww man, I *knew* it! Another fuckin' zebra story! Yeah, love is color blind if you *physically* blind, and I'm like, yo, fellas! How long we gonna let these yodies bag our jewels?! Word, they swirlin' and we ain't doin' shit about it! Black men of the world *Unite...*

...with black women.

(This has been a paid public announcement for the M.A.N. Mad-Ass Niggas)

She turned back and her eyes is welled up wit' tears. "He filled my head with so many things. So many promises...words. Progress. Civilization. How my country would prosper if the native element, with the help of America, would raise up against my father for the sake of democracy! So many words. He even said he *loved* me and I *believed* him."

Ay, dig... The pain in her voice and the rhythm of the tears... That did it. I just hugged Ma to me again, but I ain't sayin' nothin' 'cause I'm vexed like a muhfucka. Yo, all I wanna do is protect Ma, 'cause I know I done did some females dirt in my day. You know, said some fucked up shit...

Yo, Val, I shoulda been there...

Sonia, I messed up your life and for what it's worth, I'm sorry.

But here I am on the reverse side of the shit, seein' the damage it do, so like they say, three strikes and you out, right? The fuck, I'm still swingin', so what the hell, choke up on the bat, and I say, "I'ma get you outta this, i-ight? Don't worry."

Whatever the hell made me say some shit like that I don't know, 'cause what can *I* do? I got a billion dollar company, New York and the American government against me—but when she looked up at me wit' them baby browns and her tear-stained face, and said, "Okay..." Ay, yo... I feel like Rocky when Adrian was in the hospital and sayin'

74

"Win." I hear music and everything, so I know somebody gettin' knocked the fuck out! My word. But first I gotta think like I never thunk before and I can't do that embracin' Ma, 'cause her rhythm is intoxicatin'. So I step back, light a cigarette and start thinkin'.

First of all, I gotta stop lookin' at this shit like it's bigger than me, you know? So what? I'm up against billionaires and international players—niggas bleed just like me. So fuck all this, what can *I* do? Naw, the question is, what *can't* I do? You know? Shit, I'm *Ghetto Sam!* If I tell you a duck could pull a truck, then get a rope and hook the motherfucka up. Say word. Plus, I ain't no dumb Donald, I mean shit, I *got* my G.E.D... I even went to college, for a week... I'm sayin', it was Howard homecoming, but still... I went to a college.

So I'm blowin' smoke rings, thinkin' out loud, like, "I-ight, now."

But while I'm thinkin', Pearl and Waterboy come back, and Pearl say, "Boy, what president you done killed? It's hotter than a firecracker out there! Police all over!"

Damn... Damn... Damn... *Damn!*

"You got the heat, Auntie?"

"Auntie ever let you down?" Pearl say, as she toss me a .38 snub and a nine. I tuck 'em.

Waterboy walk up to me and 'Lani and say, "You a real queen? Like, um, like the Queen of Spades or Queen Latifah?"

She smile. "I guess you can say that."

"Well, um, I got, um, I got you somethin'. Here." He hand her one of those pinwheels the wind blow and make spin, and a little plastic crown. He wanna put it on her head, so Ma bend down and he put it on her. She don't know what to say. She wanna kiss him but his face kinda dirty, but she find a little spot on his forehead and give him a peck.

Ay, yo, Water's face light up like the Fourth of July. Word up, I know how he feel; 'cause Ma lit *my* rocket back at the Chinese spot...

Down boy, down... Y'all excuse me.

Anyway, Water run and go tell Pearl 'Lani kissed him, Pearl smile and give him a piece of pie.

"He's... He's so sweet," she say, touchin' her crown. I blow on the little pinwheel and make it spin. Then she ask, "Why's he...what's wrong?"

"His mother was a dope fiend." Her jaw drop. "Never been this close to what them mountain flowers of yours can do, huh?" I leave her to marinate on that...

So, yo, after showin' Waterboy a few card tricks—he love them shits—and playin' him in tic-tac-toe which he won five games to three, I settle down for a quick wink. I'm lyin' there, not knowin' how long, not asleep but not awake but conscious. Thoughts flowin'. I hear Pearl and Fulani talkin'. I crack one eye on the low and I see Pearl braidin' Ma hair. Long-ass braids, kind most shorties gotta yoke a horse for, ya'm sayin'? They talkin' and laughin'. It's hard not to laugh wit' Pearl 'cause she got a way of puttin' things, you know, so it's hard not to like her or feel comfortable around her, even if the surroundings is less than comforting.

They talkin' about me now. Pearl givin' her the lowdown on my life story.

"May I ask how you met Sam?" Fulani ask Pearl.

Pearl chuckle, "Runnin' from the police. I don't know what that young'un got against turnstiles and tokens, but I swear he never use 'em. Well, this particular day wasn't his and some ol' Transit cop see him and start chasin' 'im. He chasin' 'im up and down, platform to platform, until Sam come runnin' down here and ask me to hide 'im. Ever since then he been comin' worryin' me."

"I can tell he really loves you," Fulani comment.

"Yeah, that there my baby; wouldn't have him any other way."

I smile to myself 'cause it's good to be appreciated.

Fulani pause, then real timid-like, she signify like,

"Does he have a, um—"

"Friend?" Pearl finish for her, then she add wit' a smile, "Wellll, let's just say Binkie is really *friendly.*"

"You mean doggish," Fulani say, the hope in her tone hittin' bottom.

"Oh, I wouldn't say that, but if he was, it's only 'cause all these young gals runnin' around callin' themselves bitches. What else can a *bitch* get but a *dog?*" Fulani nodded to the jewel Pearl just dropped on her.

"Back in my day, if you called a woman a bitch, you better have your knife out, ready to do some cuttin'! But nowadays, women-folk ain't folk like they used to be."

Fulani like, "In my country, we say loose women, iba. It means fever."

"Hmph. Honey, over here, we just call them heifers, ho's." She and Fulani laugh as Pearl finished a braid and began on another, sayin, "But Binkie is a good man—that is, for a good woman. Ain't many like 'im. Now, don't get me wrong, he a handful, though. Why, I remember..."

No need to go any further 'cause all you gotta do is think about the shit you done got into over the years, probably still getting into, add an escapade or two the average man wouldn't dream of and voilà! My story, in a nutshell.

Anyway, I'm thinkin' like Wesley Snipes in *New Jack City,* this shit is bigga than Nino Brown. Word. I'm thinkin' about Waterboy, matter fact, *all* the Waterboys of the world—so many like him, so many gonna *be* like him. Fucked up for life by a choice not even they own. Right now, in hospital rooms, in incubators, in wombs, still in they father's nuts... How many families been broken up, how many grandmothers cried and prayed, prayed and cried, put up the whole family's wages for they grandkid's bail. All my peeps doin' life bids, crazy long crack bids, even on death row. How many cats got they brains blew out, *blew* brains out, crippled for life, stray shots, dead babies, black girls lost...

THE FUCK?!

And the *whole* time, the whole motherfuckin' time, these Goddamned, these God-please-*damn* these crackers, been givin' it to us the whole time! The whole time and then take our loot, our lives, our souls, then point the finger at us! I remember when the cat in San Diego linked the U.S. and contra to crack in L.A. and everybody started makin' noise. But deep down, ghetto heads always knew, you know? We knew but we didn't know, *I* didn't know, until now—until it's right here in my face. I'm like, my word to *God* they gonna burn! Fuckin' burn... I ain't no revolutionary or activist, naw, fuck dat; I guess I'm like Rosa Parks—I'm sick and tired of bein' sick and tired...

But for right now, I'm at a loss, so I let my thoughts drift from internal to external and pick Pearl and Fulani convo up again. Now 'Lani tellin' Pearl about Amantu and shit, all about the water and the air.

"...but when my mother died," I pick up 'Lani voice mid-sentence. She kinda choked up but gruffed to go on. "She died during the rainy season, when everything seemed so gray. I would sit in the palace courtyard and despise the rain. Despise its dreariness, but my nursemaid Njide once told me not to hate the rain because it is rain that makes things grow. She told me to plant the seed of my mother here, in my heart, and let the rain allow it to blossom. I was so young that I didn't understand her wisdom. But when the rainy season ended, and the sun shone anew... I still couldn't understand, but I could *feel* her understanding, you know?"

Pearl just smiled and nodded.

"It was as if I could see my mother's smile blossoming in every flower, her embrace in the warmth of the breeze, her laughter in the call of the nza."

"N-who?"

Fulani chuckled, then answered, "*Nza*. It is a small bird, but its plumage is very bright and very beautiful and it has this majestic call. It sounds like..." then 'Lani made some ol' funny noise and her and Pearl start laughin'.

"Yes, Njide showed me so much because Father

became so protective after Mother passed. Njide was the only one who would take me to the market with her because she knew I loved the smells so much. I would beg her to take me to the lagoon or into the bush to pick the wild berries she made sweets from. The real sticky kind that would smear your face. Amantu is so very beautiful, I wish you could see it."

That's when Pearl say, "Chile, it sound so pretty. Sho' wish they never woulda took us from the Motherland. Ain't you got no pictures?"

THAT'S IT!

Yo, I jump up so fast I startled 'Lani and Pearl.

"Binkie!? What's wrong wit' you, boy, jumpin' up like that!? Scared me half to death— and you know my heart."

"My fault, Auntie," but I'm still pysched, "my fault, but yo, I got it!"

"Got what? Whatever it is I don't want it if it make me jump 'round like that," Pearl say, and 'Lani laughed.

"Naw, not *what*—it. I got it! Yo, 'Lani, your father said he stepped to you wit' some flicks or somethin' of you and your partnas?" She kinda look down on the floor and say, "Yes, that's why I left."

"I know, but look, who is in the flick wit' you?" I'm thinkin' to myself, please *please* say— "Myself and Phil Chambers," she said, completin' my thoughts and grantin' my wish. But she still don't get it.

"Why?" she ask me.

"Okay, now follow me, i-ight." I catch my breath 'cause my mind is racin' and I'm speed ballin', pacin' and shit like a mad scientist. It's alive! "Okay, you said Banktel was the go-between for you and the U.S., right?

"Right."

"And Chambers put you and New York together for Pier 57, right?"

"Indirectly. Yes," she reply.

So I mumble to myself, "So that means U.S. is once removed and New York a distant cousin."

"Huh?"

79

"Nothin', I'm just ill wit' the similes. Okay... When deliveries was made, who did the pickup?"

"Jaffe handled that end. But I do know he had some guy named Chino make most of the pickups. I just handled the money." Fulani explained.

Chino?!

"Did you say Chino? Spanish cat wit' a dead eye from Harlem?"

"Yes, why? Do you know him?"

Yeah, I know that snake-ass motherfucka. Chino been settin' niggas up for years. Real sheisty Cuban character. He bust his gun, but he snitch. Just the kind of middleman Tucci would need to hook this type of shit up and keep his hands clean...

I love it when a plan comes together. "Yeah, you could say that," I tell 'Lani.

She like, "But what does that have to do with the pictures my father has and how can they help us when my father is looking for me *because* of them?" I could tell she totally confused.

"I'm gettin' to that. Now, the way I see it, Philly boy threw them slugs 'cause, number one, you murdered Jaffe and he don't know why. Number two, you and me all over the news wit' Jaffe in the trunk and *then*, somehow he know your father scooped me up and he probably think I'm some kind of mediator between you and the king. He get scared and go to Tucci. They decide you gotta go 'cause this international shit scares 'em." Ma face still a mask of confusion, so I try and relate back to prior events.

"Okay, remember when we went up to the cop on the horse?"

She like, "Yes, he was preparing to draw his weapon and—" I cut her off.

"But why? You said it was Chambers' people at the door, and even though police lookin' for us, ain't no way he coulda recognized us in the dark in that split second it took him to react."

Pearl just finishin' her braids, so she stand up and

say, "So you're sayin' Phil wants me dead and Tucci wants me dead and the only proof of my involvement with them are those pictures?"

"Exactly."

"But it just shows us talking, sitting at a table. It can't prove anything."

If she had any hope, it just aired out. But I say, "But your father *has* to have more than just pictures. He wouldn't come down on you just over a lunch date. Think about it."

She answered, "But...but I'm wanted for treason and drugs. I told you what my father does to drug dealers."

"But you his daughter."

"You don't know my father."

"Yeah, well, I'm about to get to know him, 'cause if he got what I think he got, this could be the best thing that coulda happened to your country." I light a cigarette.

She add, "Whatever it is, we have less than two days to get it together."

"Pardon self?"

"The UN, the peace troops, remember?"

"Yeah, yeah, right. Then we better get it crackin'. What time is it anyway?"

Pearl say, "'Bout nine o'clock."

I'm like, "In the *mornin'*?! Y'all let me sleep all night?"

Fulani tell me, "More like tossed and turned all night."

"And you needed the rest, boy," Pearl add, like the mother to me that she is.

Fulani turn to Pearl and ask, "Ms. Pearl, how do you know what time it is down here anyway?"

"Be down here long as I have, you get to know the rhythm of thangs. The rumble of the train, the smell in the air. Reckon it's like them ancient folk tell time by the sun." Fulani nod.

"Yeah, well, we better raise up," I say.

Pearl ask, "And how you 'spect to do that? Them streets is crawlin' wit' police. Not to mention them undercovers and a bunch of official-lookin' folk."

So I'm thinkin'...what would James Bond do? Probably break out some invisible paint and sashay the fuck outta here. Fuck that white boy. Never did like no super crackas nohow. Then I think, what would Shaft do? Yeah, my man Shaft. Cool motherfucka, afro always tight, talkin' that ol' slick shit. Hmm. I look at Pearl in her multilayered outfit of discarded wares and Fulani standin' next to her in her robe. They both about the same height, probably the same size under all them clothes Pearl got on. Hmm...

"Auntie, what size you wear?"

Fulani catch on instantly. "Oh, no! Uh-uh, *no.* Nothing against you, Ms. Pearl, but those clothes? On me?"

"You got a better suggestion?"

Now she whinin'. "But they smellll baaad."

"And you somewhere dead gonna smell worse." That got her attention.

That's when Pearl break in, "I understand, baby. Don't nobody wanna stink, Binkie. I just let it get like this to keep folk 'way from 'round me. I got some mo' things right over here." Pearl run over to her fashion corner and Fulani give me this look that I shoot right back at her like, shop 'til you drop. She go on over to the corner.

Now for me. Waterboy heavier than me but shorter. He sittin' on the mattress, rubbin' his eyes after just wakin' up. Fuck it, won't be the first time I wore some high-water bell-bottoms. My mother still got them flicks, too, from when I was five. Still extortin' me, too. The money I give her probably enough to pay her rent wit'.

Anyway, I'm switchin' wit' Waterboy and yo...you shoulda seen Ma tryin' to color-coordinate rags. If she had to wear a garbage bag, she'd probably be tryin' to find a matchin' purse and shoes.

Women...

She finally settle on some shit, and was about to take off her robe when Pearl say, "Binkie. Turn your back."

"Come on Auntie, I—" I started to say I already seen

that, but Pearl ain't wit' no sh—I mean, stuff like that. She like, "I mean it, Binkie. I don't know what you young folk *done seen*, but you ain't gonna see it *here*. You too, Waterboy." Fulani find this little chastisement amusin'. So me and Waterboy turn toward the train tracks.

"Okay," Pearl say. We turn around. Yo Ma, the *queen*, is flossin' in a ripped purple and white, well purple and dirty white dress wit' jeans underneath and a blue parka coat wit' dog fur around the collar. I bust out laughin'!

"Stop pickin' at the chile," say Pearl.

Fulani like, "I feel ridiculous."

"Yes, but you look marvelous. Pop your collar," I'm teasin'. She look like the token black girl on "Hee Haw." So she like, "Well, you're not so hot, either. Is it supposed to rain?" Then she point at my pants. Shits is kinda high—not kinda, they *are* high, halfway up my shin. I try and sag 'em, but damn, they already past my ass; any lower, they'll be around my knees!

Pearl laughin', even Waterboy laughin', so I turn to Water. "What you ha-ha and hee-hee'n at, Water? These *your* clothes."

He say, "N-not anymore," and then he pull *my* hood to *my* hoody over his head, like the deal was closed.

"He still has on his sneakers," Fulani say.

"Oh, you snitchin' now?" I ask, sarcastically.

That's when Pearl jump in. "She right, Binkie, you can't be runnin' around in them clothes wearing brand-new sneakers, too." Yeah, she right, but payback is a mother. So I give my 'Didas (sorry, Run) to Waterboy and put on his, I don't know what kind, but they two sizes too big, lookin' like clown shoes on me.

That's when I feel *it*. Somethin' *movin'* in my pocket. "Uh, Water...um, why is my pocket movin'?" I'm almost scared to ask. He shrug his shoulders guiltily.

Pearl say, in her parental tone, "Water."

He say, "Mr. Fred," like me and Mr. Fred buddies and we kick it all the time.

83

"W-who is Mr. Fred?"

"My mouse." He say it like, who else could Mr. Fred be?

Yooo, I *hate* mice, but I can't hurt nothin' Waterboy love, so I say, "Could you *please* get Mr. Fred, Water?" I'm stiff as a statue as he get him out, pat him, then put him in his—I mean, *my* pocket.

Fulani is buggin'. "Don't tell me Mr. Hardcore Street-Man is afraid of a little mouse?" She laughed.

"I'm glad you havin' fun while half the world is breathin' down our necks."

"You started it," she responded, soundin' like a little girl. I hand her the snub nose .38, but she tell me, "I'm better with an automatic," in a matter-of-fact tone.

"You better wit' an automatic? Who is you, fuckin' Rambo?" That one got me slapped upside my head by Pearl. "It slipped," I tried to explain. But back to Ma. "Look, I got this. Just take the snub."

So she like, "*You* got this? No, *we* got this. Like you said, we're in this *together* and I'm telling you I'm better with an automatic." Then she look around and say, "Okay. You see that bottle across the tracks? First one to hit it gets the nine. Deal?"

Is she challengin' moi? "Yeah, i-ight," I say, then add, "ladies first."

She chuckle like, "No, I think you better lead this time, because after me, there'll be no bottle left to shoot," then she smile, all pretentious-like.

"Ooh, aren't we the cocky one... Okay." I cock back the nine...

Fire...

Miss. Fulani giggle. Pearl, too. Water got his fingers in his ears, so I say, "Little rusty, that's all." I fire again..

BOOOSH! Bottle smashed. Mission complete. I turn to Ma and hand her the nine. "Now what are you gonna shoot?" I give Waterboy a high-five before he put his fingers back in his ears.

Now dig... I *broke* the bottle, but my word, Ma

emptied the whole clip and I swear she broke all the *pieces* of the bottle 'til it was nothin' left but fuckin' dust.

I-ight, *she* gets the nine. I tuck the snub while Pearl hand 'Lani some more shells to reload. Time to bounce.

"Auntie, where you park your car?" I ask.

Fulani turn to Pearl, who's wearin' Fulani's robe over her wares by now, and ask, "*You* have a car?"

I just smile...

CHAPTER EIGHT: RICHES TO RAGS

As I pointed to Pearl's rusty ol' shopping cart, I gave 'Lani a facetious bow and said, "Your chariot awaits."

"My chariot?! Un-uh, oh no. You said a *cart!*" Fulani screamed.

"Car, chariot, pushcart. It got wheels, what's the difference?" I'm lovin' this.

So she fold her arms, like, "Nope. I'm not riding in *that*. I put on these...these *clothes*, and I hated that, but I will not stoop so low as to get in *that*."

"Okay, we'll just walk the thirty-somethin' blocks to the Consulate duckin' bullets."

"Why not?" she ask in mock defiance-slash-stubbornness.

"Fine with me but, uh, have you *seen* yourself lately? I mean, do you really wanna die wearin' *those* clothes? To be shown on TV, newspapers and magazines worldwide?" It was a little low, I admit, but when all else fails, a woman's vanity is a viable tool in expert hands. She stopped. Thought. Looked around. Looked at herself.

"Well, how will it look with me in the cart and you pushing, anyway? Don't you think *that* will draw attention?"

"Not if you get in and shut up." I already had that part figured out. She climbs in and I start pilin' the cart wit' trash, anything I can find. I'm *really* lovin' this. She steady cussin' while I'm whistlin', and in the end, it looked like a cart piled wit' trash.

"You know I won't forget this. *Binkie.*"

Ohh, she wanna play the name game, huh? Okay... So I say, "Forget what? And you need to be quiet because trash doesn't talk."

I can tell by the way the cart is shakin' she fumin', while I'm smilin', ear to ear. Besides, a person need a little shit in they life when they get too much sugar, and I'm about to give her all the shit she can take.

I'm rollin', tryin' to find all the potholes, uneven sidewalks and gaping cracks in the street. When I get to the curb, I don't go down the ramp; ohh, nooo, I bang right down off the curb. Oh, she *really* cursin' now, in every language she know, probably in a few she *don't* know. Nothin' that a slight bump into a light pole won't cure.

"I know you're doing this on purpose!" she fumed.

"Shhh, I told you, trash doesn't talk. Oh, look! A cop! Be quiet." Ain't really no cop, just a very big pothole. "'Scuse me."

So as we bumpin' along I'm thinkin', damn, if somebody woulda told me I'd be pushin' a cart in the middle of New York, I woulda never believed them. Now look at me. Even though it's a scam, but still... And I'm thinkin', what if I really *did* have to do this, you know, for real? I'm seein' other homeless cats and before when they would ask and I'd give, now they just nod like, hold it down. You know, like we twin souls. So I'm like, how the fuck is so many people forced to live like this, when a cat can go to Vegas and trip six digits and not miss it? It's the American way...

Fuckin' bastards.

I mean, look at Pearl... I be tellin' her, fuck this, come stay wit' me. She be like, "In Jersey?" Then she start singin', "I'm a native New Yorkerrrr."

She happy, you know, and I guess if you look at it from her point of view—no rent, no bills, shelter and food—then I guess you *can* be happy. But why do people *have* to be happy under these conditions? I'm lookin' at Benz's and Lex's cruisin' by, and I'm like, yeah y'all chillin' now but, uh, a whole lot of rich people gonna be fucked up after today. I bet you *that*...

Oh, there go a nice pothole.

"Oops, excuse me, precious," I say.

"Fuck you," she replied.

Least it was in English....

That was fun, but back to business 'cause then shit got a little sticky. Now, to me a cart is a cart. We used to steal 'em all the time from the PathMark around my way. But to homeless people, I guess them shits is like whips is to us. 'Cause some ol' cat wearin' about six trench coats pull up on me like, "Hey! Hey you! Ain't that Minnie Pearl cart?!"

Huh? Talkin' to me? I look around to see if any cops around... Yep. Damn. One over by the hot dog stand, but I gotta stop 'cause I know this ol' dude gonna make a bigger scene if I don't. I stop and turn around and see him full-speed comin' behind me, pushin' his cart.

"Hey! I'm talkin' to you, let's not get ugly!"

"You talkin' to me?" I ask, like I don't know.

"Damn right, I'm talkin' to you! What you doin' wit' Minnie Pearl pushcart?!"

I look down at the cart, then at him. "Man, what you talkin' 'bout? This ain't no Minnie Pearl cart." I glance over my shoulder at the cop. He still eatin' his dog. So far so good.

"Nigga, I ain't crazy! You think I don't know Minnie Pearl cart when I see it?! You think I'm crazy?!"

Okay, you got aluminum foil wrapped around your head like a space-age turban and a stuffed teddy bear peepin' out your pocket, so should I really answer that? That's what I'm thinkin', but I say, "Naw, man, it's all a misunderstandin'. See, Minnie Pearl loaned me the cart to, uh, pick up groceries. Yeah, that's it."

He look at me. "I knew it! I knew it! I know Minnie Pearl cart anywhere, and I know she don't be loanin' her cart out to nobody neither! Now give it here!"

Then this nut actually grab the damn cart! I wanna

punch the muhfucka in his face, but I'm tryin' to cut back on my black-on-black violence. So we tusslin' wit' the cart, back and forth, and that's when I see the flatfoot comin' across the street...

Damn!

"All right, all right, what's all the commotion about?"

I'm tryin' my best to avoid eye contact while the homeless cat explain to him, "I'm glad to see you, officer! This man is a thief!" he say, pointin' straight at me.

The cop turn to me. "A thief, eh? What's your name, buddy?"

But before I could answer, the homeless dude cut me off. "He done stole Minnie Pearl cart, talkin' 'bout Minnie give it to him but Minnie don't be givin' her cart to nobody!"

"Wait, wait, who's Minnie Pearl?" The cop asks.

So I cut in. "It's all a misunderstanding. There is no Minnie Pearl. This man is clearly inebriated." 'Cause you could smell the Thunderbird in his eyes.

So the cop say to him, "Well, where's Minnie Pearl?"

"Ask him! He the one steal her cart!" he say, staggerin'.

"Did he steal anything from you?"

"No, but—" the dude start to say, but the cop cut him off.

"That's all I needed to know. Beat it! Both of youse!"

The homeless cat stumble off, mumblin' somethin' about goin' to get Pearl, but my asshole got tight when I started to push the cart away.

"Hey, wait a minute," the cop say, and I got my hand three inches from the trigger. "Don't I know you from somewhere?" he add, squintin' at my face.

"Uh, yeah... Yeah, I guess you do. I'm here all the time."

"Oh," the cop say, but before he can combobulate, I turn the corner on two wheels...

*****

That was close, but now we a block from the Consulate and the spot was swarmin' wit' police! Of course, the average Joe wouldn't know it, but uh, any cat wit' his ear to the street know a cop in the dark. 'Specially feds. They stand out in a crowd like a nigga at a Nazi rally. Ain't no real problem, though, just call and boom, we in. But... I ain't got no change.

"Don't tell me Einstein has figured out the universe, but can't tie his shoes," Fulani quip from the cart.

"Shut up, 'fore I *tie* you to a car bumper and be done wit' the whole thing."

Hmm. Thirty-five cents. Shouldn't be that hard. Here come a guy now, well-dressed Brooks Brothered white cat. "Excuse, me sir, I need thirty-five cents to call my broker. Kinda lost my shirt on those First Union ventures." My humor fell on unsympathetic ears.

Ahhhh, my man, ol' Robin Harris-lookin' brother, God bless the dead. "Saaay Jack, I—"

"Fuck out my face," he tell me, and keep steppin' wit'out even breakin' his stride.

Oh, mama mia! Look at Boricua! "Que pasa, mami? How's about a—" Damn. What a middle finger mean in Spanish? Must be the same as in English, 'cause I still ain't got no change.

Oh, my Arab friend at the phone booth... Okay, gotta time this just right. Let him pick up the receiver, drop the money and... "Abdullah! My friend! How long has it been, huh? Two, three months?!" I hug him for effect. "Oh, you're lookin' good, ha?" Hug him again, but this time he ain't confused, he's repelled.

"Who are you?! Unhand me!" he say, and pushes away, wipin' his clothes and turns the corner, leavin' the phone off the hook.

My man. I press the jack and the money returns. Voilà! Problem solved... Oh, almost forgot. "Ay, 'Lani, what's the number?"

"555-3871."

5-5-5-3-8-

"71?"

"71," she confirms.

7-1. It rings...again...again, then a woman picks up and I say, "Yeah listen, this is uh, this is a friend of Fulani's. The king is expectin' my call."

"You're who?"

Damn, why they always let deaf people be operators?

"Look, I need to speak with the king, it's about Fulani. Please, it's urgent." I'm thinkin', hurry up, just in case the feds got the Consulate's lines tapped. I hear the phone get cuffed. Muffled voices.

"Hello?" It's the king's voice.

"Your kingship, it's your friend from Jersey."

"Yes, I know."

I'm lookin' around. "Is this a safe line?"

"A who?"

"A safe line. Can we talk?"

"Oh, yes, yes," the king say.

A police cruiser rolls by, so I switch hands and turn away. "I know somethin' you don't."

He reply, "Yes, I'm sure you do. Where are you?"

"I'm around and I'm tryin' to come see you, but the feds got the spot flooded."

He like, "Flooded? Oh, yes, yes, I understand, the Federal agents, yes, yes. Can you make it to the service door? There's an alley off the side street which leads directly to it."

Yo, I'm lookin' right at it. Cool. "Yeah, it'll take me a minute, though."

"Fine, fine," he say quickly, but I remind him, "Ain't you forgettin' somethin'?"

"I don't think so."

Politicians. I tell him, "A word start wit' m and end wit' a lot of o's."

He pauses. "Well, I never said...is that your price?"

"Naw. The price is your ear."

"I don't understand."

"I know, and I can't explain right now, but before you decide on Fulani, I need your ear."

Long pause...

"How long will it be before you arrive?"

"Just keep an eye out." I hang up, wait a few minutes to see if there's any fed activity... Cool, we out.

Fulani speaks. "What did he say? How did he sound?"

"Well, I didn't hear no sharks in the background."

So I'm comin' through the alley, pushin' the cart and I catch a déjà vu, right, 'cause I see my old graffiti tag name sprayed on the wall. *BANG T.N.T.* T.N.T. stand for The Newark Tagger. Damn, I get around. Anyway, the alley lead right to the rear of the Consulate and there go my old friend Gorilla Man, and he wearin' that same cheesy-ass grin. I push the cart up to the door and he say somethin' to me, but it's in his language. I don't know what, until Fulani say, "Here, in the cart."

He shocked to see Fulani push out all that garbage and climb out brushin' herself off, and we go inside. They stop at the bottom of the stairs and Gorilla Man about to frisk 'Lani, so I slap his hand and say, "Ay, yo, partna, she is *still* the king's daughter."

Gorilla Man musta thought about that 'cause he let her go and turned to frisk me, but I ain't no king's daughter, so I say, "Um, if you feel any wetness, don't worry, the doctor says *all* the sores aren't contagious," then I cough. Yeah, disease always have a certain effect on the healthy. He didn't frisk me. Instead, he pointed up the stairs, so me and 'Lani ascend wit' Gorilla and some other cat behind us.

We get to the next floor, hang a right and span a corridor, until we reach a set of double doors.

My man knock and I hear somebody say somethin', I

guess meant, "Come in," 'cause that's what he did. Office mad plush. The king standin' in the middle of the office and the English-speakin' cat from earlier sittin' in the chair cross-legged, right over left, chillin' wit' a drink.

The king look at me, then at his daughter dressed in rags and whatnot and he say, "What—" but I cut him off.

"Long story, your kingship, but we here, safe and sound." I look at Fulani. She got her head down like she shamed, but I could tell it ain't 'cause of how she dressed. He nod to me, then turn to Fulani.

"Fulani."

"Father." They greet each other, but it's real formal. So then he say to me, "You have done well, my friend, my country and I thank you and you will be rewarded. Handsomely." And before I could reply, the English-speakin' cat approach me wit' a briefcase and flip the lid...

Ay, yo, talkin' 'bout *Presidents'* Day...

So for a split second, I'm pimpdaddyhustle-stackmoney, and I think, what the hell, wit' dat kind of cake I could move on up like the Jeffersons. Fuck, what should I care if a brick or two come in the country? Fulani was right, Cuba won't quit, Indonesia won't quit... Fuck am I thinkin'?! Naw, if I take that, I'll be an international crime stopper while the *real* criminals get away. Besides, I owe this one to my father.

Long story...

Anyway, this whole mental bout of chess boxin' took all of five seconds between seein' the loot and sayin', "I...yo, I don't want your money," although I shoulda said I won't *take* your money, 'cause I damn sure want it. The English cat stepped back in amazement but the king just smile like, "I see," then he look at Fulani. "I see your charms haven't failed you."

Fulani don't speak, but I'm like, ohhh, this cat think I'm pussy whipped and I ain't even smell it! So I start to speak, but he said, "I know my daughter is beautiful, and as I have said, she can and has had this effect on many. But you must understand the gravity of what she has done.

She has betrayed her country, she has betrayed the crown and she has betrayed me, not only the king but her *father*. She has intrigued, plotted and connived until she has succeeded in sinking her own country in civil turmoil, pitting brother against brother, friend against friend—"

This time I cut him off, "And daughter against father."

He says, "Yes, and daughter against father. And for that she must be punished for the sake of justice. I have always been dead set against foreign intervention or foreign aid. It is like poison injected into the veins of the dying, sapping them lifeless, and she disobeyed me.

"I have an avid loathing against drugs and its dealers. I have fed men to sharks and, knowing this, Fulani relied on blood ties for leniency. Well, a wise man once said, if my own daughter Fatima stole, I would have her hand cut away! This, my friend, is justice and Fulani has left me no choice, but—" so I stop him again to remind him, "Your kingship, excuse me for stoppin' you. But I asked you for one thing over the phone, and that was your ear. To listen." I paused to see if he was, then I went on.

"Yo—I mean, your kingship, you may think I've flipped out—I mean, have become, um, infatuated with your daughter for whatever reasons. Her beauty, her riches, whatever. The truth is, I'm big—I mean, I do like your daughter but not 'cause of what you think. Naw. You see, I got love for all my people just like you got love for yours, which is really one in the same." He nod in agreement, so I continue. "And, no doubt, I was upset to find out the source of the supply was comin' from Africa. But...yo, you said Fulani has an effect on men. Okay, granted. But what kind of effect has she had on you?"

That got his attention. He say, "Effect? What do you mean effect? She's my daughter, of course—"

"Your daughter or your princess?" I ask, cuttin' in. Then I add, "Remember what you told me when we met? How you took her all over the world. Had her schooled in the ways of the world. France, London and what-not. But did you ever take her swimmin'? Or just take her out for a walk? 'Cause you know what she was learnin' when she coulda been swimmin'? I'll tell you. She was learnin' everything you just charged her with. Intrigues and plots, translated: politics. Bottom line. That's what you wanted her to learn, wasn't it?"

He kinda tensed up, 'cause a hit dog will holler. The king said, "Do you mean to imply it is *my* fault my country is in turmoil, and my daughter a traitor?"

Gorilla Man moved a step closer to me, so my hand moved a step closer to my .38.

"Naw, I ain't *implyin'* it, I'm *sayin'* it! Hell, yeah, it's your fault, but I say that wit' all due respect. 'Cause I know, yo, I know how it is wit' these shorties out here wit' no father figure, my word. I'll take you to Harlem, Brooklyn, Detroit, fuckin' West Bumble Fuck and I'll show you projects full of Fulanis. Five and six kids and they still fuckin' gettin' high and shit. Now just imagine if they had the power of a whole country! How the hell they gonna control a country and they can't even control themselves?!" I know my tone done broke some international etiquette, but fuck it, if it's goin' down let's get it over wit'!

"I've heard enough!" the king say, then he give Gorilla a nod, which I guess meant, "Get this nigga outta here," 'cause Gorilla collar me up... But yo, he don't know this barrel headed straight for his kidney.

He shocked, Fulani shocked, the king in a—how you say—a state of consternation, and I'm watchin' this sneaky-ass English-speakin' cat. I tell him, "I'll put it in him so deep, it'll come out and hit you twice, nigga."

He caught my message and froze up, so I turned my attention to the king, "Yo, this just for my protection, i-ight? Now, I said I wanted you to listen, and that's all I'm askin."

Long...tense silence.

The king motion to Gorilla, he back away, ain't no cheesy grin now; he lookin' like he wanna kill me. The king say somethin' and the English cat and Gorilla leave.

"You can put away your weapon—unless, of course,

you want to shoot me," he say wit' a smile.

So I put the .38 up...slowly. He say, "I admire your valor, my young friend. You have yet to cease to amaze me. First you succeed in eluding international security forces with the simplicity of a vagabond, then you reject a million American dollars. And now, to be heard, you have brandished your weapon at the risk of certain death." That's when he moved his formal robe aside to reveal the gun he had on me the whole time, held at gut level...

My knees went weak. But he put his gun on the table and look at Fulani.

"Is what he says true, my child?"

She didn't speak. Head still down.

"Fulani, please. Is this true?" he reiterated.

She said, "I do not blame you, Father, for my transgressions are my own, but... My intentions...my intentions were to make you proud, to show you I had learned well. I learned so many things I thought you did not give a chance and would be good for the country. But later, I sought not your approval, because I no longer stood in your court. I stood in the world court and it was contrary to everything I knew or believed... But I made my choice and so the blame is my own."

The king turned away and gazed out of the window. "No. No, I must agree." He turned back to me. "My young friend is right. I have suspected as much for a long time, but guilt is an isolation sometimes. Your mother tried to tell me many times, God give her peace. She told me, but what could I teach you? A girl child? It was easy with your five brothers before you, but you... My only daughter... And then your mother died. I only wanted to give you the best, to prepare you against the hegemonic and capitalistic monster and I, like a fool, sent you into the monster's den. I...I don't know what to say. I have wronged you, but this does not change the wrong you have done. People have *died*, Fulani. People *are* dying, *our* people and I cannot stand by and—" I had to cut him off.

"Sir, again, I'm sorry, but hear us out on the solution

and *then*, when lives ain't bein' lost no more, then you can decide what to do wit' Fulani. As you said, the people—*justice*—comes first." I can be kinda articulate when I wanna be.

I turn to Fulani and tell her to explain to him the setup between her, Banktel and the government extended back through New York, and he listenin' intently. He heard how she got involved wit' Jaffe and why she killed Jaffe. How she met Phil Chambers and why she met Phil Chambers. The drug shipments and, of course, what was 'posed to take place at the UN tomorrow morning at nine.

That's when he stepped in, like, "Yes, I am well aware of the UN developments. I intend to address the council in an attempt to quell their desire to intervene, but even with you at my side, Fulani, I'm afraid it will be hard to fight America's so-called humanitarian efforts."

"It might be easier than you think," I say.

The king reply, "How so?"

"Listen, remember you said, you had pictures of Fulani and her business associates, who turned out to be Uncle Phil and friends?"

"Yes, but those pertain to drug activity, not covert American operations," he said.

"Naw, yo," I correct him, "you got everything you need right there. You do have more than pictures, don't you?" I asked him.

"Of course, surveillance of my daughter is extensive. I have video tapes, audio..."

So then I say, "Okay check it. See, how I see it, the drug thing, that was just a scam, you know, a setup to hold over 'Lani's head and keep the strings attached, á la Manuel Noriega. But dig, why not hold it over *their* head? Blackmail work both ways, 'cause what they got knowledge of, they ain't 'posed to know, ya feel me?"

He, the king, look off in thought, so I go, "'Cause look, they fuc—I mean, they messed up by tryin' to consolidate against y'all, all the time hidin' behind a major corporation, but they all one and the same."

Fulani catchin' on, but she still skeptical. "But the pictures, the talks, it could be construed to be about anything."

"Yeah, true, but Uncle Phil is on front street, so if we could get him to understand he's the most vulnerable... Play one off against another, then we'll get it right outta the horse's mouth."

"And how do you propose to do that?" the king wanted to know.

I shrug, like it's all elementary. "'Cause it's a domino effect. Fulani told me Jaffe moved through a cat named Chino, who been workin' for NYPD for years as an informant. I figure we lean on him he'll lean on Tucci, 'cause he sold too many heads to the feds to do a bid of this magnitude. Once he fingers Tucci, we play a little divide-and-conquer and play Tucci against Chambers and Chambers is who we want 'cause he the direct link to the U.S., got it?"

Y'all still followin' me, too?

The king nod, but he still a little blurred. "Suppose this Chino person refuses to cooperate, or Tucci refuses to give us Chambers?"

I light my cigarette. "Then we screwed...but suppose they *do*?"

Everybody in silent contemplation until Fulani say, "Father, what else do we have to lose? I got us into this, and if you will allow, I—" she look at me and smile, "I mean, *we* will get us out."

He clasped his hands behind his back, paced a few steps, then turned to me and said, "All right. What will you need?"

"The tapes. Audio and video... And a car. Oh, and some clothes," I say, lookin' down at Water high-waters floodin' my shins.

"Take Joseph's car, and I'll also have him get you some decent attire."

"Who?"

"My interpreter, Joseph." He talkin' bout the English-speakin' dude. The king picked up his phone, then I turned to Fulani.

"Look, I'm gonna need you to stay here, while—"

"No, Sam."

"'Lani, listen—"

"*No*, Sam. This isn't your fight—it's mine, and I intend to be there every step of the way," she say, standin' firm, arms akimbo.

"You *are*, but the first thing you need to do now is hold some kind of press conference so everybody know you safe and ain't been abducted or some shit, you know? That way, you can lift the bounty off my head and I can breathe a little easier, ya'm mean?"

"I see your point, but..." she sigh, like, "okay, okay, you're right, I do need to clean this mess up. Hopefully, seeing my father and I together will help our cause in the UN. But why can't you wait until *after* the press conference?"

I crush out my cigarette in the ashtray then tell her, "'Cause, it's gonna be like roaches when you turn on the lights—they all gonna scatter. Tucci, Chambers, everybody. Time ain't on our side."

The king hang up the phone, and say, "Everything has been arranged, Mr. Black."

I turn to him. "Thank you, sir," then I say to 'Lani, "I'll call you, i-ight?" I start for the door until I hear, "Sam?"

"Yeah?"

"Be...be careful." I flash her a smile and a wink, then bounced out the door...

Ohhh, so Joe is a player after all, huh? I'm talkin' about the English kid, Joseph, who's BMW baby-blue drop top I'm currently pushin' down West Side Highway on my way to Harlem World. Beige leather interior wit' the TV in the dash. I'm watchin' that flick *True to the Game*... Ill flick. I dug the book, too. Some cutie from Philly wrote it... Anyway, where was I? Oh yeah, I was tellin' y'all 'bout the drop. I just wish Joe had the same taste in clothes as he did in cars... I'm sayin', smoothed-out R&B style just ain't me, fuckin' linen and all that, but fuck it, when in Rome... I throw on the Gucci lenses and hit the exit for Uptown.

So boom, I park the BM a block from Chino's spot, just to be safe. I tuck the snub and hop out, keepin' my eyes peeled in all directions. When I turn the corner, I see the nigga Lex parked in front of the building so at least I ain't gotta track this cat down. Only problem I ran into was the buildin' was one of them spots that a motherfucka gotta buzz you in. I'm lookin' at the buzzboard but ain't no last name ringin' no bells wit' me. Fortunately, some delectable little Asian dish was on her way out, so I caught the door. As she passed, I tilt my frames for eye contact, wishin' I had more time than I do...

Gotta note this buildin' down on my list of things to do... Anyway, when I get to his door, I notice it's cracked... Hmm. I put my ear to it, listenin' for movement. All I hear is some mellow salsa groove playin' low, so I knock... I knock again...

"Chino?"

No response...

I know the cat gotta be home, so I look around then pull out the snub and cock the hammer. I push open the door, real slow, like, "Chino? Chino, you in here? This Sam, yo." Still no answer so I step on in.

I can see this crab-ass nigga been livin' plush off of other niggas' blood, 'cause crib is laced. As I come up on the kitchen, I peep around to see it's spotless and unoccupied...

Where the fuck is he?

I step through the leathered-out living room and see where the music is comin' from. A CD on the stereo... Somethin' ain't right. I turn it off, hopin' to get a reaction from somewhere. "Yo, Chino," I say louder. "Nigga, where you at? This Sam."

I'm scopin' the hall, headed towards the rear of the apartment, and since I turned off the music, I can hear somethin' sound like...runnin' water? Maybe this cat in the tub. So I head for the bathroom and knock on the door. "Yo, you takin' a bath?"

Still no response, but since the door is cracked, I push it open and peep inside...

Damn.

The sound? Yeah, it was runnin' water. The reason it was runnin' was the tub had overflowed and it was runnin' all over the floor, and in the tub... Chino and some chick, butt-ass naked, covered in blood and shriveled up.

I guess Tucci ain't as dumb as I thought. I look down at Chino... All that dirt finally caught up wit' his ass. Damn shame about the girl, though. To all y'all shorties fuckin' wit' these kinds of niggas, let this be a lesson to you 'cause girlfriends get it, too. Say word.

Well, so much for Plan A, huh? Yeah, no question, that's why I'm backtrackin' up out this joint, wipin' everything I mighta touched on the way. I'm sayin', my prints is on enough shit as it is, you know?

Just to be safe, instead of goin' back downstairs I went up and out on the roof. Skipped roof to roof, and came out the building around the corner on the block where the drop was parked. I sighed and lit a cigarette... Without Chino, Tucci is clean as a whistle; but without Tucci, Chambers is untouchable...

Or is he?

I picked up the phone and called Fulani.

"Sam?" Is the first word she say when she answer.

"Yeah," I say, blowin' out smoke. "Bad news."

"What?"

"Tucci beat us to the punch. Chino dead."

Silence on the other end, then she say, "It's just as well. I talked to someone close to me and Phil. They informed me that Phil is on his way out of the country."

"Going?"

"Mexico. He's planning on leaving tonight at 6."

Hmm.

"You say 6, huh? Think you can get hold of a limo?"

"What for?"

I smile, like, "We need to pick up a very important person at 6."

Fulani catch on instantly 'cause I can hear the smile in her voice. "Done."

"I'm on my way," I say, then I hang up and dial another number.

Now, remember when I told you them Bronx niggas is troublemakers? Yeah well, I'm in trouble...

"What up?" Mick Benzo say, pickin' up the phone.

"Yo Mick, it's me."

He say wit' a chuckle, "Me? Me? Not the *me* from the newspaper and "News at Eleven" *me*? Not the world's most wanted *me*? Not the—"

"Ay, yo, you gonna let *me* talk or what? I got a problem."

I hear the cat laugh. "Your problems I don't need. Remember your last problem got us banned from all Olympic sporting events, *indefinitely*?"

Yo, how was I supposed to know you ain't 'posed to put out the torch? After I lit the blunt... Honest mistake.

Anyway, I tell him, "Just meet me in midtown at *exactly* 5:45, i-ight, in a van, Avenue of the Americas, on the north side of Banktel headquarters. You got it?"

He like, "Yeah, yeah, quarter to six, Avenue of the Americas, north side in a van. What up?"

"We gonna kidnap the richest man in America."

Mick laugh fo' real at that, then say, "Yeah, right. Not even *you* would try some shit like that."

"Just be there, ready to drive, i-ight?" I hang up, hop in the drop and head back to the Consulate...

CHAPTER NINE: BOOGIE DOWN DESTRUCTIONS

So, yo, after gettin' back to the Consulate, changin' clothes and tellin' the king what I'm up to—oh yeah, and I got Belinda back—me and Fulani head over to the Banktel building to try and head ol' Philly boy off at the path. It's a long shot, but like they say, always bet on black. Sam Black, that is...

Anyway, I'm sittin' there in the front seat of this limo, in my chauffeur getup, in front of Banktel headquarters, waitin' on Mr. Monetary himself. Fulani in the back, sittin' real quiet...too quiet. She lookin' at the gun Pearl gave her, turnin' it over and over in her hands. So I'm watchin' her in the rearview, watchin' the glint of the steel match the glint in her eyes and I know what's on her mind. "Ay, dig, 'Lani, you know dead people can't talk, right?"

Yeah, she understand, but she still lookin' at the nine. I can just imagine what she thinkin' 'bout doin' wit' it, 'cause the only thing worse than a woman scorned is a woman *betrayed*. But she i-ight, considerin' what we need Chambers for. Long as she don't air his ass out as soon as she see him and get past initial compulsiveness, I figure we'll be i-ight.

So I'm checkin' out the limo, playin' wit' shit. Openin' and closin' the roof, flippin' stations. Ain't like I never been in a limo before, I'm just bored waitin' on this motherfucka...

Whoa! There he go! Right on time. I adjust my cap in

the mirror, hop out and go around to the back door and open it. When he reach me, he say, "You're not my usual driver. Where's Frank?"

"Frank? I don't know, all I know is I was told to be in front of Banktel at 5:30 and since I'm 'posed to get off at five, I ain't exactly happy about takin' up Frank slack, whoever he is. But I'm here, you're here, but if you want Frank..."

I'm hopin' this cracka don't ask for no license or no shit like that, but from the nervous twitch in his eye, I can tell he tryin' to take the first thing smokin' up outta here. After a few seconds, he sigh real hard, one of those impatient, arrogant-ass, rich sighs. "No, no need to complicate matters when I'll only be needing you momentarily. Do you know how to get to the Newark airport?"

Oh, by the way, I do know where Frank is. But that's a whole 'nother story. Don't ask, on the grounds it may incriminate me; just know you'd be surprised how many limo drivers are illegal aliens... But back to Chambers.

Just as I opened the door and Chambers ducks his head to get in, he sees Fulani. "Hello, Phil," nine held at gut level. So I give him a little shove-slash-kick, well, not really little 'cause I tried to put my whole foot up his ass. I just did it discreetly, so not to be noticed.

Once he was in, I shut the door and jog around to the drivers' side and climb in. I look back and Fulani is bitch-smackin' the cat. Long as she don't kill 'im, fuck it—let her get the stress off. He all like, "Fulani, why are you—*smack*—beating me?—*smack*—*smack*—Please—*smack*—let's talk about it."—*smack*—*smack*— I pull out and turn the corner. A block away I see an all-white delivery van. My man, Benzo—I can always count on my dogs. So I ready Phil, psychologically, for the transfer.

"Hey, Phil. Can you hear me? Okay, as you can see, Fulani is extremely upset, and also extremely armed, and you know how volatile women can get. Now, what we need to talk to you about is really reason enough to leave you leakin' vital organs in the middle of the street. So I think it's in all our best interests that when we reach the van over there, we get in it as easy as possible. You readin' me?"

"Yes, yes, but why—" —*smack*—

So I pull over and hop out. I open Fulani's door and she get out wit' Phil by the collar and the joint to his gut. We cross the street and the van side door slide open. I see my man Twin sittin' in the back. Me, Fulani and Phil pile in as Twin close the door.

When Twin realize who we got, he sound off, like, "Oh, no. Aw, man, ay Mick! This cat done kidnapped the richest motherfucka in the world! Aw, man!"

Mick shrug his shoulders and say, "Yo, I told you who I was goin' to get, and you *know* how Sam do."

"But Phil Chambers?! Man, we goin' *under* the jail! I don't wanna be a player no more!" Twin say.

I say, "Um, are we gonna just *sit* here and wait for trial or you gonna get us outta here?"

Benzo pull off. I look back... Coast is clear. Pun still buggin', though. "Come on, Sam, what could this guy have *possibly* done to you?" He ask.

"Why don't you ask him? Phil?" I add, turnin' to Phil.

Phil like, "I haven't *done* anything! I demand to be released! Fulani, please. I-I-I don't understand."

"Naw, Phil, I think you do understand," I tell him, "so we're just gonna talk a bit."

"Talk? I have nothing to say," he huff, all indignant-like.

"Yeah, that's right, you probably all talked out." I look at Big Pun, like, "Yo, Twin, I bet you ain't know, not only is Phil here a multi-billionaire and own the largest bank in the world, but in his spare time he rap, too. Yeah. Matter of fact, how 'bout you pop in this tape, Mick, and check it out? Hottest shit on the street."

So Mick pop in the tape of one of Phil and Fulani's conversation and yo, it musta been bangin' 'cause everybody noddin' they heads to it...

Well, that is, everybody except Phil...

*****

STARFLEET DESTINATION: FAT JOE'S GARAGE, BOOGIEDOWN BRONX

It used to be a chop shop for stolen cars, but now Joe and his peeps hook up systems, throw on rims and bulletproof whips and shit. So we pull the van up in the garage. I send Fulani upstairs wit' Twin so she can cool out and talk to Twin's wife or somethin', anything, 'fore she beat this cat brain-dead. We take ol' Phil over to the farthest corner of the garage where Joe and Fathead playin' checkers... Well, really they arguin' and usin' checkers as an excuse. Me and Mick sit Phil down. Joe look at Phil, then at me, like, "What the?! Phil Chambers?! Ay, yo, Sam, what—"

"Long story, Joe. I'll tell you in a minute."

So Phil, surrounded by myself, Mick Benzo, Fat Joe and Fathead, said, "What is the meaning of this? Why have you brought me here?"

"Come on, Phil. You heard the tape. I mean, you *was* the tape, so let's not beat around the bush, huh?"

"What tape? What bush? Ay, yo, Sam, don't tell me you kidnapped Phil—" Joe try to ask again, but I cut him off.

"Drastic times call for drastic measures, i-ight? Just bear wit' me." Then I turn back to Phil who said, wit' a smug little grin, "The tape? You call that some type of evidence? Of what? Ha! Fulani's got you duped. Our relationship was strictly *personal*." Then he smile like I know what he mean. I felt like yokin' the cat up but instead...I chilled. I threw on my cop voice, the one they use on us so much, and seein' where I was goin' wit' it, Mick fell in it right wit' me.

"You fucked up, Phil."

"Yeah, Phil, fucked up," Mick echoed.

"The jig is up, we know everything."

"Everything, Phil."

"But we can help you, Phil. *You* can help you, Phil."

"Yeah, Phil, help yourself."

Phil's head goin' back and forth like a Cameo song; between me and Mick and I can tell he gettin' dizzy, but tryin' to keep his composure.

"But I haven't done *anything*."

"That's what they all say, Phil. Truth is, you goin' down. Doesn't matter now if you cooperate or not. Only thing left is whether it's hard or soft. You can take the window or the stairs," I tell him, like Jack of Spades. Then I start runnin' shit down to him like, "We got tapes, videos, receipts, the whole shebang, Phil, the whole shebang. We know you were the middleman for the government and Fulani. We know you arranged the shipments of drugs in large quantities to New York from Amantu, with the consent of New York *and* the government."

That's when Joe say, "Drugs?! Drugs?! I knew this cat ain't get all that paper keepin' his hands clean. Greedy motherfucka. It ain't enough he gettin' billions; naw, he gotta keep floodin' the hood wit' that garbage!"

I hear somebody in the garage say, "And this comin' from a man they used to call Joey Crack."

Joe fire right back, "That was then and this is now. I did what I had to do! Drugs don't make Joe the Don, anybody think different we can take this shit outside!"

No response. Point taken. Joe's bravado went unchallenged.

Now here go Fathead, "This remind me of a Western I—"

"Not now, Fathead."

Phil takin' all this in and I guess he think he fuckin' wit' the Bowery Boys 'cause how we argue amongst ourselves, and he get that ol' billionaire confidence back, stand up and say, "Look, you guys. You're barking up the wrong tree. Really. Whatever Fulani is involved in has nothing to do with me, and *if* it did, which it doesn't, what you have is merely circumstantial."

I ask, "Circumstantial, huh?"

"Yes, circumstantial," he say, real slow, like he talkin' to a kid... Damn, I wanna yoke this joker up. Count to ten.

1...2...3...

Phil continued. "Listen, why don't you call me a cab and we can forget this ever happened? No hard feelings. Honest. Matter of fact," he pulls out his checkbook, "let me compensate you for your efforts. Really, it was very noble of you to save the damsel in distress, when in actuality, it's the damsel *causing* distress."

I answer him by sayin', "Is that right? Yeah? Well um, check it... Circumstantial, huh? You know, Phil, you might be right. I mean, what court in the world would believe Phil Chambers—owner of Banktel, benevolent philanthropist, international player—would be involved in a plot with the United States and New York City to smuggle drugs and take over a small African country for oil rights, huh?"

"Exactly," he responded, smug grin and all. "So who should I address this check to?"

I say, "Naw, Phil, I think you better save your money, because, well... I just thought of something. Now granted, this plot is a hard pill to swallow. Granted. But you know the media loves this kind of thing. Eats it up. And the *public*? Especially the *black* public? You know we always lookin' for a white man to blame our troubles on. You know how niggers do. And, well, imagine what the public would say if Banktel was even *hinted* towards drug trafficking. All the schools, universities, non-profit organizations, et cetera and so on would cry, "Get Banktel out of our towns!" I can hear the chant now. Boycotts. Not to mention your partners. Nobody wants to be close to controversy, you know? And wit' this monopoly thing hangin' over your head in the courts already... Whew! Imagine the stock prices. Down the drain. Then maybe me and my friends here could get up some loot and buy up the stock, we'd make a killin'! Joe, what you think?"

Joe just smile and pulled out a wad of money,

followed by Mick and Fathead. Phil gulped and I continued.

"And then, we'd be in *your* boardroom, at *your* country club, drinkin' forties and eatin' chitlins 'cause you *know* how *niggers* do."

He paused, then asked, almost in a whisper, "How much?"

I put my hand under my chin and say, real thoughtful-like, "I don't know. I mean, I really don't wanna get involved, you know, not after America finds out *you* made these tapes to blackmail *them* to try and get this monopoly thing up off you. You do know that's how it'll be worded, don't you, Phil? And I don't wanna be nowhere around when ol' Uncle Sam gets angry, 'cause you *know* how America gets when she angry. Remember Kennedy, dontcha, Phil? He made America angry, too. Boy, I'd hate to be you right about now... But there is a way. There is a way that not only could you weasel outta this, but might even *benefit* by it." I stopped to see if Phil was grinnin'. He wasn't, but I was.

"Yeah, you know, a man's conscience is a powerful thing. Powerful. Stop a man from sleepin', even. You got a conscience don't you, Phil? Of course you do, and see, yours coulda told you it isn't right what America is *makin'* me do to Amantu. It just isn't right! And even if I lose my business, gosh darn, I've got to do what's right! This is you talkin', Phil. But no need to worry, you won't lose your business. Because the funny thing about black people— well, people in general—is they forgive. They forgave Clinton, why wouldn't they forgive you? You could probably get, um, Phil help me out here. What's that 'im' word? Spelled like I-m-m—"

He say, "Immunity?"

"Yes, that's it, Phil! Immunity! See? We here, we thinkin' alike! Yes, immunity. And then the public say, oh, poor Phil. Shame on big bad America, and now America can't Kennedy you 'cause if they do, then they'd be admittin' you were right. And you *know* how America hate to be wrong."

Then I got up close to him and put my arms around his shoulder like you'd do any sucka you was about to con or pick his pocket. "You see, Phil, your old friends put you on front street. Played you—played you like a sucka, usin' you to do their dirty work. What kind of friend is that, Phil? No friend at all, if you ask me. So you need new friends, Phil. Good friends, friends like us...and Amantu."

So Phil say, "You? Friends? You, who kidnapped me? Assaulted me? Friends?"

I holler back, like, "Well, Phil, there was really no other way 'cause we couldn't get an appointment. But don't look at it as a kidnappin', it was more like saving you from yourself. Openin' your eyes to a dangerous—albeit, beneficial—situation. An offer you can't refuse... I mean, it's better than a few government-issued slugs, right, Phil? But you think about it 'cause the ball's in your court now."

I walk away, lightin' my cigarette, when I hear Fathead say to Mr. Monetary, "You like Westerns?" Only a matter of time now, 'cause after talkin' to Fathead, he'll be ready to talk to anyone *but* Fathead. That's when Joe step to me and ask, "Yo, *now* can you tell me what the fuck is up?"

I was about to when the garage door opened and a green BMW pulls in wit' a cat drivin' and a girl in the passenger seat. I see her, she see me and recognize me, but I can't place the face. Not until she hop out, screamin' on me like I snatched her purse.

"So *here* you is! Here you is, huh? No, you *didn't* go runnin' all over town wit' some African bush bitch and ain't even call me! I ain't *give* you my number for my health, you know, so what's up wit' *dat*?!" Then she fold her arms over her chest. Joe chuckle, look at me then fade off, leavin' me wit' Lil' Miss Ball of Fire.

Now if Ma *know* who I been wit' and what I been *doin'*, then she should know I wasn't in no position to reach out and touch nobody. But do she say anything about that? Do she say, what happened? How are you? I heard the cops is tryin' to bag you. No. All she see is who I'm wit'...

Women.

So I try and smooth shit out. "Yo, Ma," 'cause I done forgot her name. This the shortie I met at Money party. "I been caught up and shit was crazy hectic. Still is, really, but—" she cut me off wit' some dumb-ass remark like, "What's that got to do wit' callin' *me*? Huh? They got cell phones, car phones—what, you ain't *ran* by no phone booths or somethin'?"

Ran by what?! Hold up... Matter of fact, if this lil' chick wouldn't had stepped to me at Money party and asked for a light, then *kept* my matches, I woulda had a light on the train. If I had a light on the train, I wouldn't had asked them kids and got blunted. If I wouldn't had got blunted and would've been lookin' where I was goin', I wouldn't had bumped into Fulani and if I wouldn't had bumped into Fulani I wouldn't be in this mess in the first place and I wouldn't be standin' here tryin to hear this broad! So now *I'm* swoll.

"Look, I said I was gonna call you, i-ight? The fuck?! You ain't the only one lookin' for my ass, I got—"

Why did I have to say it like *that*? Shortie fired off words like an uzi on me. "*Oh?!* I ain't the *only* one?! So what you tryin' to say? I'm sweatin' you?! Oh, no, sweetheart, TamikaRaseekaMarieBarell don't *do* no sweatin'! You want sweatin'?! I'ma *show* you sweatin'!" Then she stormed off and got back in the car. The driver was already waitin', so they bungee.

Mick saw the whole shit, so he step to me. "What was that all about?"

I light another cigarette. "Nothin'. Some chick I met at the Tunnel, that's all."

"Maybe we oughta relocate. You know how shorties can get when they heated."

So I look at him, "Who, Ma? She just blowin' off steam. I'll give her about an hour and call her. You worry too much. She ain't *that* mad..."

Famous last words.

*****

One hour later.

Phone rings once...twice...three times. No answer. I hang up. I'm thinkin' Shortie Flip-Out done forgot all about that shit. She flossin' wit' a cat wit' a BM and he gotta be crab to let his girl jump out screamin' on another man for not callin'. Yeah, she chillin'. Probably got the cat to take her shoppin'. Now they up in a suite in Manhattan, sippin' bubbly. I'm the farthest thing from her mind right now.

That's when Fathead step to me. "Chambers wanna holler atcha."

I walk in the little office in the garage and go in. Chambers say, "I've weighed my options."

"Good for you. And?"

Chambers said, "What I know or don't know depends on three things. Number one, I *definitely* get immunity. Without it, no deal. Two, this whole thing about clearing my conscience was my idea."

I'm thinkin', just like a cracka—wanna take the credit for everything, even hangin' his own self.

"And three, I'm still in on any Amantu oil rights that may be."

I respond. "As for number two, you can say Santa Claus told you to do it for all I care, but as for one and three, I think you know shit like that, I got no say in. I'll pass the word along, but uh, for a man in your position, I'd take what I could get."

I walked out and left that note in the air, and told Fathead, "Fats, take the cat upstairs and feed him. Keep him outta the way 'til mornin'." Then I stepped off, I needed to holler at 'Lani 'cause I ain't seen her in awhile. I think about tryin' Shortie Flip-Out again but I say, fuck it, she i-ight.

I head upstairs and I'm thinkin', yo, can it really be this simple to thwart some government shit like this and get away wit' it? But then again, why not? Maybe they just make it *seem* like ain't nothin' you can do so you don't *do*

112

nothin', you feel me? But if it's this simple... Yo. Anyway, we'll see tomorrow.

Twin's wife said Fulani on the roof, so I head up there. It's gettin' dark, you know, the sun makin' its westward dive and Ma standin' there silhouetted. I almost forgot how utterly stunnin' Ma look, you know, 'cause I ain't really had a chance to look at her in a while. But, yo, shortie is lovely and I'm thinkin', I could really get used to wakin' up to a face like that, if only...

Long story.

She standin' there lookin' at the Bronx, so I walk up to her and she say, "You know, from up here the Bronx isn't that much different from the villages outside of the palace. I mean, you see that woman coming out of that corner store? Just like the women in my country when they leave the marketplace. Same expression, same gait. I used to watch them. My people and I admired them—even envied them— because of the simplicity in which they lived. Our country is relatively poor in comparison to other African countries, but you could never tell by the people.

"I see much of the same spirit here. I-I-I never realized who would receive my...shipments. I mean, I knew but I didn't know, you know? Not until I met your friend Waterboy. At first I was repulsed, until I realized why he was how he is. Then it was like I was repulsed by *myself*. Can you understand that?" Fulani asked, turnin' to me.

I don't know what to say. It just seems Ma been doin' a little soul searchin', so I just say, "Yeah, but you, like you said, you ain't the only one pushin' that shit. You didn't know, well—"

Her serene aura turned crimson quick, and she spat, "Why must everyone always make excuses for me?! Huh?! Why?! Why can't you just say I fucked up? It's like, if I blew up the entire planet, you'd probably say, at least there's life on *other* planets!!"

Damn. I was just tryin' to be helpful. I think I'll keep my mouth shut and sit on the edge of the buildin'. After a minute, she sat down next to me, and go, "You know, don't you, that after this I'm going back to Amantu indefinitely?"

Is it okay to speak?

"Yeah, I know."

"And what will you do?" she ask me.

"What I been doin'," I tell her.

"Which is?" she ask, still probin'.

So I shrug, like, "A little of this, a little of that."

Then she flip again!

"Damn, can't you *ever* give a straight answer?! Why all this vagueness?! What are you afraid of?! I ask you a simple question and all you can say is this and that?"

If this chick was a roller coaster I'd be screaming, stop the ride! I'm ready to get off! 'Cause I don't like a lot of questions, 'specially about myself. I stand up and say, "Look, I got complex reasons for simple answers, all right? And anyway, instead of worryin' about what the fuck I'ma do, you need to be worryin' about how the fuck you gonna face your country wit' blood on your hands! 'Cause of you, a whole lot of muhfuckas is dead, dyin', i-ight? While you playin' global chess, that shit is happenin'! It's not a game! Yeah, you fucked up, you fucked up bad and if it wasn't for me you'd probably still be fucked up. So you need to recognize and stand on your own two feet 'cause I ain't gonna be there next time!"

I'm out. I turn and head for the steps, when I hear. "Sam." I don't even turn around, I just respond like, "What?"

"Thank you."

Women... Go figure.

So it's almost zero hour to the next mornin' and I spent the night tellin' Twin, Joe and Mick everything I done told y'all up to this point. For the umpteenth time, I find myself explainin' this shit. Maybe I should just write a book, huh? *The Adventures of Ghetto Sam*... picture that.

Anyway, all Twin kept sayin' was, "But she was

naked?!" So you know what part he was stuck on. Fathead and Phil Chambers did have somethin' in common. Westerns. So they kept each other outta my hair. Fulani, she just chillin', reserved but polite. I can tell she anxious to get this over wit' when she keep askin' me, "Do you think the UN will believe us?" I just shrug it off and blow out a smoke ring. She put her finger through the ring as it rose and said, "I'm sorry about the roof. I-I didn't mean to be so—"

"Nosy?" I complete her sentence.

She chuckle lightly, "Yeah, I guess I was. But I was only doing to you what you've been doing to me."

"Which is?"

"Figuring you out," she said.

"Oh yeah? And what have you figured so far?" This should be good.

"I'll tell you if you let me ask you one question." I give her the "okay" nod. "What's her name?"

Damn! Ay, yo, remember I told you earlier about the linen of a lie and how, when at a loss for one, always answer a question wit' a question? I-ight then, check this.

"Her who?" I know she heard my voice crack, 'cause shit, I heard it.

"Oh, come on, Sam, I see the way you look at me, how you responded to my kiss... Don't think I haven't been noticing. But it's like, there's something—no, *someone,* holding you back. Am I right?"

...Remember Shortie Flip-Out in the BM? Yeah well, apparently she remembered, too, 'cause she sent me a message to let me know I was on her mind.

"Come out with your hands up!" is what the bullhorned announcement bellowed from outside the garage, so that pretty much told the story. Besides, nobody else wit' animosity knew I was here. I guess y'all and Fulani gonna hafta wait on that answer, huh?

"Ay, Sam! The fuckin' place is swarmed! Cops *and* feds everywhere and it don't look like they here to arrest!" Twin screamed.

I turn to 'Lani. "I thought you took care of this wit' the press conference?!"

"I did!" she holler back, nervously.

"The fuck?! Police don't watch TV or somethin'?!" Damn! Think...think...think... Can't hit the roof 'cause wit' feds come snipers. Back door covered, front door covered... The fuck?! Man, we need a tank...

Lightbulb!

"Yo, Joe! What you got in here Armor All-ed down?"

Joe say, "The gray Lex in the corner and the Hummer up on the rack."

Now, remember I told you Joe hook up systems, rims and shit? Remember I also told you he bulletproof whips, too? Voilà... A tank!

"Okay, check it," I say, turnin' to Twin, "Twin, why they call you Big Pun?"

"'Cause I like to crush a lot."

"I-ight, that's exactly what I need you for. Joe, get the Hummer off the rack, and Twin, you grab the tow truck and run a block for us."

"Run a block?"

"Yeah. When we ready, I want you to smash through the garage door and crush into a cop car in the way, and we'll be right behind you in the Hummer. Don't worry about the charges 'cause once this bomb drop, a few crushed cars will be the least of New York's worries."

Twin like this kind of shit. "I feel you," he say, givin' me dap then headin' for the tow truck.

Outside the bullhorn say, "This is your last warning. Come out with your hands up!"

I turn to Joe. "Ya ready?" All I hear is automatic pistols click-clockin' the reply. We all pile in. Joe drivin', Benzo up front, me and Fulani in the back wit' Chambers between us. He scared to death. No need to front, 'cause I am, too. Fathead in the back-back, wit' a Mac 11 pointed through the gun turret slit in the window. A ghetto armored truck. Twin in the front wit' the tow truck. He look back at us as Joe give him the nod and Twin floor it...

Garage door everywhere!

Cops duckin', dodgin' and shootin', but Twin low in the seat. He manage to clear us a path between a S.W.A.T. van and a fed car. We out!

I look back and Twin done hit a tree. Cops swarmin' him and tryin' to light us up. Bullets bouncin' off like Superman chest and Fathead sharp-shootin' out tires, so only two cop cars and a fed made it clean out of the pile-up...

It's on!

"Ay, yo, Joe, *drive* this muhfucka! Mick, pass me the celly!" I gotta call the king and let him know it's been a change of plans. I told him he need to get as many cars as he can muster and drag the streets leadin' up to the Bronx through Harlem, 'cause ain't no tellin' how far we can make it.

So we rollin'. Four more cops jump in the chase, sirens wailin'. Fathead manage to take out two, causin' the fed car to flip over the first car that jackknifed. But just when we about to hooray the shit, six more come through and a ghetto bird hit the air.

"Aw, man! They callin' out the 'copters, yo!" Mick said, lookin' through the bulletproof sunroof.

We just got into Harlem, then we back in the Bronx, then we in Harlem again 'cause Joe whippin' this shit like a pro. He even made a cop crash into the front of a liquor store. These motherfuckas everywhere like roaches!

"Hit Broadway, Joe!" Mick yelled.

Joe swung a hard left and fishtailed into a parked car. Now shit *really* get hectic. I guess the cops realized we pushin' a tank, 'cause the next batch of cops, when they started shootin', windows started smashin'!

"Oh shit, they got penetrators!" Fathead hollered, duckin' down. Matter of fact, *everybody* got lower 'cause cats know they playin' for keeps. So now we got a whirlybird up above, penetratin' bullets all around and up ahead... The *thickest* roadblock I ever seen! No side streets to hit, can't ram it, can't back up so Joe come to a screechin' halt.

Oh, my God, we're going to die! We're going to—"

—*SMACK*—

That was Phil yellin' and me smackin'. I tried to draw blood from his ass.

"Motherfucka, if you scared get in my pocket!" I tell him. You know this coward motherfucka actually tried! "Get the hell off me!"

So cops is gettin' out they whips, guns drawn and pointed. So I hold Phil up by the collar. "Yo, we got Phil Chambers! You hear? Phil Chambers! One more step and—" I was answered by a barrage of bullets. So much for the hostage angle, huh?

So we all low, cops like, "Come out—"

"Yeah, yeah, wit' your hands up, we know already!" Mick hollered back, then he said, "You know if we get out, they gonna light us the fuck up, right?"

"So, what up?" Fathead ask.

Joe said, "This what up!" Then he hold up his Desert Eagle .40 caliber.

"Fuck it," I say, and look at Fulani. She ready. Then I smell it. What the...?

"Ay, yo, the white boy done shitted on himself!" I screamed.

Joe like, "Fuck him! It's do or die now!"

So just as we ready to bail out and go down guns blazin', all I saw was black limos, Lincolns, Cadillacs and vans, in total about twelve vehicles comin' from everywhere!

"It's the cavalry! It's the cavalry!" Fathead yelled out.

Sho' nuff. Yo, you shoulda seen all them Africans pull up and surround all them cops wit' guns you 'posed to only use in wars! My word! 5-0 ain't know what to do, until one of the Africans said, "That vehicle contains His Majesty's daughter, the princess. If you do not cease and desist, it will be viewed as an act of aggression against the country of Amantu, and we *will* reply in kind!"

Yo! Them cops was fucked up. The feds just dropped they heads and waved to the police to lower their weapons.

Ay, yo...

By now, a crowd had gathered along Broadway and when them cops lowered their guns in defeat... You shoulda heard the cheers and yells from that jet black and golden bronze crowd! Word up!

I had to get a better look, so I climbed through the sunroof and perched myself on the roof and I'm thinking...

Eleanor Bumpers.

Abner Louima.

Amadou Diallo.

Patrick Dorismond.

And all those in between, this one's for y'all! Black Power! Yo, not even a mile from the Audubon Ballroom. Malcolm woulda been proud, and yo, *speakin'* of Malcolm...

Hmm...

CHAPTER TEN: DETROIT RED & HARLEM BLACK

We missed the nine o'clock deadline.

I mean, after the chase and New York's top brass being called to Harlem to straighten out the situation, it took us a minute to get to the UN building. So as we entered the Great Hall, we heard the American delegate saying, "And this is why we propose the sending of peacekeepers to Amantu."

We caught the tail end of his presentation, but we caused quite a stir walking in. Me, Fulani, King Mofusu, his advisor, five of his guards, Phil Chambers and three cats from the Bronx. The king's advisor spoke first.

"Stop these proceedings! The war in Amantu is no more! I bring before the Council King Mofusu and his daughter Fulani, heir to the throne and alleged rebel leader. As of today, the government of Amantu and the rebels have reached an accord!"

The American delegate, realizin' what was at stake, blurted out, "It's a sham! A sham! A-a-a cover-up within the royal family to repel intrusion and continue to manipulate and oppress the native Amantians!"

The advisor smiled, "A sham? Gentlemen of the world, I'll tell you what's a sham. The sham is America's façade of concern and humanitarianism. We have concrete evidence and an eyewitness willing to testify, under immunity, that the U.S. government and the city of New York used a major corporation to smuggle illegal drugs into

New York. We also have evidence that paid provocateurs entered Amantu to stir up civil strife and unrest. This is the real cause of civil war in Amantu!"

The American delegate turned crazy red in the face, as the ooh's and ahh's went through the assembly like a wave. The American cat said, "I object to these allegations, unless and until they can be substantiated!"

The chairman of the UN was like, "Sir, where is your witness and what is this evidence you alluded to?"

The advisor gingerly—I say gingerly because Chambers was still smellin' like shit—guided him forward. "I bring before the Council Mr. Phillip Chambers, owner of Banktel Corporation, who, of his *own accord*," the advisor said "own accord" wit' an irony you had to understand to detect, "has come forth, and in my hand are recorded phone conversations, videotaped meetings and shipping documents for the Council's review."

More ooh's and ooh's as the chairman looked on. The king cleared his throat and spoke. "Mr. Chairman, Amantu would like to be heard."

"You may do so at this time," the chairman replied, wit' a nod of courtesy.

Fulani stepped forward to address the peoples. "Representatives of the world, hear the cry of Amantu! For the past eighteen months, my country has been ravaged by civil unrest, due in part—a *major* part—to my own naïveté. It is also due to foreign manipulation and intervention—namely, the United States of America. It is true, I am solely responsible for my participation and will continue to suffer long after justice has been served, but I ask you—I *implore* you—do not punish my people for my crimes by inflicting them with more bloodshed and sending in troops. These troops' main goal is to depopulate the countryside and stake out shares in Amantu's newly-found oil reserves. I know this to be true because, as I have said, I too am responsible.

"But Amantu is not the only country being puppeted. My experiences have made me privy to information concerning many of the countries you represent and many of you I see before me. So I ask you to rescind on the American proposal of UN troops. I also ask you to search your own hearts, your own conscience and purge your precious lands of the cancer that is America. Thank you."

Ay, yo, it was total silence. You could tell mad cats was feelin' it 'cause they was noddin' they heads and smilin', like, you go girrrrl. Other cats had red faces. I guess those was the puppets 'Lani was talkin' about.

But dig, just as the chairman was about to speak, I thought, aw, what the hell.

"Um, yo—I mean, excuse me? I would like to be heard, too."

The chairman, Fulani and Mofusu looked at me like I was crazy. The chairman like, "And who are you? What country do *you* represent?"

Represent? Now he talkin' *my* kind of language. "I represent Newark: the Brick City, and I got the Don from the Bronx wit' me."

Joe say, "What up, yo," like this was Madison Square Garden and not the UN.

I spoke.

"Listen, about thirty years ago a man named Malcolm X wanted to politic wit' y'all about the conditions over here in America. He was comparin' our lot wit' a lot of third world countries. He said America was the biggest hypocrite in the world 'cause they front like they all for peace abroad while it's a war goin' on in their own streets. I'm sayin', right here in New York, while y'all poppin' bottles a man named Amadou Diallo was shot *forty-one times*... They hit him head to toe, he even had gunshot wounds in the bottom of his *feet*... Even firin' squads don't carry out executions like that. Just like thirty years ago, just like now, ain't nothin' changed. Cats is still dyin' and it seem like nobody care.

"Now, I don't know a whole lot of big words; probably, longest word I know is motherfucker, but I do know if America wanna be a uncle then he need to start bein' a father to his own, you know? So recognize, 'cause if America do it to us or to Amantu, they'll do it to you. Bottom line. So listen to Ma—I mean, Princess Fulani, 'cause she right and anybody think different, me and my mens from the Bronx will see anyone of you muhfuckas in the street right now!" I threw that last challenge at the American delegate and looked him dead in the eye, but just like a sucka, I made him study his shoes.

The chairman cleared his throat and said, "Uh...yes. Very, uh, well-spoken, Mr..."

"Black. But my friends call me Ghetto Sam, brother." Yeah, 'cause the chairman, he a brother and I could tell he was feelin' what we was puttin' down.

So anyway, after a whole lot of political mumbo-jumbo, of which I understood nothin', we bounced. Basically, they put a freeze on the proposal 'til the UN send a commission to Amantu to investigate the situation and see if America gonna get served. But you know America, them some slick-ass cats, and like cats, they always seem to land on their feet. Yeah, well, not only is the streets watchin' but the world too, so, yo... We'll see how that go.

As for Tucci... He got rid of Chino just in time to duck the bullet, so he got away...for now.

Oh, and Chambers... Banktel's stock dropped like Mike Tyson's opponents back in the 80's. But it was only temporary, and you know what they say, one man's loss and all that. Anyway, who wanna buy some Banktel stock street corner-cheap? Don't matter to me 'cause what I paid, I'ma flip profit regardless.

But I'm gettin' ahead of myself.

Joe and them shot up to Central Booking wit' the king's advisor to get Twin out the bing and just when I thought it was safe, 'Lani say, "Two more stops before we go to Amantu."

"We?" I ask, 'cause that type of French I understand.

"That's what I said, isn't it? And it's not debatable; it's an order from the queen," she say wit' her hands on her hips akimbo, lookin' straight delicious.

An order, huh? Yeah, I danced for Latifah when she ordered me to so, yo, who am I to buck royalty? As I opened the door to the Navigator, I ask, "I-ight, where to?"

"To get the gold and the pearls."

Gold and pearls?! Ay, yo, what else is this girl into?...Here we go again...

About the gold...

Remember the Q4 got found in Jersey City? I-ight, well, that's where she had the payment for the last shipment stashed, on the docks. Get this... Fifty million dollars in gold! I almost flipped when I saw them oil barrels filled wit' shine. Talk about bling-bling... Where was I? Oh yeah, Jersey City. That's where she was headed the night she met me. To grab her gold and vaporize, but Tucci had some cats waitin' to body her. They ain't know where the gold was, though. Check how Ma got away! Yo, *she swam the Hudson.* Anybody know the Hudson know that's the nastiest, slimiest, toxic-iest river around. She swam all the way to NY!

I was like, "Swam?"

She echoed and confirmed. "Swam."

Damn. I'm surprised she ain't grow another arm or some shit in that radioactive shit. I asked her why she got paid in gold and she say because she ain't trust American currency. No doubt. Ma may be naïve, but she a thousand miles from dumb.

So we load up the shine and I'm like, "But where the pearls?"

She just smiled...

"*Minnie* Pearl?! Go to Africa?! I can't even get her to move fifty feet to Newark. Aw, man, you must be smokin' more than la or somethin'."

·124·

But 'Lani say some shit like, "Woman's intuition."

Yeah i-ight, woman's intuition, is what I'm thinkin' as I drive to Pearl spot. We go to her layout but she ain't there. It's mid-afternoon, though, so I know exactly where she at...

Central Park. That's where we found her, pushing Water on the swing. I pull the Navigator over and I'm tellin' Ma, "Yo, I *know* Pearl, she gonna start singin' "Native New Yorker." Pearl ain't goin' to no Africa."

So 'Lani like, "What would you like to bet?"

I should take the bet, is what I'm thinkin' as we slide up on Pearl. Pearl hug 'Lani but she swing on me. "Boy, where's my Belinda? You get her back yet?"

"Um, yo..." I just shrug shoulders. Truth is, y'all know I got Belinda back, but uh...

So Pearl like, "I see y'all dressed regular. Binkie, pull your pants up, don't nobody wanna see your black tail. Nice big car and y'all ain't duckin' no bullets. I reckon everything musta turned out all right."

Fulani say, "Yes, it looks like it. Listen, I just wanted to stop by and say thank you and I'm sorry for the way I acted back—"

Pearl just wave her off and said, "Ain't nothin', baby. I gets fed up wit' it from time to time myself." Fulani look at me, but I still ain't convinced.

"Well, that's the other thing I came to say. You know how you asked me if I had any pictures of my country?"

"Yeah."

"Well, um, it looks a lot better in person," Fulani timidly suggested.

Pearl say, "In person? You mean like *go* there? To Africa?" Here it come... *I'm a native New Yorkerrrr...*

"Yes. I mean, think about it, Pearl. I know you've got your freedom and all but, well, I would be honored to have you and Waterboy in my country. Really."

125

Pearl sorta looked off right, so I'm thinkin', she tryin' to say it so she don't break 'Lani's heart. Damn, I knew I shoulda bet.

Pearl says, "It sho' would be nice to see for myself where my blood run from. See the Motherland up close and personal-like... I don't know..." she say, turnin' to Water and askin', "Water, what you think?"

Water clappin' his hands, talkin' bout, "Africa! Africa!"

What?!

"Well, I guess he said it all," Pearl say, smilin' that snaggletooth smile. Waterboy is clappin' and Fulani lickin' her tongue at me like, I told you so.

Glad I didn't bet...

CHAPTER ELEVEN: THE DAY THE SKY RAINED GOLD

I knew I shouldn't have sat by no damn window... Look at all that shit down there. Rivers look like cracks in the sidewalk. Aw, man... Brothers ain't supposed to fly, we 'posed to *be* fly. But here I am, on the king's private jet. It's me, Fulani, Water, Pearl, Fat Joe, Twin, Mick and Fathead. Oh, and fifty million in gold coins.

Fulani ask me, "You okay? You're not airsick, are you?"

"Naw"—just sick of the air—"naw, I was just thinkin', you know, 'bout the gold."

"Yes, I can understand. You and your friends will soon be very happy and very rich."

"Yeah. That's just it. Them coins, we can't take 'em and you can't give 'em. 'Cause they ain't yours to give or ours to take."

She like, "You mean—"

"Yeah, I mean...it's blood money. I mean, I wanna get fat like the next gully cat that's starvin', but yo..." I ain't know what else to say.

"Well, what do you expect me to do with them? Give them back to the U.S.? Throw them into the sea? Come on, Binkie, now the money can be put to good use."

I just look at her, then nod towards Waterboy. "Good use? Tell that to Water 'cause if anybody deserve it, it's him. Go 'head and give him a whole barrel full and tell him that's for him being born and abandoned. You think it'll be

127

enough to compensate for his life?" Fulani looked down at her hands folded in her lap...

Then it hit me. "But you know what? I got a better idea. How far to Amantu?"

"Within twenty minutes, why?"

"Just come on," I say, takin' her hand and leadin' her towards the rear of the plane.

It took me a minute to convince Ma it was the right thing to do. All she kept sayin' was, "You're crazy, you know that?" But I been knowed that. I finally convinced her, though. When I told Mick to grab a barrel, he thought I was nuts, too, 'til I explained where it came from. Then he was wit' me.

See, what we did was, when we got over Amantu, we slid the door open, braced ourselves and dumped barrel after barrel out in the skies over Amantu, until every barrel was empty. Twin went crazy! I thought he might jump out after it, 'cause he kept sayin', "First she was naked and now *this*!"

But, yo...seein' all that shine fill the sky like that... It was a beautiful thing. The coins glitterin' and sparklin' in the sun, lookin' like the glitter on Michael Jackson's glove. Only the sky was the glove and the shine, the sparkle. And dig, I'm thinkin' about Frankie Beverly and Maze, that song "Golden Time of Day"... It was beautiful like that, and you know what? It felt beautiful.

Life is good...

Amantu was a sight fo' real. Make Hawaii or Bermuda look like Coney Island wit' a makeover. I had forgot there was places in the world without projects, but still a lot of black people. A few spots had been burnt out 'cause of the fightin'—villages and stuff—but besides that, everythin' was fly as Eden. You could still hear occasional gunfire in the distance, but without the U.S. and wit' Fulani's word, most of the rebels ceased fire. The ones that didn't wasn't no match for the king's army. They still a long way from gettin' back to normal, but at least they on the road to recovery.

They even had a ceremony for us, too! Fulani ain't tell me about that. It was some shit like when them medieval cats got knighted or a purple heart, or like Princess Leia did Han Solo and Luke Skywalker at the end of *Star Wars*, 'cept ain't no wookies—just Big Pun.

Imagine that.

Four cats from the BX and one from the Brick, grimy hoodlums, goin' to be honorary members of the Amantu Elite Forces. It was mad fly, Fulani lookin' all regal in her royal garb, purple and gold, and barefoot...

My foot fetish... Damn.

They sang mad songs wit' some fly rhythms and beats, shit make you nod to this. But, yo, African drums ain't no different than hip-hop drums, but then again, they are one in the same. Say word.

Oh yeah, I forgot to tell y'all about the locusts. Before we had got there, the locusts had came which, unlike Egypt, to Amantu it was a good thing 'cause they eat them shits. Ay, yo... I did, too—that is, until 'Lani told me what it was.

I was like, "Locusts?!"

"Locusts."

"Bugs?!"

"Bugs."

Fuck dat, I ain't eatin' no damn bugs. I mean, I mistook a roach for a raisin in my bran once, but shit, that was a mistake. Taste like chicken, too...

Anyway, at the festival, they had some type of wrestlin' match that the Amantians is big on. Sorta like WWF without the choreography. They tried to get me in it, but two men grabbin' each other in contorted positions ain't my type of hype—I'm better at shootin' dukes—but Pun got in it. The object ain't to pin your man, just make his shoulders touch the ground. Shiiiit, they couldn't even *move* Pun, let alone drop 'im, so he won by default.

Fulani had Pearl lookin' good, too. Pearl was wearin'

an all-yellow African getup wit' the head wrap. Far from the rags she used to find. She insisted on cookin', too. While the other women were makin' yam foo foo and eatin' kola nuts, Pearl was fryin' chicken and cornbread. Hey, you can take the girl out the city... Y'all know the rest.

To make a long story short, everything was goin' good... Too good. 'Cause I was gettin' comfortable and Ma was startin' to sink her hooks in me. Not that she was tryin', but uh, the moon does have a magnetic pull, ya feel me? So after a few days of celebrations, I tell her, "Yo, it's that time," reluctantly, and she made the arrangements—reluctantly.

Last I saw Water I told him, "Yeah, Water, you gonna be happy here."

He say, "Happy," then ran off to finish playin' wit' his newfound friends.

As for the king, he came back just before we was about to go. When he found out he said, "Leaving? So soon?"

I say, "Yeah, Your Kingship, I—"

He cut me off to say, "Please. Call me Mofusu. You have earned it." Then he flashed me his kingly smile. He went on. "I am not so old not to know spring blooms in the blossoms of youth. What does Fulani say?"

"Well," I started, slow-like, "We ain't really talked about it, you know? I told her I gotta go," then I shrug my shoulders, and I guess he understood, 'cause he nodded and said, "You, my young friend, are of a dying breed. I wish you well and whenever you wish, please don't hesitate to call on me as you would an old friend, or on Amantu as your second home."

Hmm. For a cat of my ilk, a country halfway around the world wit' no expedition law is a wonderful gift, indeed. I guess the king knew that. He offered me his hand and I offered mine in return.

Now the whole time, Gorilla Man been standin'

behind Mofusu, eyein' a nigger wit' a crooked grin. So when the king walked off, Gorilla Man step up and said, "I glad...how you say, I glad I not kicka off...kicka off on your ass."

Say *word*!

"You know, festivals in my country sometimes last for days, sometimes months, sometimes even years," Fulani signified, and gave me that smile I remembered from when we first met.

I'm like, "Yo, ain't nothin' I'd like better than to stay here wit' you for days, months and years, but truthfully I'd only be gettin' in your way. You know? I mean, you got a lot of catchin' up to do, makin' up to do and findin' the 'u' in 'you.' All that gonna take some time. Besides, I got a lot of prior commitments on my side of the tracks, you know?"

She just nodded her head as tears welled up in her eyes. I feel mine in my gut, so I say, "But um, if you ever in New York, run me over again." Corny, I know, but dig, I'm doin' everything in my power not to boo hoo like a baby in front of 'Lani and what do she do? ...Hug me. Hug me, like it's no tomorrow... Damn... I feel the shit trickle down my cheek.

After a minute, which seemed like forever (*forever fo'eva* eva *forever eva)*, we broke the embrace and she looked in my face.

"What's that?"

"What's what?" I ask, frontin' like I don't know.

"Tears," she say, and wipe one off my cheek, but I pull back.

"Yo, chill, 'fore them knuckleheads see you."

"Too late."

"Huh?" I say, then turn around. Fat Joe huggin' Twin, Fathead huggin' Mick Benzo, then they rub they eyes like they cryin', then bust out laughin'. "Aw, man, you see what you done started? I ain't *never* gonna hear the end of this."

Ma find it amusin', but I know them cats. If they ever catch me just chillin', bein' my introspective self, they'll say some ol' fly shit like, "What's wrong? Baby miss Fulani?" And the bad part about it is they'll probably be right.

So just when the Jeep to take us to the plane come, here comes four of the most beautiful little girls you ever seen, wit' the biggest eyes—like the souls of the four little girls that got killed in that church in Birmingham in '63 done came down from heaven. They approach me and Fulani. Three carryin' a really, really big wooden bowl and the one in the front started talkin' in Fulani tongue.

"They have something they want to give you," Fulani said, then she translated as the little girl stepped forward timidly and began to speak.

"Before you came, our nights were filled with death and fears, and our days running from our nights. But with you, the Most High sent us peace and rained gold from the sky. That is a blessing and will help us in the hard times and replace our lost crops. So in the name of the Most High, we present this gift to you."

After that speech, all them BX heads had tears in their eyes. Ma too. The little girls stepped up and placed at my feet the biggest bowl of gold this side of the rainbow. Twin's eyes got big as plates and Fathead said, "It's gold in them there hills!" Always the comic...

Fulani smiled as Joe and them loaded the gold in the Jeep. I tried to give Fulani one last hug, but she took a step back, slowly shaking her head no." Yeah, I feel you, Ma. I might not let go, either.

As I turned to walk away, she said, "I finally figured out a name for you." I turned to face her and she say, "Zauj Nafs. It means mate... Soul mate."

Ay, yo, I been called a lot of things, but...

FINAL WORDS

So there it is, in a nutshell. How, no matter *who* you are, or *where* you are, you can get your point across—you know, make your voice heard. I'm sayin', just look at a ghetto cat like me. I took on half the world—and *won.* Which is how I came to be sittin' here on the Ivory Coast, feelin' the breeze and singin' Jungle Brothers classics in the real jungle, two or three coconuts filled wit' shine, wonderin' if I shoulda stayed wit' Fulani. What y'all think?

Naw... Not now, anyway, maybe not ever. I don't think neither one of us is ready for that. But hey, you never know what the future holds, right? Yeah, no doubt. To the future.

So as I'm sittin' there about to light my cigarette only to find I *still* ain't got no match, wishin' I had two sticks, a magnifyin' glass or a volcano would erupt...anything... And I think, maybe I should buy a lighter. Naw, it'll take the fun outta smokin'. You can get into a lot of shit just askin' for a light. Besides, I ain't seen my Mom Dukes in a minute and I'm late on my blackmail fees. And, yo, I need a few ends so I can cop the new Tribe called Quest when they get back together...

Wishful thinkin'? Yeah, but hey, a brother can dream, can't he? After all, that's what life's all about...

We'll holler...

The Adventures of Ghetto Sam

THE GLORY OF MY DEMISE

The Glory of My Demise

This is for all the poets, thinkers, geniuses—all who died unbeknownst in slavery—for all the trees that fell in the uninhabited forest and reverberated...silently.

The Glory of My Demise

PRELUDE TO A THOUGHT

Tell *no one* of this...what I've seen, what I've done...

But I hope you understand, I *had* to tell someone...and you—yeah you—you been wantin' to know...dyin' to know...

Literally.

Dyin'. And what have you learned? You write books about us, try to psychoanalyze us. Pigeon hole us, lab-rat-monkey us, and then you go home, driving in your Lexus LS or Suburban to suburbia or wherever the fuck they keep the rock you crawled out from under, and you listen to *it*, thinkin', boy am I glad *we* don't have *it*.

But that ain't *it*, and you ain't safe. *No one* is.

Let me tell you something. Those that don't know can't tell you—and those that do, won't.

Period.

What they say is pain, it ain't pain. You can't bottle pain, you can't Memorex tape pain, you can't prostitute pain on every corner or market and sell it. The streets can tell you that, hungry eyes tell you that, *Malcolm* tried to tell you that, but you still ain't listen and you still ain't heard a word! Okay, fuck it. You really want *it*? I'ma take you there, right now. Naw, fuck that! Fuck wifey, your kids, your dog, your two-car garage, pull this shit over, now! Pull over!

Feel that?! You feel that?! Look at you now. Blood runnin' down your face like water. That's real, right?! It ain't comin' out your books, your studies or your speakers no more, is it?! Naw, it's comin' outta you... Fuck you mean, how I get here?! Don't worry *how* I got here, I'm here 'cause you called me and I ain't goin' nowhere until I teach you one thing...be careful what you ask for. You might just get *it*.

CHAPTER ONE

He screamed, "Life's a bitch and then you die!" and then he jumped off the roof, like he thought he could fly...

I was there. I saw the whole thing. I was comin' out of the store wit' papaya Goya and a chew stick. I had just bought a pack of Newports wit' my last two dollars, and the only reason I got it, 'cause Nanny let me go for the difference. But I seen it. I heard him. I looked up and he was looking up. Towards the sun. Looking...at death. And he...he ain't really jump, he just leaned into it to embrace *it*, or rather let *it* embrace him. And on the way down, my word, he was smilin'. Not no happy smile, not no crazy smile. Naw. Like a man who had just found the answer to his biggest problem...

Life.

Like right before you bust a nut. Fuckin' ecstasy. I'm talkin' about the smile 'cause I can't explain the feeling, the thought. Just the smile. I wasn't the only one to see it. His daughter seen it, too. Well, she saw as much as three year-old eyes would let her see, let her understand. But I know she didn't, 'cause who can understand death, you know? Once you go, who can you tell? What I'm asking you for, you don't know no more than I do.

You know what her name is? Eternity. He named her Eternity 'cause he said through her he lives on. No matter what, she *is* 'cause he *was*, you know? But her mother call her T.T. Why, no matter how beautiful a name *is*, no matter how deep, niggas gotta make it so simple? Like Eternity is

141

too much to comprehend or say.

He had just come home from upstate. Three joints. That means years, three years. Nothin' major, just part of survivin'. But you don't understand that, do you? You still caught up in the American Dream, huh? Yeah, well, wake the fuck up, 'cause here we are, where dreams come in bottles and bags. And a job? What can I do wit' a ninth grade education, a record and a black face? Don't even mention school. You know what? My eighth grade teacher...I *fucked* her. Word up. You think I'm lyin'? I fucked her right there on the desk. So how much you think I learned? What she tried to teach, I already knew...

But what I don't know is why. Or maybe I do, just too easy to understand some shit like that, when I 'posed to be freaked out on seein' some shit like that, you know? But I'm not, and that's what scares me.

But yo, at the wake, everybody was there. Ere'body. My man had mad love. His baby mother was there, Eternity's mother. Her name, Jewel. Yo, she was fucked up, but what you expect? She loved that brother, for real. I mean, for real. Been wit' him since before I could remember, but I was there when they met. Naw, I know, I know. It was '86. I know 'cause LL had just dropped "I'm Bad." Met her at the block party they be havin' every summer on our street. She was dipped. Fly-ass red bone in a pink and blue Dapper Dan Fendi suit, wit' pink and white Reebok Classics. Hoop earrings wit' her name through 'em and *mad* shine. I ain't know whether to rob her or throw rhythm. We was all young but her older brother Sammi was gettin' money on the South side. Year after dat, some cats caught him on his porch and wet him up. Now he in a wheelchair and shit in a bag. He still gettin' loot, though. I respect that.

Yeah, so, my man stepped to shortie and bagged her and they been troopin' ever since. She even did his bid wit' him, the whole nine. You don't find many shorties willin' to stick by a cat when he upstate, so she earned her birthright, Jewel.

Eternity was there but she wasn't there 'cause she ain't know what was goin' on. She was pullin' on Jewel, callin' Jewel, but Jewel was incoherent so I took Eternity...

Come here, girl. Hey baby, lookin' just like your daddy wit' them green eyes, 'cept he only had one green eye and the other, gray. What? This stick in my mouth? You want my stick? Okay, here. No, I'll hold it 'cause you might swallow it. Good, ain't it? Taste like cherries, huh? Can I have my stick back now? No? Well, there go my last chew stick. Here come your Aunt Val. Val is Jewel's sister. They got the same mother but different fathers, that's how come Val's dark and Jewel is light. Ay, Val. Ay, take Eternity so I can pay my respects, i-ight? Val and me always been cool, she like a sister to me.

But anyway, everybody was goin' up to the casket leavin' shit wit' my man. My man Rags left him a picture of all of us on 42nd Street in '89. Me, my man Rags and Bang, God bless the dead. Then came 'Dre. He took off one of his nugget rings and put it on my man finger. Then came Tinkle. He used to sex that and she never lost the sensation. She put a rose in his grip and kissed him on the cheek, whispered in his ear and stepped off. I thought Jewel was gonna flip! But Ma carried it like a queen. They loved the same cat and they both understood their positions. I respect that.

They pushed Sammi up in his chair and he fastened a platinum figaro around his neck wit' a medallion that had a picture of my man and Jewel imprinted in it like a sculpture. Word. Then it was my turn. I looked down on him.

Jeweled.

Dipped.

Dead.

He had on a burgundy and beige Polo velour suit wit' some beige Wallis. I spoke. The words...they ain't important 'cause that's between me and him. I left my watch and fastened it around his wrist. What you mean, why? So he could count the minutes until I joined him.

143

I love you, nigga.

As I left, I looked around the room and looked for his family—or rather his mother 'cause she all the family he ever had—but what I expected was confirmed. Absence. Probably don't even know her only son is dead. Not that she didn't care. Just indifferent. What y'all scientific tight-asses call it? Desensitized.

So much heartbreak in one life, one more heartache don't even register, no matter how big the hurt. So I slid and on my way out the door, I took in faces. Mad faces. Cats I ain't seen in years. Eyes meet, heads nod, pounds was exchanged. I know all these crab-ass cats ain't come to show love, 'cause where they was at when my man was biddin'? They ain't go see 'im, send him no dough, no kicks, not even a fuckin' letter, like, hold it down or keep your head up, type shit. None of that shit. Bitch-ass motherfuckas. All they did was try to scoop Jewel while my man was biddin' but she brushed 'em off like lint. Now I wonder how many of these vultures got the same idea in they rusted-ass minds and son ain't even buried yet. They did it while he was here, fuck stoppin' them now? I hate motherfuckas. Let's bounce.

Yo, you got some change on you? I gotta stop by the store and get a couple of dutches. You smoke weed? I ain't think so. Just gimme the change.

{As we walked away from the dead man's wake—I say dead man because I still don't know his name, nor do I know the young man accompanying me and vice versa—but as we walked through the dimly-lit streets towards a neon-lit store, the scenes that I saw were...disturbing. Appalling. Tenement buildings so old, so dilapidated, that you couldn't tell the occupied dwellings from the abandoned ones—}

Ay, yo. *Yo.* What you writin'? Notes? For what? When

you gonna learn, yo? Can't you understand that this shit can't be explained? Your little sociology class or psychology or whatever other "ology" ain't prepared you for this. Yo, gimme that shit, lemme see what you sayin'. The *dead man's* wake? That's all you call him? Or what, you wanna know his name? Earl. Here, write that down. E-A-R-L. Earl. You got that? I-ight, now erase it 'cause that ain't his name. Yeah, I know what I said but what do it matter? He could be Earl, Mike, Lloyd—but to you, he still gonna be another statistic. Another number to add to your data on what percentage of black males commit homicide, genocide or suicide. Just the dead man or better yet, *a* dead man. Ain't no "the'" to dead, 'cause death ain't singular. Just wait right here while I go in the store.

{I don't know if it was the sudden fall breeze rebounding off of the water, or the feeling of eyes everywhere but no one in sight, that sent a chill through me. But whichever, I quickly followed "my guide" into the store. I stood by the door as he exchanged pleasantries with the middle-aged Puerto Rican gentleman behind the counter. The Hispanic storekeeper spoke of the death of his friend and I strained my ears to hear the name, but the Salsa music and the heavy accent camouflaged the syllables. He never acknowledged me, although the Hispanic man, from time to time, glanced in my general direction. At me or through me. I couldn't tell which but it was so casual, so naturally fluid that I felt...invisible. He paid for his purchase—two cigars— with my change and walked out the door, still not acknowledging my person or presence, but his departure told me to follow. So I did.}

You see that wall right there? That's where they puttin' it. My man gettin' his own wall, his own piece of the world. That right there is like...like...like a bust of Caesar or a portrait of a president, you know? Whenever a cat die around here, if he wasn't no crab or coward, he always get a wall. Like that. See that? That's for my man Tone that got murdered. God bless the dead. It's kinda dim now 'cause the rain and shit...and wind. But it's still vivid in my head.

Naw, it ain't graffiti, why you always usin' ill-fittin' words? You know, you think like a computer, you can only compute what you've been programmed to, and you act accordingly. Just know this: every killin' ain't a murder and every word spray-painted on trains or walls ain't graffiti. It's a memorial. Everybody had 'em! Memorials. Even graffiti. The Egyptians had it but they was called hieroglyphics. Alexander had it, Napoleon, too. Every conquerin' army had it, 'cept what we call a tag, they called a flag, you know? National colors. They stuck it in the ground after a battle. They might as well've tagged, "Alexander was here," you know? Even the backwards-ass cave dwellers had 'em. Look at America when they went to the moon, what did they take? They flag. That's they tag, they piece of graffiti, so is it so surprisin' in a modern-day city, when the people seem invisible and they voices ain't heard, that you find words, names, places everywhere, on anything, *especially* if it's movin' and you not?

Like a message in a bottle, so somebody somewhere'll read it and say, they *did* exist! Why'd I say invisible? I didn't, some cat named Ellison said that shit but I knew what he was talkin' 'bout long 'fore I heard him say it. It's like, yo, you ever notice why brothers always wanna wear big hats and funny suits and drive long pink Cadillacs through the city? The same reason they wear big slave-like gold chains and play they radios in the car full blast. To be *heard.*

Fuckin' recognized. Everybody do it. Y'all do it. You paint your hair green and purple and your parents say stuff like, "They goin' through a phase," or, "They're tryin' to find an identity." What about when a whole race tryin' to find an identity?! What you call that? Growin' pains?! The fuck. We been growin' for four hundred years and we still ain't grew up! Look at church. People shoutin', screamin', hollerin' and callin', hell, it's like a party! Call and response. Say Hooo! Ho! Say amennn! Amen! Holler. Holler back. Same thing. It's like they think *God* don't even hear 'em! Imagine that.

Even the Creator Himself turn a deaf ear and a blind eye? I don't think so, but they damn sure do. Been feelin' like that, gonna *keep* feelin' like that. But look at y'all. Y'all go to church, quietly nod. Weep a little bit. Ain't no hollerin', no cryin', so y'all either know God there or you scared for Him to know *y'all* there 'cause all the shit you done. So y'all stay real quiet so you don't disturb Him or somethin'. Either way, you know you bein' heard. Bein' seen. So that's why I say invisible. Just ghosts. I don't know, man. But yeah... Yeah, that's the wall. My man's wall. God bless the dead.

CHAPTER TWO

What? You ain't never climbed a fire escape before? Scared to get those Armanis all scrapped up? Come on, I wanna show you somethin' up there...

{As we climbed, or, as he climbed, my mind was flooded with apprehension. What did he want to show me on the roof of an abandoned tenement? What was there that couldn't be brought down here? Did he want to push me off the building and show me, firsthand, what his friend must've felt? Couldn't be. Not that I thought he wouldn't, but you see, despite my schooling and profession, I'm by anyone's standard what would be called a big man. Not imposing, but large nonetheless. I'm 6'2" and 239 pounds. I played college football. Linebacker at Dartmouth College. So I didn't think this young man of 5'8", maybe 160 pounds, plus at least fifteen years my junior, could force me off of a roof in a life or death struggle. Not when opposing teams couldn't even move me off the line and the prize was only six points. My thoughts went back to the blow he dealt me in my car. I had been hit harder. Much harder. In Irish bars.

But the blow...it wasn't so much the blow or the force, but the desperation I felt he conveyed through it. A last-ditch effort for someone, like he said, anyone, to listen to what needed to be said.

I was shocked back into reality as he said, "You gonna stand there scribblin' or are you comin'?"

I looked up at him, the building, the crescent moon as

148

it hid behind the shadowed disc of the sun, who seemed to ask, well? Are you?

I grabbed the bottom rung of the fire escape ladder, which was probably seven or eight feet off the ground, so I had to leap to grab it. It moaned under the pull of my body weight and I thought it would give...
But it held...and so...

I climbed.

Higher into the night air. I felt him above me. I looked out over the urban sprawl and I thought of the glorious cities of Babylon, with its array of golden gods and hanging gardens, the great pyramids in Cheop, or is it Giza? Egyptology was my worst subject. Or the institutions of Timbuktu, and here were its people, its descendants, centuries later, living in anything but their formal glory. The utter abandonment of self shows in one's surroundings, and this...this squalid display of human degradation told stories. Many stories. Eight million stories.

I climbed higher and something funny happened. Nothing of concern, just a testament to the line I had crossed.

A cat.

The cat, known as feline, timid, set to run at the least disturbance...this cat. Gray or just dirty white in the moonlight, not big, but certainly not a kitten. The type of cat I might buy my daughter for her birthday. This cat was sitting in one of the corners of one of the many fire escape landings I had passed. The eleventh or twelfth, I had stop counting. But this cat was gnawing on what looked to be the remains and entrails of a rat.
But that wasn't what intrigued me. It was that, as I approached, it didn't even respond to my footsteps, aside from a quick jerk of its ear...

Quick, but lazy.
Unconcerned, but apparent.

Nor did I get its attention until I was quite close to it, and this cat looked up as if to say, "What? You expect me to run?" and went back to its meal. I surmised that here, nature itself was not...was not natural... Not the same. The cat had

149

somehow hardened or naturally adapted to an arduous situation.

We finally reached the top, seventeen or eighteen flights up. Maybe twenty, but you could see down below the streets we had just left, alive with movement. Talking. Laughter. A gunshot, or a car backfiring...far off a siren.

But in contrast, to the left, the dazzling spectacle of the metropolis of...the city I knew. With its neon-lit skyscrapers and...the skyline was breathtaking. Pristine. Alluring. He paused to allow me to get my bearings and scribble in my ever-present note pad. The sights. The sounds.}

Well, this is it... Where it all started...and ended.

He did it right here, where I'm standin'. Spread his arms like this, and screamed at the top of his lungs, "Life's a bitch and then you die!"

And he did it. Lookin' down like I'm doin' now. I can still see him there... Blood everywhere. Comin' out of his ears.

Damn.

Let me sit the fuck down, I'm gettin' queasy just thinkin' about it. Like the feelin' you get in your stomach when you're riding a roller coaster, 'cept he ain't come flyin' back like no roller coaster...

You can sit down. Here, sit on this crate while I roll this blunt...

You ever heard Redman's "How to Roll a Blunt"? Came out in '92... Yeah, well, he was explainin' in detail how you do this shit, just like I'm doin' now...Talked about how you split it like this, wit' your fingernail or key or somethin', dump out all the tobacco and fill it wit' izm...weed. Marijuana to you motherfuckas. Anyway, you even it out, then roll it like this. Lick it. Then...hold up. You got some matches? Damn. Don't tell me we up twenty-one floors without a match...I had some earlier. Damn. Gotta be a lighter up here, many crackheads be up here. Look around. Here go one. I know it's dead. Damn. Sure is. But if

I could find another one...here we go. Just gotta light 'em both together and it usually... Bingo. Blunt lit, mission accomplished. I learned that from a basehead. Yo, them baseheads is some resourceful motherfuckas, but I guess when you ain't got shit, you just gotta make the best of it, huh? Yeah, I know that's right...

{As he smoked, the tension around us began to dissipate...not entirely, but at least it lost the choking reel of thickness and wafted to a tolerable "misty" level...}

Yo, why is you always writin'? Huh? Fuck you writin' now, "he's getting high"? Shit like that? Don't write—listen. I brought you here for a reason. This ain't one of your books or a thesis or dissertation you scholarly motherfuckas be publishin'. Let me see your pad... Lemme see. Now watch it.

Bye, bye pad...

Look at it flutterin' in the wind, like a hit bird flappin', like a muhfucka tryin' to stay afloat. Why I do that? Yeah, I *know* what I said, I do got somethin' to tell you, but it ain't got nothin' to do wit' words, you know? Never mind, I'll explain that later... For now just know, yo, I want you to feel us before you judge us, understand our quality of life before you criticize...

Like, people always be complainin' about rap songs and they explicit lyrics. Yeah, I know, of course, it's other shit goin' on around the way than drugs, guns, murder, money and sex. I mean, babies born every day or somebody graduate or get married, or just a block party or a cookout, but no matter what, that shit's always in the back of your mind, you know? Always. If a cat make it big or whatever, go to college, make a name for himself, they always say *despite* his childhood environment, you know what I'm sayin'? Or when a baby born, most of 'em to unwed teenagers, you automatically think, what hard knocks he gonna have to face? Will he see age 21? It ain't like that for y'all. I mean, everybody got they worries, but while y'all worry about *bein'* doctors and lawyers, most of us wonder

151

when we gonna *need* a doctor or lawyer... Or bein' President? You think that go through the mind of an 18 year-old girl from the projects? I wonder if my son'll grow up to be President? Hell no, he ain't! It just be, I wonder if he gonna *grow up*.

Period.

You know...even at parties. Heads 'posed to be chillin', kickin' it wit' dimes...that's a girl, a dime is a girl... Anyway, kickin' it wit' dimes or what have you, but it still be there, hangin' in the air like a rain cloud waitin' to wet shit up... Cat get drunk, high, or just wit' too many muhfuckas, thinkin' he got an army and all of a sudden, he don't like this cat 'cause he got a new whip or he pushed up on his shortie and there it go... So it's always there, even if it ain't spoke, it's thought, you know? So I guess that's why cats say what they say, but it be mostly for y'all, for the cameras, 'cause we already know...

Damn, yeah, I just said it be other shit goin' on but let me put it like this. What else went on in 1929 besides the stock market crash? I'm sure *somebody* was born, *somebody* was happy, but did it make the books? Every book written around that time had somethin' to do wit' the Crash or the Depression 'cause that's what made the environment. It *was* the environment... Everything else was just a product of... Every era is dominated by some event or events, you know, and art of they time imitated that, you feel me? Just like now. So forget the name of this city. Names don't matter 'cause every place is the same. New York, Jersey, Ohio, Compton, Fifth Ward, everywhere projects Love and Hate. Life and death, same tug o' war goin' on daily.

Who will win?

This is where I grew up, where all of us grew up, and like I said...

Where it all started.

On the roof top... Me and my man... Smoked my first blunt up here, got my first piece of pussy... I'ma tell you somethin' I ain't never told *nobody*, not even my man.

'Member that shortie, Val? At the wake? The one who took Eternity? She was my first. Word up, I was hers, too. We was like eight and her pops had these porno flicks and shit but that ain't why, the real reason was 'cause she had Atari, and back then Atari was the shit! She was, like, the only one I knew who had the shit... Anyway, we was playin' Pac-Man... Yo, *that* was my shit! I knew every pattern, but who didn't?

We used to go to the pizza parlor and jug the coin slot wit' a paper clip and put mad credits on the machines and play all day. I know my man used to empty his machine, like, "Damn, where all the quarters?" But word, I was the best... Naw, I ain't gonna front. My man, he was the best. And this kid named Ali, he was nice, too. But besides them couldn't too many others fuck wit' me. So anyway, Val lives downstairs from me in that building over there on the fifth floor, and when she got it, I was like, yo, shortie got Atari! So I started, you know, buyin' her candy after school or writin' her notes in class like, will you go wit' me and then draw two boxes, one for yes and the other for no, and I'd be like, check one... Now I ain't really, what you would call, *like* Val. I mean, I was eight, fuck I know about girls? I guess she was cute, but you seen her and she fuckin' beautiful now and she ain't change 'cept her ass fatter and chest bigger. Back then, she was all bones. But her eyes... You know a person eyes don't never change. You might get fat or lose weight, but the eyes...never change. Knowin' that shit there kept me outta mad jams... Anyway, I was talkin' about the note. She marked yes, but what I shoulda wrote was, can I go wit' your Atari, 'cause when I got the note back, that was all I was thinkin'. Oh shit, it's on! Word...

Damn. Blunt went out... Hold up.

I-ight. So check it. I start goin' over her house. Met her pops, her little brother Freddie. He in the juvey now... That's the juvenile facility upstate. Anyway, yeah that's my lil' man, wild as hell... But yo... Man, this weed be havin' a cat zonin', like you drivin' and you got a destination but every corner you see you like, let me go this way, 'cause it look interestin'. So you make a right, then another right and another right, and before you know it, you right back where you started! So where was I... Oh, so I'm wit' shortie, in her house, matter of fact, that's when I first found out her pops ran numbers. My mom used to send me wit' little papers and money but I ain't think nothin' of it. So we playin', and I'ma tell you somethin', Val was beatin' me, 'specially in Pac-Man, but it was her game so what you expect? But we played. Played Space Invaders and shit, but now I'm bored, and I see the videotapes under the TV... "Yo," I'm like, "let's watch a movie." But she like, "Them my daddy movies, he told me not to touch 'em." That's one thing about Val, she wasn't hard-headed, but I was a little mischievous-ass knucklehead, and I say, "Your daddy ain't here now, how he gonna know?" Although you know if somebody been in your shit 'cause you know how you left it. That's how my mother found out I was smokin' her cigarettes. Beat my ass, too...

Anyway, I wanted to know what the fuck was so secret on those tapes. Tellin' me don't is like tellin' me do, same thing. My mama always said if somebody wanted to kill me, all they had to do was send me a bomb wit' a note attached sayin', "Don't open." Shit. Next thing you know, *Boom!* Nigga everywhere...

But in a way everybody like that, all you gotta do is look at Adam and Eve.

Don't touch this tree.

And here we are now. Guess I'm just true to my roots. So I talk her into it and we put the tape in. First thing I see is some ugly white broad and an uglier black dude. They talkin', but you could hardly hear 'em, so I'm like, fuck kinda movie is this? Can't hardly hear, motherfuckas ugly as hell... I thought it was the tape so I fast forward, but you know how you fast forward but you don't press stop and everything on the tape goin' fast? That's how it was goin' when I started seeing clothes come off and the man start humpin' like a jackrabbit. So I cocked my head to the side and press play and yo, these motherfuckas fuckin'! On TV! Now mind you, I was only eight and I ain't never seen no shit like that. Well, not on TV. I heard my mother and her boyfriend or walked in on 'em 'cause I had a nightmare or whatever, but I ain't never seen it on TV.

And the shit they was sayin'?! Fucked me up. That's when I feel my little jones growin' in my pants and Val lookin' at the screen, eyes big as plates, talkin' 'bout, "Eww! Turn it off! 'Fore we get in trouble." But I'm like, chill, 'cause I'm startin' to enjoy this shit, watchin' what this cat doin'. And she watchin', too. So I say, "Shit. I could do that," or somethin' like that. She say somethin' like, no you can't and then we hear a key in the door and her father come in! I pressed stop fast as hell and sit down, but my jones still standin' up! Yo, I know he seen it! And besides, you could tell when little kids be up to somethin', so he ask, "What y'all doin' in here?" Val like, nothin' we goin' outside then we run out and leave the tape and everything in the VCR!

Years later, when I started sellin' weed for him, he used to tell me he knew what we was up to 'cause he found the tape, but yo, I never told him what I'm tellin' you about what we did *after* we went outside.

So we come up here. This always been our spot 'cause it always been abandoned. They had some riots back in, like, 1967, before I was born, and the National Guard came through wettin' heads up, wit' dogs, tear gas and set this shit ablaze. Gutted the whole building, but they never tore it down, just left it standing. Like a warnin', like as if to say, "Y'all niggas act up if you want to, remember how we came through and deaded shit in '67? Don't get fucked up..."

That's what they was sayin', you know, but we was young and all we knew is we had a building all to ourselves. Well, us, a few drunks and rats. Mad big-ass rats, but yo, it was our palace, you know, rats and all. We played hide 'n seek and all that, but the spot was the roof.

155

So me and Val came up here. It had been rainin' so nobody was out, but it's still kinda drizzlin'. We quiet for a minute, then I say, "Yo, you see them people? What they was doin'?" She like yeah or whatever and I add on, "Let's do that. Let's do the nasty like they was." She all like, hell, no! I ain't! Sayin' shit like that, but see, I know how to get to motherfuckas, know how to push they buttons, 'specially back then 'cause all you had to say is, "You scared. You a chicken. You a punk." Nobody wanna be a coward even if they is one... So she like, "I ain't scared, not me, I'll show you." So she drop her pants.

Now *I'm* the one scared, but my jones, he get to standin' up again...

You don't need all the eight year-old details, 'cause that's all it was, two little kids not knowin' what they doin' but bein' grown. She made me put my word on it I wouldn't tell nobody and I didn't. I guess that's why we so close, 'cause of that bond, that trust, you know? But sometimes, she still kid me about it or I'll tease her. Like when she had her first son, I was like, "You sure he ain't my seed?" She be laughin', talkin' 'bout, "And I bet it's the same size, too." Yeah, Val, she cool peeps. Real cool. Matter of fact, she the reason me and my man got fly in the first place. He had come from Florida that next year and he wanted to play Atari, too... So he started pushin' up on Val, buyin' her candy and shit like that. Now even though I ain't consider her my girl or whatever, still people *thought* she was, and that's all that counted. What everybody thought. So I couldn't have some ol' new jack pushin' up on my shortie. And he was a pretty boy, too?! Oh, *hell* no...

Yo, we fought, like, every day for a week. Fightin' everywhere. After school, in the playground, at the store, at the rec center. Every day, 'til we was like, fuck it. I respect this cat. A lot of cats I know got tight after they fought, not outta fear, 'cause sometimes you win, sometimes they win, but you realize, yo, he holdin' it down just like me. Fuck we fightin' for? We got down and held each other down.

That's why I wish brothers fought more... Naw, I ain't

156

mean it like that, I mean, fight instead of pull a trigger. Any pussy can do that. You got four year-olds shootin' people by mistake... It take heart to step to a cat like, I got somethin' on my chest or you got somethin' on your chest, fuck it, air it out, you know? Then you still breathin' tomorrow, but a gun... Somethin' permanently damaged or decayed...

Anyway, we stopped fightin' and the three of us just played Atari. I don't know if Val thought she had two boyfriends or we had one girlfriend, all I know is we played Atari. After that, if you seen me, you seen him, like twins. Me wit' my braids and him wit' his waves. I always had braids 'cause my mother told me she ain't have no money to be gettin' my hair cut every time it decided to grow back... We was some cool little cats. Kept fresh sneakers. My shit was the shell-toe 'Didas, I thought suede Adidas was beyond wack, it was fuckin'...sacrilegious, yo. Everybody know Adidas is leather and Pumas is suede. But my shit was' 'Didas and his was Pumas. Any color. Gray on burgundy, gray on black, white on green. When the baby blue and white shits came out, he was the first wit' them shits, him and this girl named Faith, but we called her Faye. She a singer now... Yeah, I had a mad crush on her...

But yeah, we kept kicks even though we was broke 'cause back then you could go in a store and ask to try on this pair or that pair, and then just dip. 'Specially if the store was crowded, you could just walk out then, but most of the time you had to run. Did the same thing wit' Cazals and Kangols, even dashed wit' a gold dookie rope. And the good thing about it was the old cliché saved us: all niggas look alike. You might hafta chill for a minute but you could always go back and gank 'em again until kids started bumrushin'... So I... Huh? What's bumrushin'? Bumrushin' is, like, when mad kids get together and do just that, bumrush a store, snatchin' stuff off the racks. Sneakers, hats, clothes, gold, leather coats, whatever—and they all had razor sharp box cutters so if you got in the way, *boom*, buck fifty... A buck fifty? Naw, this ain't got nothin' to do wit' no dollar and two quarters, but a hundred and fifty stitches, 'cause a box cutter hit you, you bleed for real.

But we ain't never get into that 'cause we was wild but not savage, but I understood. I mean, imagine you starvin' and it's a meat market right there. Won't feed you and ain't no way to get money, and you got mad heads wit' you just like you. Starvin'. Like DMX said: *Robbin' to eat and it's at least a thousand like me mobbin' the streets...* That's for real, yo...

But all we wanted was some fly kicks, a few Lee suits, nothin' major. Just so when we went to school, we ain't get laughed at or picked on 'cause you got on your brother's clothes from last year, you know? And yo, I ain't *have* an older brother, I had an older sister, so you know what kind of predicament I was in. But my man, he was the only child so he had it a little easier...

Back to school...

That's where I really started to see how shit was, what girls look for and how to get it, 'cause no matter what, that's what we live our lives for anyway, to love and learn. Just depends—what you love dictates what you learn to obtain. For most cats at the time, it was girls. The clothes, the jewels, and later the cars and money, all boil down to one thing: women. Somewhere in every sad hustler's story it's a female involved somewhere. The Power U—that's pussy in plain English—is a powerful thing. That shit done started wars.

Look at Helen of Troy...

So we in school, lookin' jiggy, geared up, you know, sti broke than a muhfucka but we learnin'—fast. The first hustle learned was flippin' coins. That's when you flip, say, a quarter and it lands on heads, then I gotta flip a quarter and matc your quarter on heads; if not, you get my quarter. Some cat pitched—meanin', whoever came closest to the wall wit' the coin won—but that take skill and I had more finesse than skil 'Cause see, flippin' take finesse 'cause you can make a coi land on what you want depending on the bounce of the surfac and the weight of the coin. You 'posed to flip on concrete c somethin' hard so you get a true bounce and you 'posed t stand up and drop the coin waist high, but cats who ain't know, I'd be flippin' on the back of coats, cause they soft, no bounce, so that's child's play... Cheatin', basically. Plus I be crouched down or leaned over so, yo, I used to bag them cats every day...that was my job. Get the money. My man's job was to get the pussy. So one day, it's like damn near time to go home. I guess I was like thirteen and I had just licked a cat for two dollars and some change all the way down to pennies, but that was candy money 'cause back then, we ain't smoke weed so the cost of living was cheaper, you understand...

Anyway, this kid Bang, God bless the dead, 'member he was in the picture Rags left in my man casket? Yeah. Bang...the way he got his nickname was 'cause he was crazy nice wit' the hands, and when he hit you, it was like a gun goin' off.

Bang!

So cats started callin' him Bang. Now I see him watchin' me take this cat fast. Every once in a while I'll glance up and see him watchin' me, leanin' on the bathroom stall 'cause that's where we used to flip, in the bathroom. He, like, in the back of a crowd of, like, five or six and my man got some skeezer hemmed up in the back stall. So I'm watchin' this cat... Not that I was scared. Not even nervous, 'cause even though I knew he was nice wit' his hands, he knew I'd fight and that's all it really take. Win or lose, long as you played the game... And plus, Bang wasn't never on no bully shit; in fact, he hated bullies. If he seen someone gettin' bullied, he made it a point to pull the bully card first opportunity. He was, like, the equalizer... But see, what I was doin' wasn't bullyin', I was just fast-talkin' these herbs out they dough, and well, that's on them...

So the bell 'bout to ring and everybody broke—'cept me, of course—and cats 'bout to leave when Bang step up wit' *one dime.* Ten damn cent, and say, "Let's flip." Well about this time, my man came out of the bathroom wit' whatever her name was and see me and Bang, not squared off, but eye to eye...

I'm like, "For a dime? Against two dollars? Hell, no." But somebody in the crowd, I don't know who 'til this day said, "That nigga scared Bang gonna take his money," and a couple of kids laugh. Now I ain't know what they meant by *take* his money, but there it is, the punk call. If I don't flip, they might've meant take my money like strong arm, so I had to flip... I-ight, fuck it, come on. Plus, not to mention, it's a *girl* in the bathroom.

So I flip.

He match me.

His dime.

He flip.

I miss.

His dime. Just like that, I'm down to a dollar eighty cents.

Now... It's somethin' about even money. I could have a G in my pocket and if I want a soda, I might ask you for fifty cents. I can't explain it, and besides, the rules of flippin' is, you don't walk until somebody broke. It's an unspoken rule, but if you broke it...

So I'm locked in to this course 'til completion.

To make a long story short, me, my man and Bang still in the bathroom an hour later, school been let out, even the janitor in there watchin'...

Yo, let me tell you... He broke me! *Flat.* Two whole dollars. I'm mad as hell, but see, he peeped my game from jump street, 'cause before I flipped, he was like, "Naw, stand up." Then he moved the coat I was flippin' on. I'm still nice like that but the cat just had a hot ten cent.

I'm heated! My man cussin' me out all the way home. No candy. No Pac-Man. Fuck it.

Next day...

Now I gotta tell you, we had another hustle which was at lunchtime when we went out for recess. There was a store around the corner and up the hill from our school, but it's a gate around the schoolyard. You seen schoolyard fences? Yeah, like that. And plus it be teachers out there making sure nobody fight or whatever. So everybody scared to hop the gate and go to the store—everybody except me and my man. So every day we take orders from everybody and charge you; like, if you spendin' fifty cents, we get a nickel. Or if you spendin' a dollar we get ten or fifteen cent. Some cats ain't got but a nickel so on shit like that, no charge.

Anyway like I said, I was heated, and the main motherfuckas got orders is the same ones I been flippin' wit', and they done heard about the bathroom incident.

I-ight, cool...

So we take up the money. Bag of chips here, two jingles there, five packs of strawberry Now and Laters.

Ay, yo, I love them shits!

Not strawberry, though; pineapple or banana was my flavor, then they made that nasty-ass chocolate...

Anyway, where was—oh, okay. We collectin' and we got like eight dollars in orders. I look at my man, he look at me...shiiittt, you know what it is. We hit the gate wit' no intention of comin' back or bringin' back shit! But what I don't know is Bang somehow got a dollar mixed up in here somewhere, 'cause he done gave a girl a dollar to get him and her somethin', but I don't know this at the time. All I know is I'm jackin' *ere*'body and I'm out. Fuck y'all, basically. So we 'bout to hop a bus downtown when we see Val's father's Lincoln outside the barbershop. He always good for a dollar or two, so we go in the barbershop while he gettin' his fade tight. Val pops a real handsome, straight-face brother wit' mad finesse.

Style.

So he give us the usual, why we ain't in school, kid me 'bout the porno tape and then we hit him up.

"Yo, let us get two dollars."

Now he finished wit' his haircut, and he like "Y'all little motherfuckas gettin' too comfortable wit' my money," but he finished up sayin', "Take a ride wit' me, and we'll talk about it."

Yo. This man ain't *never* took us in his car, matter of

161

fact, I ain't never been in a Lincoln before, period. So I hop up front after arguin' wit' my man, and we agree he get the front on the way back...

I-ight, cool...

Off we go...

Yo, my word, I'm in heaven! The Lincoln was all black wit' beige leather interior. Everything was leather, even the dashboard. It had them electric seats that slide forward, backwards, tilt, all at the touch of a button, so I'm slidin' and tiltin' my little ass off, 'til he told me quit fuckin' wit' the seat, so I did. He caught me in an awkward position, too, kinda tilted forward, damn near standin' up.

But I was still chillin' as we rode through the streets I probably done walked a thousand times over, but now I was ridin'...like a prince. Ghetto Prince, and I knew—well, I *thought* I knew—this what I want. I wanna ride like this. My man in the back, searchin' the ashtray for cigarette butts, he found what we thought was a cigarette wit' no filter, but we'll get to that later. 'Cause for now, I'm chillin'. Music playin' some ol' school shit...

Yeah. I remember it like it was yesterday. We pulled up to the worst projects in the city, way 'cross town by the waterfront, and Val's father get out at this bar across the street. Now he ain't said nothin' 'bout nothin' 'cept, stop fuckin' wit' the seat, since we got in the car. He gets out. I did fuck wit' the seat, just so I could get back straight. So me and my man arguin' 'bout it's his turn and I'm tellin' him, we might go somewhere else so wait 'til he come out. So we steady arguin' when Val's father and another cat come out talkin'. Wasn't no frowns, no loud talkin' or nothin', but you could tell the man was tryin' to explain something that Val's father wasn't really tryin' to hear. He wasn't frowning, like I said, but his gestures. He was smokin' a cigarette or a wood-tip cigar, I forget, but just when I thought everything was cool, the man laughed, Val's father laughed. He turned to us...smiled...hit his smoke... thunked it down, and wit' the same hand he was smokin' wit', hooked this dude so hard, me and my man stopped arguin'—yo, we stopped talkin' *completely*—while Val's father beat this guy until he was damn near unconscious...

But he kept kickin' him...

I suddenly remembered my seat, thought about what he'd told me, what I was seeing now, and instantly put that shit back up in the air, best I could like it was.

After that, Val's father leaned down, went in my man pocket and whatever the content, put in his own pocket and walked back to the car like he'd just stopped to tie his shoe. He got in and we pulled off. Never once did my man say anything else about the front seat.

As we rode, I tried not to look as him, like I was scared he might be thinkin' I'm tryin' to get a witness description. And when I say I was scared, I was *scared*. A motherfucka couldn't have melted me and poured me on anything he said don't touch or don't do.

I put my hands in my lap.

What could make a man flip like that? From this smooth Billy Dee-type to a ragin' bull, and not *once* raise his voice, curse or nothin'...

I knew then that you never know what a cat might do. Sleep on no one. I watched him—driving, singing whatever tune was on the radio—but the heaven music was gone, at least to my ears. All I could hear was, don't fuck wit' the seat.

I *folded* my hands in my lap.

Yo, my man? He put the buttless cigarette *back* in the ashtray.

We drove in silence, except for the singin', until he got to my buildin'. He went in his glove box, reaching across me... I flinched—not visibly, at least I don't think so 'cause I still remembered, even if you scared, *never* show it. So let's just say my asshole got tight.

He went in the glove box and that's when I saw *it*— the gun—for the first time. Black. Revolver? I don't know. I just knew the shine and it was only a few seconds until he got out what he tossed in my lap, a manila envelope, but my eyes lingered on the glove box, and through x-ray vision

I still saw the gun, point-blank range, lookin' down its barrel. I learned another lesson. Not only do you not know what this cat or that cat might do but you never know where it could be comin' from—*it* could be right in front of your face and you never know.

Don't sleep.

His words brought me back to reality.

"Take this and see what you can do wit' it," he said.

I looked down at the package and thought, do wit' what? And as if he was readin' my mind, he said, "It's twenty nickel bags. A hundred dollars. Sell it."

"To who?" I heard my man say from the back seat. Val's father just laughed and was like, "Whoever want some weed. Smoke it, give it away, I don't give a fuck. But when I see y'all in a week and y'all ain't got no money, you better not ask me for another dime."

I knew he meant it.

We had got too old for that Uncle B shit, that game was played. He was tellin' us, be men or get the fuck from around me. We got out the car and he drove off, 'cause by then, he and Val had moved out of the projects.

We took the weed straight up here and forgot all about the eight dollars that jingled and jangled in our pockets all the way up the fire escape.

Until the next day.

Next day. Hundred dollars. We had a hundred dollars—or the *potential* for a hundred dollars—in our pockets and we felt like kings. To go from broke to a hundred dollars for two thirteen year-olds was some captivatin' shit. Imagine how much candy a hundred dollars could buy? We was crazy naïve 'cause the cost of livin' was about to go up and the streets was the landlord. When we get to school, mad heads was grillin' us...oh, that means lookin' at us real angry. I forget who I'm talkin' to sometimes. But we ain't give a fuck, we had a new role model: Uncle B, or Grand Daddy as everybody called him. Grand Daddy had opened up a whole new door and we was 'bout to slam shut this one. Except for one thing.

Bang.

Remember I said Bang had a dollar in this candy thing? Well, first thing on the schoolyard before class, here he come. "Ay, yo, I want my fuckin' dollar." The whole school out there and they listenin'...watchin'. And when a man curse... So I respond like, "Ay, yo Bang, you ain't give me no fuckin' dollar." I'm tryin' to play it cool, but at the same time, he cursed so I gotta curse but instead of sayin' "Fuck you talkin' 'bout?" which I know what would happen, I tried to be diplomatic and save face at the same time. So I used his name like, yo Bang, and just threw the curse in at the end like, here, take that shit back. I still don't wanna fight but far as I'm concerned, the dollar was dead, so yo, whatever's whatever...

His next words told me he ain't really wanna fight, either, but Bang was like that wit' everybody...like the law— hard.

But fair.

So he go, "I gave Kim a dollar and she said she gave it to you." Here go Kim, "Yep, I gave it to you!" I wanted to smack this chick. But I looked Bang in his eyes, knowin' whatever I said, the conversation was over, either he gonna accept what I offer or I'ma see what he really know...

"Check this, kid, I don't know nothin' 'bout no Kim or no dollar..." Kim started to speak but Val eye checked this chick so cold, she froze me...

My words lingered...

"...But uh, what I need to talk to you about is a whole lot better than candy money...a whole lot better, and I figure, wit' what I'm 'bout to do... It'll be in your best interest to come wit' me and rap a taste on some things."

So there it was. Ride or die, but since my mouth wasn't bleeding and my back wasn't dirty, I figured we was gonna ride.

I exhaled.

I later found out that Val heard Bang was vexed wit' us, so she casually dropped in her conversation, within earshot of Bang, that we had been wit' her father yesterday.

So Bang put two and two together and came up wit' what, four, you know. Val... I smile when I say that name 'cause she so real. Know when to say when, when to say why and when to just don't say... If it wasn't for Val that day, I don't know if my diplomacy would've been so well received. And she never let me live it down, yo, especially when she mad at me she say shit like, "I shoulda let Bang kick your ass," or if I argue wit' my girl, 'cause she loved wifey so much, I had to ask her, "Yo, is y'all fuckin'?" And she come back wit' some ol' fly-ass remark like, "She need somethin' besides your ol' eight year-old shit." My man could never figure out this eight year-old reference between me and Val. He knew somethin' happened when we was eight, but what he ain't never know and I never told. I gave Val my word, so even though my man my man, my word my word, you know? So yeah, anyway, Bang always swung wit' older cats 'cause he had, like, five brothers. He the knee baby. And he knew what to know and we knew where to get it, so we woulda probably had linked up regardless...

So we showed Bang our treasure in the bathroom and you know what this cat do? This cat laughed! I mean, not no giggle, chuckle or snicker, this motherfucka laughed from the gut. Yo, if we walked in the bathroom like kings, we walked out like peasants. He said somethin' like, "Y'all fuckin' wit' Grand Daddy and you ain't get but twenty nickel bags?" Me and my man looked at each other, dumbfounded. What's wrong wit' this cat? both our eyes said to each other, this more money than we seen in our *life*. Then Bang asked us what we 'posed to bring back. Bring back? This our shit... He got serious then...

"He testin' y'all," them was his exact words. Then he told us to meet him after school. As we walked out the bathroom, a cat comin' in asked me to flip 'im...

I didn't even look back...

Bang lived two blocks from school, in a house wit' five

brothers and two sisters, his grandmother and his father who was in a wheelchair...don't ask me why 'cause I ain't never ask him and he ain't never tell.

So anyway, when we got to Bang's hangout spot, we knew why he laughed. The twenty nicks was gone in less than two hours. Now yo, to have twenty nicks and the *potential* to make a hundred dollars is one thing, but to *have* a hundred dollars, so easy and so fast, for two little happy heads... It was like meetin' the girl of your dreams and she promises you the night of your life, and the next morning...

Ahhhh...

Say word. Especially sellin' nicks, 'cause cats be havin' a lot of one dollar bills, so we damn near had a hundred dollars in ones and that shit is thick. Well not quite a hundred, more like eighty-somethin' and mad change. Mostly quarters.

Me and my man was in heaven, but Bang brought us back to earth. "Yo," he said, "this ain't shit. We can make five times as much before Friday."

Five times? Five times what? A hundred? That's—I had to carry zeroes back then—five hundred?! Now it was Bang's turn to put us down.

He continued. "My brother know this Cuban cat sell weed. We could get a pack for seventy-five but we gonna have to give my brother something..." Say no more.

Take me to Cuba!

To make a long story short, by the time we saw Grand Daddy on Friday, we had two hundred and eighty-five dollars and we all had new kicks that we ain't even steal!

Felt good, yo... Real good.

We walked into Grand Daddy's new apartment overlooking the river and threw the money on the coffee table. He just smiled.

Val was in the kitchen but it had a bar-like front, so you could see her from the living room as we lounged on the plush, leather L-shaped couch. I spoke to her, but she didn't even lift her eyes from whatever she was doin'. I figured she ain't hear me.

"What up, Val?" I repeated myself. I hate repeatin' myself, feel like a cat ain't listenin'. "I *said* hi, you deaf?" I ain't expect that 'cause I never got that from her before, and here I am two hundred and eighty dollars richer, pops puttin' me down, I'm 'bout to be like family, and she got a 'tude? Must be her time of the month, I thought, 'cause I heard people say that's when women get ill...

Again, Grand Daddy ain't say a word. I was learnin' slowly that he led by examples, 'cause he told us to chill and watch a movie wit' 'im... It turned out to be *Scarface*. As soon as it came on, Val made her anger very clear, when she sucked her teeth *loud* and stormed out. I heard a door slam down the hall. Damn. Periods make 'em crazy like that? I came to realize after much thought, years and experience that Val didn't want us sellin' drugs for her father. She didn't want us selling drugs, period, him either, 'cause she had seen a lotta young cats just like us took up wit' her father and now they dead, in jail wit' years reachin' other millenniums or on witness protection. But here we are, thinkin' we the mens...watchin' Al Pacino and Manny... I was Al. I know my man felt the same way. We watched as they came over on the boat...got sent to the refugee camp...murdered the cat in the white suit...worked at the burger stand when Omar told Tony he could make five hundred unloading weed...

Five hundred...

My thoughts went back to Bang and his words, "...five times as much." He wasn't here 'cause we wanted to *tell* Unc before we just brought another cat to his house. I didn't think cats like Unc were the type you surprised... Damn sure weren't the type you disappoint. Examples had been made.

Point taken.

So as Tony rose to fame, so did I. When he bought the Porsche, I thought, Benz. When I saw Frank's girl, I thought, Val. When Frank said, "Don't get high on your own supply," I winced and my man did, too, 'cause we had already smoked our first joint not ten minutes after we left the Cuban wit' Bang brother. We was curious. "Why people pay five dollars for some grass?" It was funny...until my man lit the joint and I knew instantly *why*... I was relaxed yet more alert, I was paranoid but feared nothin', I forgot my next word and last thought but spoke fluently for the whatnots, all at the same time... So there we was in Grand Daddy's living room watchin' the man I wanted to be, or *thought* I wanted to be, on screen. I saw his mistakes. He said he was slippin', I knew he had slipped. He had slept, and I knew, don't sleep. So you see, what I'm tryin' to tell you is, I no longer wanted to *be* Scarface. He died. His sister died, his man died.

Fuck that...

Naw... I was gonna be smarter. I wasn't gonna sleep or slip.

When the movie was over I was still mesmerized, and when I spoke, I could swear my first words back on earth came out Cuban slurred. Maybe it was the weed...

Grand Daddy spoke slow, but he always spoke slow to make sure he was understood. I guess he hated to repeat himself, too.

He said, "You wanna be like that, don't you? You want that life? I'ma give it to you but always remember, you Scarface. You and you, but I'm Sosa. Not Frank—I'm Sosa. Please don't ever mistake me for Frank."

That was it. No more words. You ever seen *Scarface*? So you know what happened to Frank, right? So you understand what Unc was tellin' us, then.

So, yo, we started gettin' a little paper. Nothin' major, but enough to make our names ring bells.

Recognition.

Remember we talked about being invisible? We wasn't no more, at least we ain't think we was. But I know now that as our gold charms got bigger, our gear more expensive, our pockets fatter, we was cryin' out for attention more and more, we was like fiends, you know?

Once is too much and a thousand times is never enough 'cause once you known, you either stay known or you get known for fallin' off. It's easier bein' invisible when you look at it like that 'cause when you nobody again, then you a *known* nobody that *used* to be somebody. But you don't really think about bein' nobody 'til you somebody, 'cause before, you like, fuck it, you know, I'm free. You follow me? Yeah. You a smart man. So yeah, there we is and ain't nobody thinkin' about tomorrow 'cause it's comin' too fast today. Bang bought a car. A little piece of Omni, but he put a system in it and that's all we needed. About this time, Jewel come through. I shoulda told you that even though Jewel and Val sisters, they had different fathers. Oh, I told you that already? Twice? My fault.

Weed, yo.

Anyway, yeah, she come from a town not too far away but distant just the same. I forget the name, but it's one of them spots on the train that you stop at but nobody get on, nobody get off, so you like, why the hell do it keep stoppin' here? She was from there and like I said, he met her at the block party in '85. I said '86? I don't know, years run together in a blur sometimes. Anyway, '85-'86 she came through.

Val introduced us and I remember thinkin', *y'all* sisters? Not that Val was ugly, you seen her. Far from it, matter of fact she gorgeous, but Jewel... Well, you seen Jewel, too. When we all met, I could've kicked it to her just as easily as my man did, but it was like, the whole vibe... Naw, her vibe said *this* the one here. I dig your profile and all, but this the one here. Besides, when Val introduced us, she introduced him first. Now, dealin' wit' as many females as I have, you notice little shit like that. It was like, this one is free, but this one here, we got an understandin'. Respect that. Plus, you don't just kick it to the sister of your first, it's like y'all say, uncouth...

So Jewel and my man got big.

Real big.

Started dressin' alike and all that shit, and yo, no

frontin', I was kinda jealous. Not 'cause he got the girl, but 'cause the girl got my man. Not no gay shit or nothin', but I'm sayin', you went to college or whatever, right? Ain't you had a friend, before you got married, and when he got married all the shit y'all did, y'all ain't do no more? Shit like that... He ain't hardly even creep no mo'. Every once in a while he might creep, but Jewel, she was his heart. So I guess when I introduced him to Tinkle, I was tryin' to break that bond. I don't know...but when I met her, as fly as she was, and she was fly...remember shortie from the funeral that put the flower in his hand? Her. As fly as she was, I didn't even try to keep her for self. I purposely picked her ol' loudmouth-ass friend Roxanne.

Hate that girl...

She a go-go dancer wit', like, a hundred kids and all of 'em loud as she is... I purposely took Roxanne so my man could talk to Tinkle. He bagged her, but not like I expected. Jewel had the cat. So me and Bang got tight...crazy tight... That's why, yo... I don' know why I was put here or whatever, but it had to be somethin' 'cause I coulda went like Bang. He died of AIDS two years ago.

God bless the dead.

But me and him, man, we sexed the same shorties raw, no hats. Hats is condoms. No hats...trains. That's group sex, you know, ménage à trois... The whole nine. I don't know, wild I guess, but yeah, Bang died. So, yo, we gettin' money lovely, Grand Daddy hittin' us splendid, but we decide it ain't enough. Fuck bein' next to the man, we wanna *be* the man. Me and Bang was talkin' about it, high—as usual. 'Member I said I'd never sleep?

I was gettin' drowsy.

"What that nigga know, we don't?" Them was my exact words, right here on this roof. Now mind you, we talkin' 'bout a man been hustlin' twenty years or better before he got knocked recently, but here we is, ain't been in this shit a hot two years and suddenly we wanna be king of the city. I guess that's how it usually works, 'cause cats usually aspire to positions that they capacity can't compute, ya'm sayin'?

So anyway, we step to my man... Yeah, yeah, whatever, just take me back to Jewel house, that was his attitude, not his words. His word was, "Whatever," and I knew it meant he wit' whatever, but I took it like I said before, impatience at being separated from his beloved.

Now keep in mind, Grand Daddy didn't fuck wit' crack, period, and he ain't want us or nobody connected to him fuckin' wit' it either, but our plan involved goin' against that whole unwritten law. We planned to get in on Grand Daddy name and bring so much blow to this town you'd think it was snowin' in July. Now mad heads was sellin' crack, gettin' loot, but we wanted to blizzard shit. But like I said, ride Grand's name until we get a foundation and then be like, "Yo Unc, I know you didn't want us fuckin' wit' crack, but we gotta make our own now," this that and the third. Basically tell 'im, fuck weed, we ain't fuckin' wit' you no more. Kinda like what Tony told Frank, set our own limits and enforce 'em, except I forgot what Grand Daddy told me.

He ain't Frank...

I'm no longer drowsy—I just lay down.

So first we had to get a connect. We went to the same Cuban who sold us the weed when we first started, but what we ain't know is the Cuban worked for Grand Daddy! 'Member I told you about the gun in the glove box and how you never know, it could be right in front of your face?

The Cuban was that gun now.

I just went to sleep.

We step to the Cuban, like, "Yo, we know you got connects. We got the money..." I think we had like ten G's, *if* we could keep Grand Daddy off our back long enough for Rags, that's Bang's brother, to go to the connect, cop, come back, set up shop, get about three words in every project, 'cause we couldn't sell it 'cause of Unc, recoup Unc seven grand and hit him off, all wit'out Unc knowin'. The Cuban like, "Come back tomorrow." First person he call is Grand Daddy, but we don't know this. I go to Grand restaurant and catch him there. Bang in the car. Now he already got the word that we tryin' to cop some yayo—that's cocaine—but of course he didn't tell me this. I run some ol' weak shit like, "This cat got bagged, he in jail, bail ying-yang-yang, give us two weeks and we'll have your money."

He smiled.

The smile I seen before he stomped that guy out when I was a young buck ridin' in my first Lincoln. He like, "You know you my man, right? You know I love you, right? I know you fucked my daughter and I ain't kill you."

He laughed.

I shoulda known then, 'cause he never outright said I fucked Val before, he just hinted at it or the tape but never he *knew* I fucked her. I sensed something but I was too high to understand the gravity of the situation, so I said somethin' like, "I never fucked Val—or her father." I wasn't lyin' about fuckin' Val 'cause what we did you can't consider fuckin', we humped, but the second part... I lied to his face and he knew. I knew. But I ain't know he knew it, and something flashed in his eyes. I know now it was rage, but he held it in check. Swallowed it—plus a little pride—and just said, "Two weeks." He never did speak much, so I knew I had two weeks. Fourteen days. Not fifteen, fourteen.

Ever since then, I regret that day. I wish I had said, "Unc, I love you, but this crack thing. It's loot and I want a part of it. I want to be you when you gone, carry on the bloodline." But ya don't leave Unc's family. Yo, I coulda done somethin' besides lie to the only man who had shown me love... Instead, I lied to his face.

Yeah, I can tell by the look on your face you thinkin', but this man introduced you into a lot of crime, he used you, whatever—but that ain't it. My childhood wasn't no sob story. No starvin' babies, no homeless shit. I just wanted two dollars one day and he gave me a chance to make a hundred. He taught me not to run around wit' my hand out, to stand on my own two. He taught me responsibility.

Just sometimes you gotta separate the message from

the messenger, you know? The Lord look out for fools and babies, and I was never a fool, *foolish* maybe, and I was no longer a baby. I'm sure if Grand Daddy would've owned the corner store, he would've given us a job sweepin' floors, or if he would've had a lawn, he would've paid us to mow it, but around here, seem like only grass is in the park, not in your yard, so he gave us the best he knew. He probably loved me and that's probably why he wanted to kill me so easy. And would've, if Val hadn't stopped him. Not really Val, but on the *strength* of Val, you understand that?

But you know the fucked up part? Instead of feelin' ashamed 'cause I lied or some sort of remorse, I almost told Bang to turn the car around and drop me off, 'cause I was gonna wait 'til Grand Daddy came out and I was gonna murder him and make it look like a robbery. Don't you see? I wasn't ashamed of the fact I lied, I just knew there was a man alive who knew I was a liar. And I *knew* he knew, he just didn't know why, or so I thought. So while he wanted to murder me, I was a red light away from murderin' him... Now who's the gun in the glove box?

The only thing stoppin' me was the only thing stoppin' him...

Val.

'Cause I knew I had to go to the funeral and she'd be cryin' and she'd automatically come to me and I'd hug her and say, "I'm sorry about your father"; all the while, the blood was on my hands, the very same hands I embraced her wit'... The same hands that comforted her pain would be the ones to have *caused* it, and I would've had to tell another lie to cover the first one and then what? Kill Val? Perish the thought. I hated it for comin' in my head, and hated my head for thinking it and I hated myself 'cause it was my head, and just like that you get a cold chill but just like that, it's gone. That's the first time I thought about death—well, my own death.

But anyway, just like that it was gone, and I glanced over to see if Bang could possibly know the chain of thought that just hit me, but he was lightin' a blunt.

Death, murder and deception had all come to replace candy money and kicks not two years before. Yeah.

I was blinded...

But one monkey don't stop no show, right? Hold up, let me take this piss...

{Mental Note: No more pad so I was glad to get a chance to collect my thoughts and digest everything he had said in the past—as I pause to check my watch, 1:45 a.m.— three hours. I was engrossed and the time had flown by. Thoughts flew through my head at blinding speeds, and sociological phrases and terms alternated and amalgamated as I tried to compartmentalize every nook and cranny, every iota of this young man's life, and then...I remembered.

I remembered what he had said about my thinking resembling that of a computer... Input... Output... Data banked? Is that what I'd become? I did not enter the profession of sociology with such...rigid...cynicism. The liberalness of the "radical" sixties had opened up doors I had never known existed before. One of which led to the urban communities. The ghetto. I thought of the taboo my father had placed on the other side of the tracks as I grew up, and my never questioning him. I guess one could say I was programmed then. First by my father, then by school, then by the Daisy Age and then by the criteria of my profession, which I always referred to as my "scholarly pursuits" over "societal concerns," maybe even training, but never did I view it as my shaping or mental molding. But why was I drawn to these people? These social dregs? Was it my subconscious American voyeur or the love for the outlaw, of which we so desperately want to emulate but just don't have the gall, the...temerity, to step out of the status quo of boundaries and become? Or was it the forbidden allure, as he said earlier, the I-don't-but-I-do syndrome, started by my father but perpetuated by society?

At first it was, until my early college years and a few friends told me of a black man who preached that the white man was the devil. I was enraged! How dare they cast a

175

collective mantle for all white shoulders to bear, mine included, mine specifically, but as I listened...to his rhetoric...his...his demagoguery, I realized the ideology was just the dressings, so to speak, the icing of this scapegoat cake, and the scapegoat was me. Not for my overt involvement, but covertly...

My silence.

I was magnetized, almost like a child to a freak show. Amazed, shocked, appalled, and lastly, full of pity... And maybe even guilt. Not guilt for a whole race as some of my colleagues clearly try and shoulder, but my own guilt, that I had lived twenty-two years at that point, and never known that such poverty and degradation existed in my own backyard, but also in the back of my mind, that part reserved for self-preservation. I wanted to know the symptoms so this contagion would not seep into my backyard, my family, my life...

My people.

I wanted to somehow be reassured that it was them *because of* them *and not us—ever.*

So I entered with this guilt. But once rejected by the very ones I pitied, the guilt turned to condescension. You need me. Arrogance. And finally, the heavy brooding of cynicism, if not only for my own sterility in the face of such adversities but for the fact that they almost seemed to not want to help themselves. To be content with the scrapes off of the table, the handouts of government subsidies, to live of off—to leech off of—America, off of me! So I regarded black people with scorn, thinking America to be so great, and the opportunity there for the taking. But how can you teach someone to read in the dark? First there must be light, and so for the first time that night, I sincerely tried to listen—to learn. I no longer wanted to think like a computer...}

Where was I? Oh yeah, yeah. Okay. So we 'posed to see the Cuban cat the next day, so me and Bang go back around the way. We see my man, and I'm thinkin', damn, Jewel let the cat off the leash? But I ain't say nothin' as he

176

climbed in the back seat. Bang was parked in front of the building. So my man like, "What up? You see the Cuban?" I'm like, "Yeah, it's on for tomorrow." He like, "Yo, y'all go 'head 'cause tomorrow is Jewel birthday."

Ay, yo...

We 'bout to make the power move of our lives—matter fact, lives on the line—and all he worried about is an extra candle from last year?! I'm sayin'... I spoke outta turn, you know; matter fact, I ain't even know I said what I said, or I *knew* but I thought I just thought it. But I heard the words, he heard 'em, and I know Bang heard 'em 'cause he looked at me like I was crazy when I said, "Fuck that bitch birthday, we got—"

That's all I got out 'fore he swung from the back seat and hit me in the mouth, and I'm smoking a blunt at the same time! So I throw the seat back wit' the little release lever on the side quick 'cause the blunt in my lap burnin'. This motherfucka swingin', Bang yellin' and all this goin' on in this little-ass Omni. I'm halfway in the front leanin' over the reclined seat and I got his right leg pinned under the seat. We fightin' like a motherfucka! Blunt still burnin' 'cause Bang had sheepskin seats and that shit done started smolderin'.

Bang jump out the car and run to the passenger side and open the door, draggin' me out. He put the seat fire out and I'm standin' on the sidewalk wit' a hole in my pants. My man on the other side in the street, cursin'. Fuck you nigga this and I kill yo' ass that, you know, the usual ghetto war mantras and Bang tryin' to calm him down 'cause I know I'm dead wrong. Bang knew it, too, so ain't no need in tryin' to convert Satan, you know? So I just lean on the car hood and light another cigarette. He walk away.

You know God work in mysterious ways and I'ma tell you why. Next day I go to the Cuban house alone, 'cause Bang in New Yitti gettin' his radio fixed that I kicked out in the fight. When I got inside, who in the living room but Grand Daddy.

I froze...

177

I had a gun, the .380 I kept everywhere, but yo... I knew I fucked up.

All he said was, "You lookin' for a connect?"

I couldn't speak.

"There's only one reason I ain't gonna kill you," then he paused. "'Cause I know you ain't got my money on you." Ten grand to Unc ain't shit, so I knew that wasn't the reason, we both knew that wasn't the reason. In the emotion of the situation, I finally heard Unc raise his voice.

"I want my money, motherfucka, today! Not *two* weeks, today! Or you better use that shit to get you the fuck 'way from here!" Them was his words, but on the inside of each syllable, behind every vowel, he was sayin' he'd loved me, he'd trusted me, he'd given me everything he could but now all he could give me was advice. He washin' his hands, and if his conditions ain't met...

Sometimes I wish he woulda shot me 'cause God knows I'd rather that than to have to tote them words in my heart all these years... Word.

But like I said, God work in mysterious ways, and why I say that is 'cause if Bang or my man would've been there, I ain't got no doubt in my mind Grand Daddy would've killed either one, just to get the pain out his eyes and at least some of his pride back that he had swallowed for his daughter. No doubt in my mind.

But it was just me and him, and just like he knew years ago I was fuckin' wit' his shit and like he knew in his car I was fuckin' wit' his seat, we both knew now I was fuckin' wit' somethin' far more important. His livelihood.

He walked past me and out the door and climbed in a gray Chevy Nova.

Never looked back.

Now, gettin' the loot wasn't no problem, except it was at Jewel house, and me and my man already bumpin' heads, but yo, couldn't keep it over Bang house 'cause he got five brothers, and if you got G's in a house wit' five brothers, who also happened to be family, somethin' bound to get missin'. Not on no stealin' shit, just they look at money like clothes, you know, if it's there, they gonna wear it. So if it's loot in the crib, then they like, I need to get this, Bang won't mind if I snatch up a twenty—a dime here, fifty there—before you know it, G's fallin' down into the hundreds! So that was out.

My house? Yo, I had got kicked out my house, but that wasn't no biggie 'cause I was always gettin' kicked out, just this time I was like, fuck it, I ain't goin' back. So I did like I do now, just float...a girl crib, a hotel, park benches, but mostly just in the projects, 'cause it's somebody always out in the PJ's, no matter what time it is. So since I ain't had no crib, that was definitely out.

But Jewel house? Perfect. So Jewel stayed wit' Sammi and his girl, Lisa. Remember the cat in the wheelchair at the wake? That's Sammi. Now Sammi was Jewel brother, but not Val brother, even though Val and Jewel was sisters, 'cause Sammi had the same father as Jewel, but not the same mother. That's some shit, huh? At one time, before he started gettin' money, him and Val was kickin' it together. So he was goin' wit' his sister's sister but they wasn't related, so it wasn't no incest but still you like, damn. You know? Anyway, Jewel was livin' there and my man had basically moved in. So since Sammi was gettin' money anyway, you wit' me so far? I-ight. Huh? What happened between Val and Sammi? Why that important? Like I said, Sammi started gettin' money and Val hated drug dealers.

Except us and her father, she tolerated us.

So here I am on my way to see my man over Jewel house. Building right over there. Apartment 151.

Sammi answered the door. "What up, Be-bop?" He always called me that, 'cause I used to clunk my Adidas when I walked. Let you know I was comin'. So we dap, which is like shaking hands except you and him bring your fist together, like...make a fist. Dap...dap, feel me? Okay, so we do that and he call my man. He came to the door, but right behind him is Jewel like they joined at the fuckin' hip or somethin'.

She speaks.

Say my name then, "What up." Simple. Anybody on the street you don't even know say the same thing. What up partna or peace. Whatever.

But in that split second between the words leavin' her lips and hittin' my ears, this cat grill me. Like, muhfucka you speak and I'll kill you. What you mean, why? Yeah it do seem simple, but it's 'cause my man know me. I don't call girls bitches. Not playin', not arguin', not in they absence, not even in general like, "bitches ain't shit," or "it be mad bitches at so and so." Naw. I don't use the term. I say chick or shortie, maybe even ho if they playin' the part, but never bitch, and he knew this. So to say what I said, which like I told you I ain't even mean to be spoke, just thought, I might as well had spit in her face. And to speak now? I'd be smilin' in her face, all the while done cussed her behind her back.

She spoke again, but my man let me off the hook and told her to go get the shoebox 'cause he knew what I was there for but he thought shit was still lovely but it wasn't.

I never told him Grand Daddy was there or how close I came to death or what went down or none of that. I just told 'im, "Shit is dead." He nodded like, whatever, like he been doin' for the past two months, like if I said, "Yo, they blowin' up my building tomorrow and they sacrificing me on the altar of some ancient Mayan god," he still would nod like, whatever. If it wasn't about Jewel, it was whatever. She came back. Gave him the box. He gave it to me, closed the door, never takin' his eyes off mine. I know I had hurt the brother but I guess I never realized it until a nanosecond before the door shut. Two for two so far. Betrayed Unc and alienated my man, my twin.

Our little clique broke up. Cats was always askin', "Where Bang? Where your man?" I'm sure they was gettin' the same thing.

So everybody settled into the new life the game had brought 'em. My man wit' Jewel, who eventually started hustlin' for Sammi, that's how he caught his bid. Bang became the ladies' man and his nickname lost its old meanin', which was for fightin', 'cause girls started saying his name like a song, "Baaang."

Yeah, yo, but we still called him Bang for Bang 'cause we ain't know the other Bang. But yo, what I'm sayin' is, everybody had found they niche, except me 'cause, like I said, I was floatin'. Sure I hit shorties—had sex—but I wasn't addicted, especially after I got burnt for the fourth time. That's gonorrhea. Yeah, four times. Don't sound so shocked, I know cats done got hit like eight times or better and still goin', so I'm par for the course, you know? I mean, especially when you hittin' shorties in a circle, which means, dealin' wit', like, four or five girls at one time. You don't tell 'em you burnin', and you get cured, then go back, cured, go back. It sound fucked up, but at least you know if another man hittin' your piece 'cause if he screamin' on her like, "You burnt me!" You know he ain't lyin' 'cause you burnt her! Yeah, I know. It's fucked up but we was young, we ain't really know what that shit can do to your body over a period of time undetected and uncured.

Yeah, I fucked, but I wasn't stuck on stupid like Bang, and I was gettin' a little paper but I could do wit'out. Yo, what the fuck was my purpose? My mama don't want me, my man, my ace, he fucked up over Jewel and shit ain't the same. You can say I was the leader of our lil' money clique, but now that was gone, so what now? The only thing I had to look forward to was football in the park on Sundays. Seem like everybody play football in the park on Sunday. Project against project, street against street, crew against crew. Yo, I done seen some real money exchange hands over them games, word up, it's like a tradition. That was usually when I saw my man or Bang 'cause you might miss one or two Sundays, but you ain't gonna miss it altogether, unless you dead or in prison.

I be watchin' TV now and I see some of those cats come outta the park who doin' they thing in the NFL, and I smile like, "Yeah, nigga learned that move on a Sunday way before *this* Sunday." I'm glad cats doin' they thing. Couldn't be me, though. I wasn't good at that, neither. I wasn't too fast, wasn't that big, either, but I ain't mind gettin' hit, hurt the fuck up. Fuck it, let's play ball, wipe the blood on your sleeve, you know? But the rest of the week, I'm slingin' coke, you know, just enough to survive. Nothin' spectacular, but I'm eatin'. Solo, no real partna, just various baseheads I had met over the years roamin' the streets four in the mornin', so they bringin' sales and whatnot. Talkin' to me, hookin' me up wit' basehead broads who do anything for crack. Not that I was hard up or nothin', 'cause I still bagged my share of, if not dimes, eight or better. A dime? Like a scale of one to ten. A ten. Like that movie wit' Bo Derek. I don't see how y'all gave her a ten, only thing dimed about her was the cornrows. So, yo, sometimes I be like, fuck it, I'm bored, it's late and there that go.

Some of the shorties be ugly but some be like females I knew from the past. Like that girl Kim who said she gave me the dollar me and Bang bumped heads over? She had turned out. I told you I wanted to smack her then and I still hadn't forgot. And it's something about havin' power over a person like that, you know? That you can get your every wish carried out as long as you got *it*.

Better than money.

'Cause you could have a cat that love money, but it's certain things he won't do to get it, everybody got they limits. But wit' crack? It's like that limit no longer exist and you'd do anything, even die for it. I seen motherfuckas snatch a pack, get caught and be gettin' the shit beat out of 'em but they never, and I mean *never*, unball they fist wit' that crack in it.

Until they beat to death.

And even then... Ay, yo, you ever felt a dead man's grip? That shit ain't no joke.

And here I am, young, wild and got all this power over other people. I'm ashamed to say what I did to degrade these people, to disrespect, tryin' to find they limit but I never did. I'm even gettin' myself involved 'cause when I don't have a hat, remember a hat is a condom, when I don't have a hat, I'm usin' plastic shoppin' bags, garbage bags, for a condom. I was playin' Russian roulette for real.

And I thought, yo. *This* is what I want, this power— or at least I *thought*, again, like a hundred times before, this was what I wanted.

Yo, I read somewhere that adversity is nothin'. If you really want to see the character of a man, give him power. I be rememberin' shit like that, 'cause sometimes I don't understand, you know, 'cause I always thought, when you down and out, you know, that was the greatest test of character. Hunger, poverty, hopelessness. But then I saw that, yeah, in adversity you gotta be patient, you gotta be humble 'cause you ain't really got a chance, but wit' power? Yeah, like they say, power intoxicates, then yo, I was piss *drunk*, you hear me?

Until one night. Not really different than the rest. I was out on the Ave., like three or four in the morning. The block is mad quiet, fuckin' desolate. I was expectin' for tumbleweeds to blow down the street like in them old Westerns.

I'm on the phone explainin', or rather, lyin' to my girl of the moment, the girl I was stayin' wit', where I had been, 'cause at the time I was stayin' wit' her more often than not, and I seen the way she was gettin'... Where you goin'? Where you been? Shit like that, so I was makin' a point of not comin' home for days at a time. I'm like that to this day, old habits hard to break...

Anyway, she bangin' her gums and I'm like, yeah, yeah, whatever, I'll be there when I get there.

Hang up.

So I turn around and it's this pregnant woman waddle up the street towards me. Now it's dead winter, I'm goosed down and Timmed up. I was dressed warm, in other words, and she wrapped in a blanket—no coat. I guess the blanket *was* her coat. Now dig, I had served pregnant woman before, and although I ain't like it, I still sold it to

'em, so here she come. "Let me get three for twenty-five."
Three is three ten dollar caps and she five dollars short.
Fuck it, it's late and I ain't really tryin' to hear the song and
dance I know she gonna give me if I tell her no. But she pull
out food stamps. Now I ain't discriminate, food stamps,
money, TV, pussy, etcetera and so on. And plus, the Korean
cat at the Chinese restaurant gave you seven dollars cash
for every ten dollar in food stamps. Her twenty-five is in
food stamps, and that ain't but like...seven...fourteen...like
eighteen dollars, so I'm like, hell no! I'll give you two for
eighteen.

Here go the song and dance.

"I done spent this much with you," blahzay, blahzay,
yo, "I'm good for the rest, I'll suck your dick," the whole
nine, but I'm like, "Yo, take two or leave it." So she say, and
I'll never forget it, "Damn... I'm sayin', I was savin' this for
my son's Christmas, but I got..."

How much she had I don't know, didn't *wanna*
know, and I can't remember now, but all I heard was "son's
Christmas."

Now I had heard of crack babies, you know, babies
born addicted, but that was too indirect for my callous
mind to grasp as my responsibility. But here go a little boy
somewhere, writin' down a list, "I want G.I. Joe Kung Fu
Grip, a remote control car, Atari..." writin' Santa, and his
mother giving away the only thing this little cat got to look
forward to. And she was willin' to give away what wasn't
even hers.

Her son's hope.

His dreams.

Power intoxicates and reality is mad soberin'. I was
fuckin' frozen. Dazed. I remember reachin' into my pocket, I
probably had, like, seven vials left and put it in her hand.
She looked at it like she had won the lottery. "Oh baby,
thank you! Thank you! I don't know why...you want the
money? Here take the—"

When she said money I almost threw up. I only said
bitch twice in my life; once I ain't meant to say it, and the

other I wish I coulda embellished it on her forehead. "*Bitch*, if you don't get the fuck away from me..." Her eyes got big as plates. She turned and walked off quick, or shuffled off, lookin' back to make sure I wasn't comin' after her...

I walked to my girl's house in a daze...thinkin'.

All this time...

All this time...

How many nights did mouths go unfed 'cause of me?

How many backs went uncovered 'cause of me?

How many nights did human beings freeze in heatless apartments 'cause of me?

The how many's was endless and lasted the whole four blocks to my girl house.

When I came in the door, she still bangin' her gums, but I'm...what you cats call it...incoherent. I walk straight to her room and stuff my bookbag wit' my clothes or as much as I could stuff, and my sneakers, Walkman and some tapes. I guess she stopped riffin' then 'cause I vaguely remember her saying her favorite line. "Where you goin'?"

"I'm leavin'," I guess I said, I don't know. She musta thought I was zombie, the way I walked, the way I talked...the way I looked through her. Probably thought I had finally went from sellin' crack to smokin' it, then she went into the, "Good, you ain't shit anyway. You never here and I could do better by myself," type tirade, the one we go through when somethin' we want we can't get and we front like we ain't want it in the first place. I wonder why people do that? Act like they don't care when they really do? I guess it's like that power I was talkin' about. Nobody wit' limits want you to have that power over them.

I don't know.

I walked out and I felt this, like, I felt crazy *free*. I couldn't explain it then, but now I know. I was no longer bound by a label, like, drug dealer, boyfriend, outcast, liar. I just *was*, you know? Maybe I ain't makin' no sense but sometimes when we let other cats define us, it restricts us 'cause in that definition is our purpose, our meaning.

Free—are you really?

185

'Cause I'm walkin', not thinkin', just floatin' and I'm like, what's next? Not the same thought of being free from a minute ago. Like I said, the flip side of all this is, if I ain't get no definition then yo, what's my function?

I was worthless.

Again, like the night leavin' Grand Daddy restaurant, death blew through me like a cold breeze and called my name.

I still had my .380... Then I saw it.

Now, you or the cops or your average Joe woulda missed it, but I knew. I saw. An all-black Honda Prelude. Stolen. It's something about a stolen car to a car thief, you can smell them shits. It could be parked but you still gonna know. I ain't tell you I stole cars? It's a lot I ain't tell you 'cause it ain't relevant to what I'm gettin' at.

It ain't relevant to *it*.

But yo, wasn't no need to tell you 'cause who didn't steal cars? I knew girls fourteen or younger that could make Richard Petty stop, duck and roll. Not so much for speed, but agility. So yeah, I stole 'em; around the time my man was Jeweled out and Bang was skeezin', I be wit' my man Tone. Brother was the nicest motherfucka around, he *never* got caught. Matter fact, he never got his car lost in a chase. 5-0 killed him one day outside his house, washin' a stolen Olds Delta '88. They pulled up and as he jumped in, they shot him in the back of the head.

God bless the dead.

Why? These grown-ass men we talkin' 'bout and they got little thirteen, fourteen year-old kids makin' fools outta them? Especially little *black* thirteen, fourteen year-olds. And when I say makin' 'em look foolish, I mean just that. I mean, yo, when we got bored, we used to literally go lookin' for 5-0 so they would chase us and we'd lose 'em. We called it "dickin' 'em." So I guess they got fed up and started sendin' out messages in the form of bullets.

So yeah, I stole 'em, and here one was right here, waitin'. First thing I thought of...

Down south.

First thing popped in my head. It was the only time I been out this city in my life like that. I remember, man, I was young as hell! Probably like seven and me, my mother, my sister and my aunt went down to North Carolina for our family reunion. First and only time, 'cause my mother and her sister couldn't stand each other, and the only reason my mother went was 'cause her mother was sick. So off we go. We ridin' and I'm lovin' every mile, I remember thinkin' probably like Columbus people, "Damn, the world *ain't* flat!" 'Cause I'm like, there is more to life than just projects.

Word.

It take crazy long to get down south, so after a few hours of playin' "my car" wit' my sister, it's like, seen that tree, seen that bridge, ho-hum, go to sleep. I wake up and we ridin' down a street, or rather, a road wit' big-ass plants on both sides that my mother said was corn.

"Corn? Like the shit we eat?" I asked her.

"Yeah, like the shit we eat. And stop cussin'."

I always cussed, long as I can remember, and my mother, she ain't never stop me, just mildly discouraged me, 'cause she cussed, too.

My grandma house is on some Roots shit, in the middle of the woods, and her bathroom was outside! Freaked me out. I don't know, though, 'cause I used to piss in the street all the time. Used to try to write my name in the snow wit' it. But I was freaked, matter fact, the three days we was there, I shit in the woods. Oh, you done that too, huh? Yeah, wit' leaves, wipe your ass wit' leaves? I guess we got somethin' in common 'cause you can damn sure call shittin' in the woods common.

But I liked it—the south, I mean. The wide-openness of it. So I guess that's why I thought of it. That, or it was just the farthest place I knew from here. In a way, I wanted to start over, wipe my slate clean.

Remember that song, "I wanna go where everybody knows your name..." I can't sing but you get the point. Well, I wanted the exact opposite. I ain't even know what I was gonna do when I got down there 'cause I ain't even know

187

North Carolina *had* cities until I seen Charlotte on TV. I guess I was gonna be a farmer...yeah, picture that, me a farmer.

I ain't know, all I wanted was out, so I jumped in the Prelude and I was out.

So I'm drivin', shit is sweet. Only thing, I ain't got no weed. I always got weed. Half a blunt, a roach, somethin'. Ain't nothin'. Fuck it, when I get down south I'll grow some, is what I'm thinkin'. So I get to Maryland, and the sun is up and it's, like, almost seven. I got gas, just got some in Delaware, tank more than half full, but I wanna stop, stretch my legs. I see a sign, ol' 'Bama-ass name, I shoulda known right then, keep goin', but naw. I had to pull off in this redneck-ass town. I ain't know it was redneck then, but I'm sayin'...

Anyway, I'm thinkin', I might as well call my aunt, get my grandmother number, plus I'm kinda hungry. So I pull into a gas station wit' a store, like a Quick Mart or some shit, and I'm like fuck it, get some gas, too. I pull up to the pump, hop up, leavin' the driver's door open, music blastin' some ol' ghetto shit, and people lookin' at me like it's jungle music. Now the only white people I knew up until then was either cops or crackheads and they lookin' at me like the only black people they ever saw was in newspapers and TV.

I get my gas, go in the store, and say, "Yo, y'all got a bathroom?" Clerk act like I'm speakin' Chinese, so I repeat myself. I told you I hate to repeat myself, so I guess the absence of sleep and this gaga-eyed motherfucka is irkin' me. So when I repeat it, I guess it came out a little harsh 'cause he just pointed. I guess that's when he called the police 'cause I went in the bathroom, pissed, then caught myself and took my gun off my waistline and put it in my pocket for easy access. Not 'cause I was thinkin' some ol' felonious type shit but...just in case. Call it street intuition. Instinct.

I come out, grab some chips, a beef Hot Pocket, a Snapple and take it to the counter. He still lookin' like he seen a ghost, so after I pay...I just say, "Boo!" He jump back a half-mile, I think the shit is hysterical and walk out.

Now my car door still open, music still blastin' but it's two phone booths outside the store and I get on one to call Auntie. Phone ringin'. I'm boppin' to the music when I see two cop cars, not speeding but you can tell they had a destination. I put my hand on the gun, nonchalantly turn around and put the gun under the phone book and hang up. I start walkin' towards the car when they pulled in, one in front of the Prelude, one in back, blockin' it. I think to myself...I bagged.

Now ain't no sense in runnin' 'cause I ain't fast and wit' my luck, I'll probably be runnin' straight to the county jail. Four cops, two to a car, get out. Not on no SWAT shit but some serious shit nevertheless.

"Take your hands out of your pocket."

I obliged him...slowly.

"This your car?"

"You can say that," is what I threw back.

"Well, is it or isn't it?" Yeah, it is. He ask for my license and registration and you and I both know I ain't had no license. So I threw him my sob story, how I was sixteen and ran away, this and that, in hopes that when the plates come back stolen I could ride this orphan Annie abused child shit. Remember.

Finesse.

So I'm in the back seat, cuffed up, goin' to the station. When we get there, they offerin' me candy, sodas and shit, and I'm like, damn, am I guest or a prisoner? Fuck it, yeah, let me get a Coke and a Snickers. I'm handcuffed to the desk, one hand free. Now, I know if you just let the police talk, they'll tell you everything you need to know, if not everything they know, period, which is usually nothin'.

First thing he say is, "Where'd you get the car from?"

I perked up.

He said *get* it, not where did I steal it, a significant choice in verbs, so somethin' tells me they don't know.

189

I relax and I run down the runaway shit and how it was my stepfather's friend's car, 'cause I know it's a older dude car 'cause of the music. Al Green and shit like that. Anyway, to make a long story short, they never found out the car was stolen. Either the plates ain't been run back home or this lil' backwards-ass town didn't connect that far. Shit reminded me of "Dukes of Hazard," station was set up like that, and all they could really bag me for was drivin' without a license. Cool. They tell me they gonna transfer me to a juvenile facility to await trial. A juvey. Yo, I know how the youth house is back home, and I know cats in B-More and D.C. will bring it to that ass, so I'm like, whatever, it's on. 'Cause I know when they see me—Tim boots, thick leather goose, Levi's, plus holdin' like three-fifty—they gonna think, "Lunch!" And I ain't never been the one to have for dinner...or *as* dinner, so I wait...and wait...and wait. I wait for six hours, until this fat white cat come in a van and pick me up. We ride past Baltimore, which was only five miles from this piss-out town—yo, I coulda kicked myself! Five mo' miles and I woulda been in B-More, and coulda blended in, disappeared, but they say everything happens for a reason, huh? I guess so, but right then all I'm thinkin' is, I'ma hafta fight half the joint to ring bells, 'cause outsiders in the juvey? Not a good combination. I'ma swing on the first motherfucka I see.

We get off at an exit and we ridin', by now it's night, and we pull up in this long ranch-style house. I'm thinkin', what's this? These motherfuckas stoppin' at home? 'Cause it looked like somebody house, but that was the juvenile spot. It was for kids who ran away and waitin' for trials on petty shit, so we go in and I see it ain't nothin' like no jail. This a house! The door came in on the kitchen right next to the living room. It was a lady sittin' at the table.

Ms. Washington.

Probably in her late thirties or early forties, but she looked good for her age. You could tell she still swing out, wit' all her gold gleamin' against her dark brown complexion. But in the living room... Yo, it was three of the flyest shorties I ever seen and two herb-ass crabs, one white and one black. They was watchin' a movie, I forget the flick.

Probably rated PG.

But later for them, Ma, what's your name? And yours, and, of course, yours. All three of y'all. One was named Mia or Myra and the other two was twins, the kind that don't look alike, Lena and Leslie. I don't remember the cats names 'cause they was pests, "Where'd you get the boots?" "Where you get the coat?" I answered it all wit' a simple, "Get off my dick," and redirected all my attention over here, on the ladies. Ms. Washington, she observin' me. I could feel her eyes on my neck, and I'm lovin' this. I got the stage, all eyes on me.

Ten o'clock came and the TV go off. Bedtime. Bedtime? At ten? Fuck it. Myra, where you sleep? So I get up to go to the back, followin' the girls, but one wing to the right was for the girls, to the left for the boys, and in between, Ms. Washington. She call me back.

"Not you. Come here, let me talk to you."

Oh boy, here we go wit' this orientation shit. No smoking, no cursin', no fuckin', shit like that. But first thing she say is, "You want a drink?"

I'm like, daaamnn. Now remember, I done fucked my eighth grade teacher, so you see what I'm thinkin' at this point.

"Yeah," I tell her on the drink. She just laugh and light a cigarette. "You smoke?" Yeah, I smoke, but where that drink at? She look me up and down, "You think you slick, don't you? Where you from? Up north, I know. New York? Jersey? Philly? Nigga, you ain't no runaway. Naw. You ain't no runaway. Where you steal that car, huh?"

Now I'm thinkin', okay, she a cop. So I go into my little song and dance, but she cut me off. "Nigga, I was born *at* night, not *last* night. I ain't tryin' to hear that shit. I know your whole m.o. You open like a book. Real slick tongue. I seen you wit' my girls over there, leather coat, how much that cost, huh? Little piece of watch on your wrist.

191

Probably got a couple hundred in your pocket."

Actually, three-fifty, I thought to myself.

Then she started runnin' it to me. The cliché shit I probably heard a thousand times before and since, about all the gangstas dead or in jail. You need to get an education, you won't be shit without one, the whole soapbox speech. But yo, I ain't *never* heard it like *that* before, from someone who been there, done that. She even knew Grand Daddy!

Aw, man, for the next few weeks, 'til I went to court and got probation, she schoolin' me to the streets, the world—life—and I'm like, finally I get a little help. I ain't gotta figure this shit out as I go, 'cause up until then, that's what I had been doin'.

She told me about books I should read, people I should know about and most important, that I should go back to school. She said she could help me.

I had heard that two other times from adults.

One I fucked over.

The other, I just fucked.

But this one...

I just fucked up.

She said she knew a children's home where I could go, in Baltimore, but I never saw myself as a child, not when I was eight, not when I was thirteen, and damn sure not then. But the thing that scared me the most was that word.

Help.

Damn, I needed it, I wanted it, but for the life of me, I just couldn't bring myself to lettin' nobody hold that...that power over me. Not even the power of love, 'cause I knew Ms. Washington loved me. I seen it in her face when she dropped me at the bus stop wit' a bus ticket in my hand. "Remember what I said," she said, and I never forgot. "Anytime. Call me. Call, nigga. I'll come *get* you," was the last words I heard from her.

I think about her a lot, wonderin' where my life would've gone had I picked up that phone before I... Never mind. I'm gettin' to that, or rather, *you'll* get to that. But for now, just know it's somethin' I'll always regret, not calling, coming, running, crawlin' to Ms. Washington. Kids need people like that. *Sincere* people like that.

Anyway, when I got back, I found out from Val that my man had got knocked sellin' for Sammi. Caught three years. Jewel was pregnant so while my man was in the tomb he had a seed in the womb. Ironic. I wrote him. He wrote back. I wrote again and the words was like old times. Just me and him. I sent him sneakers, he sent me flicks—pictures, that is. He asked me what I was doin'; nothin', I told myself, just like always.

It seem like every time that breeze come through and I hear my name and I was at my last, somethin' else popped up. This time, it was Ko-Ko, my girl. Real girl, not like Roxanne or the chick I split on.

Like Jewel.

Her real name Tonya, Puerto Rican, she teachin' me Spanish. You'll meet her. She got her name in the youth house 'cause she loved Cocoa Puffs. You know the bird that be sayin', "Coo-coo for Cocoa Puffs?" Yeah, that's her, only cuter. But I ain't tell *her* that, not when we first met, 'cause I knew she knew already. I remember the conversation word for word. She was walking down the street and as she passed me I was like, "You ain't cute."

"'Scuse me?"

"I said, you ain't cute. Damn, you deaf, too?"

So she said, "So why you talkin' to me then?"

"'Cause I know all day, cats been gassin' your already big head up. Yo, shortie, come here, check this and all that, so I'm just tellin' you, in your best interest, you ain't all that so sit the fuck down somewhere."

"What?" she said, 'cause I guess I piqued the Boricua in her.

"But I can help you."

"Help me?"

I'm like, "Help you get over the lonely years, 'cause ugly people need love, too."

"I know *you* know," she say, 'cause she got a smart mouth.

"So what you sayin'?"

"You ugly."

"So why you talkin' to me then?" I said, and ended the conversation where it started. We been together ever since. Ain't seen her in like a week, though. You know, old habits...

So my man came home, couple of weeks ago. I seen 'im once or twice and we promised to get up but he went home to Jewel and I went back to my thing, floatin' and, occasionally, Ko-Ko.

Last time I seen him, he was walkin' this way and he had this look. Kinda glassed-over like you could hear him, see him, but you couldn't get too close, you know what I'm sayin'? I asked 'im, "Where you goin'?" Top spot...that's what he said 'cause that's what we call this place of ours. "Yo, meet me on the top spot. Yo, where Bang?" Top spot. So I said, "I'll meet you up there."

"Naw, gotta think...be alone." That's what he said. I need that, too, so I understood, or at least I thought I understood. So I say, cool, you know, beep me. Oh, you got a dollar? I'm short on some cigarettes. He gave it to me.

That's the last thing he ever gave me.

He never said a word. He coulda told me somethin', anything, like I'm tellin' you. Just one word. I woulda jumped for him. My *word*, I woulda jumped for him. Just tell me why, yo, *why*, let me handle it, let me...

Where my cigarettes at?

{Mental Note: Throughout the night, he had stood, sat, teetered precariously on the edge of the building. He talked with words but expressed himself with his hands—every sentence was punctuated, every afterthought hyphenated, every heartfelt point emphasized with the physical fluidity appropriate to the season. I absorbed it all. Absorbed it like a sponge. He had strung his life together for me like a string of pearls, interwoven like a tapestry, until in the end, I could

194

see the shapes that formed the angles of his perception he had so masterfully stitched together. The soliloquy he had spoken that took hours seemed to span only minutes, and as he finished, the sun had just begun to rise in the east, as if to say...

And then there was light.

But why?

What about him or what about me, made me, or him, or us, so important? All I could think of was perhaps he wanted me to know everything it had taken to mold him, shape him, prepare him for what he had felt in that instant he saw his friend embrace death. Everything that flashed through his mind in the time it takes a man to fall twenty-one stories to the ground.

Some say that when faced with death, their whole life flashes before their eyes. I had just learned that this same spontaneous reflection can occur when another's death is flashed before your eyes. In the thralls of death we think of life.

As he finished, as if to himself, he said, "He could've said something." I get the impression that it wasn't because he would've stopped him, or as he said, jumped for him. No. It was as if to say, "Why didn't you take me with you?" The agony of never quite finding where you fit in, your niche, discovering only to be abandoned, beckoning but never receiving...loving, only to find that the only thing he ever wanted was always in front of his face.

A friend.

But now, he had lost his only chance for eternity.

I slept.}

CHAPTER THREE

*{Mental Note: I awoke, seemingly days later...
months...even years...from a sleep so celestially deep,
cerebrally suspended, I thought, could I be...?*

*The sounds of honking horns and cars badly in need
of new motors answered my question. To my drowsed ear,
the chirping of the birds sounded like quarrelling—sharp
bursts of rapid-fire chirps, with none of the lightness I
remember from camping trips high in the mountains. He sat
there, with his legs dangling over the edge of the building, as
if he was just sitting on a stoop three feet above the ground
and not the twenty-one stories we had ascended... The way
Otis Redding must've sat on the dock of the bay.*

*He was unbraiding his cornrows one by one, until half
of his head stuck out in every direction imaginable, in little
spiked tufts. It reminded me of a weapon I've forgotten the
name of—that chain and iron spike ball that medieval
knights brandished to demolish the defenses of the enemy—
but sitting on the edge of the building, he was anything but
chained.*

I stirred.

He turned. Spoke.}

Oh, you back, huh? Yeah, I was sitting back, taking
my braids out, listening to the sounds of blackness, yo. I
love this place. That might sound crazy to you 'cause how
shit is, or how you think shit is. And you might say what I
feel ain't love, just that I learned to accept it, but naw. The

ghetto... It's like a girl, you know, that you know ain't no good for you, cheat on you, set you up, just straight up shit on you, but you keep goin' back to her 'cause the sex is the bomb! That's the thrill, that's her claim to fame. It's why motherfuckas write songs for her, it's why cats be even dyin' for her. Only live by her or wit' her, set they watch by her...

You know she don't give a fuck about you, but she keep callin' you, just to see what crazy shit she can make you do for her next.

She cold.

Ain't never gonna change, but hey, you knew what she was about from jump street. You hungry? Man, it's too early to be thinkin' about eatin', it ain't but...oh damn, forgot I blessed my man wit' my watch. What time is it? Eleven seventeen? I don't even think about food 'til I get some money in my pocket—then my stomach speak up like, don't forget 'bout me! 'Cause he know I'll spend that shit on get-high or wifey or some kicks. But fuck it, come on. I know just the spot.

{Mental Note: As he descended the fire escape, and I after him, I felt a tinge of envy.

The top spot.

Not only a place to grow up, but a place that grows with you; and as you grow, you begin to find new solace in it. No, I never had a place like that. Sure, I had my treehouses, my secret hiding places. Under the porch, in the crevices of the attic, but you soon grow out of the confines of these small places, if only physically. It is as if the treehouse says, you have outgrown me, now you must go. There is no more room for you here, so you begrudgingly trek on, still psychologically yearning for its simple comforts. But there are always other places, other sentimental attachments to which we latch and unlatch, like nostalgic suitcases. Like the fishing trips to the lake which, even to this day, Dad and I still take. That is, when he feels up to it, when the climate permits, and when my prior commitments don't conflict and

197

all these preconditions coincide. But in a small way, you can say I grew up at the lake...but not with the lake. For one, because of the physical distance, the lake being an hour away from my house. I never had a place I could just run to with every new discovery that my youthful excavations had uncovered. A constant in the young world that is constant change. I had my stability supplied in other areas of my life. But how, I wondered, to have such a place, to take it all there, like a prize and examine it, discuss it, turn it over in your hands and watch it shine. Feel it grow warm, only to realize it is alive itself, and it bites you—not hard, but sharp, but even the bite itself was a thrill. Why did it bite?

And in a way, you want it to bite again, because everything else about it had become mundane, and soon you are trying to make it bite, or if not bite, at least snap at you...for the thrill or out of sheer boredom, and when you've grown numb to the bites, you fling it into the wind. Headfirst, into the abyss, to find out what else it could possibly do before it descends into oblivion.

No, I never had a spot like that. Mixed blessings, I suppose.

We descended the fire escape.

Back down to earth—literally.

I instantly had a flash of recollection. My wife. My life. My world.

Now, I must digress here only to tell you that as we speak of this incident, or these incidents, they have already transpired, and therefore I speak as a man with the luxury of hindsight. What I knew then as I experienced this...this journey...is not the same as I now understand it, or at least grasp it. So forgive me where I pause, or lull, and neglect to record the obvious but it is all in the name of effect. But as I said, I've digressed.

Now, at this time my thoughts turned to my wife and the anxiety she must be feeling because of my unexplained, uncharacteristic absence. I reached for my cell phone only to find it was dead. I assumed it was the battery. Then I thought, my car? Where had I left my car? I only vaguely remember driving home after a long night of research I was doing for my latest book on suicide in the inner city, its rise and its causes, when he...appeared?

No, he had to have been in my back seat.

But how?

Why didn't my alarm go off? Then I smiled, as I remember him saying, "Yeah, I stole cars." But why, when I noticed him, was he in my passenger seat? How did he climb out of the back without my noticing him?

The last thing I remember, I was at a red light. Maybe he jumped in at the light. No. It couldn't be, because I always lock my doors. It's as routine as putting on my favorite radio station for comfort or my seat belt for safety. In this twenty-first century world, it had become just as much a part of driving as steering itself. Had I forgotten? I shook off the how's and they were replaced with just as many why's. Despite how he got in, why had I so totally abandoned my own life to find out about his?

What did he want to tell me?

Why me?

And why did he say I called him?

When I looked up from my query, I realized I had lost pace. I saw him standing at the bus stop, asking another man for a light. He lit, the man passed on. I approached, and suddenly the why's and how's all made sense. Simply, I was intrigued; more than merely curious—but that alone, as they say, killed the cat.

I accosted him, "You said I called you?"

He just smiled. Inhaled the smoke, exhaled in French fashion, mouth to nose, a ring formed and floated away, and he responded.}

You gotta crawl before you walk. But yeah, you called me. Why you? Let's just say I read your books. I read your articles, too, 'cause like I said, I read a lot. Partly out of cold winter nights when I be in the library and partly 'cause what Ms. Washington had told me. But the more I read, the more shit I didn't know; it was like, the more I learned the dumber I was for it, you know? I started wit' Donald Goines 'cause I could relate to the titles. Shit like *Dopefiend* and *Street Players*... And as I read, I saw my world for the first time from the outside, 'cause it's hard sometimes to see the picture from inside the frame. But the way Don presented it, I kinda understood it better. The good and the bad. I think when motherfuckas write, they give certain characters they own characteristics—you know, the flaws of the writer, the morals of the writer—and then the writer take the character wit' the flaws he don't want no more and he kill 'em. It's like killin' that part of themselves.

Check it out, next time you read a book, see if it ain't true. You might not realize it, but motherfuckas do it. *You* do it. In your book, *Stolen Moments*? I could tell you don't like liars, but who do? And another thing, you don't like men who depend on women. That told me that you got a strong sense of manhood. Responsibility. Maybe it's psychological, but all of 'em do it.

I read *Moby Dick*, mostly 'cause of the title. Then I read Henry Thoreau, *Walden*. I like the cat, 'cause here was a white man, two hundred years ago, sayin' shit that a motherfucka like me from the projects could relate to! Shit like, "In an unjust society, the only place for a just man is prison." I thought about my man and I was like, yeah, my man just. Only thing put him there was the fucked up system, so I wrote him. He said he been readin', too.

A dream deferred...

But you, I read and read and read and sometimes I'd fall asleep readin' and I be dreamin' about all these motherfuckas walkin' around the library, talkin' and laughin' and they be dressed like how they used to dress. Like you might get some English cat wit' them buckle shoes and high-water pants come to his knees and a wig and shit. Or pirates wit' wooden legs, Arabs wrapped in white cloth and bejeweled turbans, and I'll be talkin' to these cats, and they be sayin' shit from out their books. Like I dreamt *Hamlet* or *Macbeth*, I forget which, and I asked him, why

200

you dress like that? And he said, "This above all, to thy ownself be true." Like he was tellin' me, motherfucka be yourself, fuck what another cat think. Yeah, I always remembered that 'cause it's true. People worry about what another motherfucka say too much, what somebody else think of them and don't even know theyselves. But anyway, I read about philosophy, science, religion. Yo, I ain't never know so many people believed so many different things. Like, some people worship cows! Cows, yo! All the while I'm eatin' a burger, and I look at the burger like...God? Naw, naw, hell no. I couldn't get wit' no shit like that. And cats worshippin' stones! Everyday rocks?! Shit I used to bust windows wit' or throw at girls while they be jumpin' rope. Only thing I really know about God was the Jehovah's Witness my mother used to duck on Saturday mornings. Turn the radio off and everything, like shhhh! And they be knockin' and knockin'. Persistent cats. Or the people went to church on Sunday morning, buying weed from me Sunday night. But I believe in God...

You?

Yeah, I know He out there seein' the fucked up shit we be doin'. But I don't wanna talk about God 'cause He the only one I truly fear. Not like fear as in run away from, but fear to offend. I wanna do right, but...well, you know how that go. Hold up, lemme see if this our bus... Naw.

Anyway, yeah, I read books, even read schoolbooks but I wouldn't go to school.

Why?

'Cause goin' back woulda meant I was wrong in the first place, like anything and everything I decided after not goin' to school was wrong, and that woulda meant *I* was wrong. Hate it. I mean, it done got me fucked up. Like, I think if I woulda told my man that night, yo, I'm sorry for callin' Jewel a bitch, shit mighta been different. I ain't sayin' he'd still be here...but...who's to say? Pride, man. A man who ain't got none is the scum of the earth and a man who got too much is a foolish motherfucka. Seem like the less you have, in terms of money, looks and talent, the more pride you have in the shit you do have. Yeah, it is good 'cause you can learn appreciation, but most of the time it get outta hand. Like, you remember hearin' about kids killin' other kids 'cause they stepped on they sneakers? Sound stupid, huh? It is, but it ain't. 'Cause like I said, when you ain't got nothin', the little somethin' you got, you put your whole self in that. It becomes a part of you. So if a man come along and, even by mistake, step on your sneakers, he ain't just steppin' on your sneakers, he steppin' on *you*! Your manhood! That's the equivalent of a man come piss in your living room! It's like, this all I got and this nigga gonna disrespect that? But the other cat, he feel the same way, if he say sorry, he sayin' he wrong and you right, that maybe he ain't deserve to step on the ground your shoe happened to be occupyin' at the time! So now you got two opposing forces feelin' the same way. It's dangerous when that happen, you know? It's like a irresistible force meets an unmovable object—they bound to bump heads, you know? But take you, for instance. You got a car, a house, plenty of shoes, so if a cat step on your shoe, you like, don't worry about it—simple mistake, right? A shoe a shoe; that shoe don't define you, it ain't all you got. But I'm sure you'd respond... I-ight then. Cats just got different limitations, that's all; so there that go. But we was talkin' 'bout books and I was tryin' to answer your first question 'bout your callin' me, more or less, when you asked me why I ain't go back to school.

Don't ask no more questions unless it's necessary for clarifications, 'cause you know how I flow by now—I like to take the scenic route when I spill thoughts, so if you point out some interestin' shit, I'ma comment.

So just listen. It's an art form to that. If you listen, you might hear what a motherfucka sayin' without words. It's all about a command of words. You can command words whether speakin' or bein' spoken to, or how we say, bein' spit *at* or spittin' on, i-ight? That's why Shakespeare get the props he do. Command of words. But if you think *he* had a command of words, you should see the average pimp, now *that's* a command of words! Could you imagine Shakespeare a pimp? "Thy yonder damsel, my money, bet' have..." Wouldn't work. Now when a pimp say it—"Bitch, betta have my money"—you get attention.

Politicians is pimps, 'cept they pimpin' thousands. Command of words. That's why Malcolm was successful. Same as Martin and Farrakhan. 'Cause they put into words what other people can't 'cause they don't have a command of words, they commanded *by* words. Stop. Go. Sit. Run. Walk. Don't walk. Smoke. Don't smoke. And they obey 'cause that's what they know the word as, through they experience. So the trick is to relate your experiences to they experience, even though the words y'all both use is the same...

Okay, maybe I ain't make myself clear... Let's say you got a...parole officer. She a middle-aged, former debutante conservative. You a young black cat. You see her and she ask you, are you working? "No," you reply.

"Well, are you looking? I've seen many jobs in the paper, so you can't say there are no jobs."

So you like, "Yeah, I been there, done that, but they turn me down, 'cause I got a jail record, I'm black and I'm a man." She say, " I *know* this, but *why* can't you get a job?"

See, she think you not tryin' 'cause she know the words jail, black and man, but if she don't know the implications that trinity represent in the eyes of the average employer, she gonna miss the whole point. You just told her why you can't get a job, but for the life of her, she can't see what in the world that has to do wit' sweepin' floors and flippin' burgers. That's 'cause she ain't never been an unemployed black man wit' a record, and since you'll never be a white woman from Hempstead, you might wanna flip, yell and cuss. But that only make it worse on you, 'cause not only do she think you lazy and irresponsible, but now she think you crazy, too!

That's being commanded by words.

Now had you said, "In this day and time, black ex-convicts who may be qualified are often not considered for employment because of society's disdain for convicts, especially black ones, just as at one time before white women, such as yourself, won the right of suffrage, they too were excluded solely because they were women, albeit white." You see what I'm sayin'? It don't always work 'cause since motherfuckas just dumb or they just don't want to understand, or they experience is just beyond explanation...

Like love...

Or if you ask a pregnant woman how it feels to give birth. She gonna tell you some impossible shit like, imagine pullin' your bottom lip completely over your head 'til it touch your neck. Impossible to do 'cause it's impossible to explain. But if you notice, only thing shouldn't be commanded by words is feelin'. Love, birth, death. That's where the art of listenin' come in, when silence speak louder than words...

Here come our bus...

{Mental Note: We rode in silence or, should I say, wordless. It was anything but silent. He looked out of the window, or at his reflection in the window, or at his reflection reflected upon the passing streets—I couldn't tell which—while I watched many bus occupants, "hearing" their stories.

Like the petite, brown-skinned teenaged girl, fat cheeked and doe-eyed, with the three college texts on her lap. Accounting, Principles of Management and Economics. Her book bag beside her, with a hint of her red and yellow McDonald's uniform sticking out. In her hand she held a baby pacifier hanging from a key chain, which she lightly fingered periodically. It all seemed to say, "Yes, I'm going to college, partial scholarship, work at McDonald's. It's hard, especially raising a child, but I'm managing, and I'm going to make it."

Or the man who limped onto the bus. Not a man with the clumsiness of a temporary annoyance, but with the grace—or if not grace, at least the ease—of a man who had adopted the handicap, birth or inflicted, into a part of his demeanor.

Or the driver—middle-aged, slightly balding on the top of his head, with the driver's cap, worn and slightly soiled, tipped back on his head. The hat itself may be the cause of the bald spot, I mused. Tilted up in the summer, fitted down in the winter. Friction. The bald spot, like the rings in a tree, which you could probably count to an even match of his years of service. He even seemed "rooted" to his seat—this route, this way of life.

Or the three teenaged boys who got on two stops prior and had passed row after row of vacant seats, just to settle in the back of the bus. I thought of years before, before these boys were even born, when Rosa Parks, too tired to move, had abolished just that. But now, decades later, her "descendants," her progeny, had opted voluntarily for what she and thousands of others had boycotted against, and it made me contemplate the irony of freedom...

I nodded to myself, and the young man with dreadlocks and the Walkman, who had been nodding to the music in his headphones the whole while, now nodded at me.

I nodded back.

Perhaps he thought we shared some kind of unspoken rhythmic bond, or maybe he thought I was nodding to my own beat in my own head. Maybe I was. The rhythm of understanding. Not that I felt anywhere near understanding this situation, but at least I understood why I was ignorant. My head was filled with a sort of victory interspersed with a smattering of defeat, because I knew this could be the closest I get to understanding...

Understanding I didn't understand.

My guide rode on quietly, never taking his eyes off whatever he saw in the window...and beyond...

People got on, got off, and I heard their stories. Apathy. Indifference. Tension. Hope. He rose, and I realized our stop was upon us so I followed. We disembarked in front of a Burger King. I remembered my hunger, which had become ravishing by this point. As we walked towards the *parking lot, I thought that perhaps this was a shortcut to another destination. I was just about to voice my protest when he turned onto the drive-thru, passing two waiting cars, and went directly to the speaker that you order from—usually, from a car. He interrupted a heavy-set gentleman in a brown Cadillac to holler into the speaker. He pardoned himself to the stunned Cadillac driver—"Pardon self, my man"—and then turned his attention to the speaker.*

"Yo sun...yo sun, what up, this me."

He said "me" as if he had an appointment...

The speaker called back. "Yo, that you, kid? What up, sun, where you been?"

He replied, "Just loungin', ya know how we do. Look, I need the hook-up for me and my man, i-ight?"

"I-ight, come around to the window." We walked away from the man in the Caddy, who wore a stunned look that seemed to say, I thought this was a drive-thru?

I found it amusing.

As we rounded the corner, I noticed a row of three phone booths on the sidewalk, just beyond the parking lot. So as he went to the window, I walked over to the phone.

My first thought was, what would I say? "Hi, honey, I got carjacked—or at least I think I've been carjacked—but the 'jacker' was extremely intriguing and wanted to tell me something, so I've decided to hang out, for research purposes."

I wonder who she'd call first—a psychiatrist or a divorce lawyer?

I didn't know what to say but knew I had to say something, as she would be distraught with my almost-24-hour absence. I deposited a quarter and dialed the number.

Nothing.

No ringing, no busy signal, nothing. The phone went dead. I hung up and waited for my quarter to return, and re-deposited it. Again nothing. I tried the second and third phones in rapid succession but every time, I got this dial tone, inserted the quarter and dialed the number. Then it happened...

206

Nothing.

The phone went dead. I tried to call the operator. I pressed "O." Dead. I noticed a fish market across the street with the address and phone number displayed on its awning. I again inserted my quarter and this time dialed the number from the awning.

"Hello, Joe's Fish Market..."

I was perplexed. I didn't speak. I could vaguely hear him repeat his greeting, then a short silence. Then an aggravated curse followed by the dial tone. Buoyed by this minor breather, thinking that perhaps the phone was "broken in," I tried my number again.

Nothing.

I hung up. It was like anything that could verify my existence, my own life, had been denied. Like there was no way out of this...this...foray I had undertaken, and the thought was suffocating. I instinctively reached for my wallet, for something familiar, anything familiar. I'm not a sentimental man so I had long stopped carrying pictures of my children and my wife. Now the only contents of my wallet were credit cards, gas cards, various cards of business associates...slips of paper I had written messages and numbers to myself...

And my license!

Yes! What could be a more familiar face than my own?

I looked at it—at the picture, at the address, at the seal of the state—and I thought, at least I'm not dead. Not unless they now had cars in heaven—or hell, whatever the case may be—and God had divided eternity into a commonwealth. I returned my license to my wallet, and my wallet to my pocket, and thought of trying the phone once more, but this time just dialing randomly, any series of numbers. I turned in time to see him approaching me with two bags, and I forgot everything but my now-raging famine...}

Ay, yo, you i-ight? You look kinda sick... Oh, the

phone? Them shits work when they want to, but yo, don't worry, you'll be home soon. For now, let's see what my man hit us off wit'. I couldn't get no sodas 'cause his manager be hawkin', so you know how that go. Come on, we can eat while we walk...

Let's see, we got fish fillets, cheeseburgers, whoppers... What's this? Chef salad? This fuckin' rabbit food, I'll leave this for the birds... Oh, you like salad? Well here, knock yourself out...

Yeah, that was my man Shameek, cool peeps, but motherfucka think he God! You understand that shit? Yeah, I guess you could 'cause, like, the Romans used to call motherfuckas gods if they did somethin' the average cat couldn't do. Like they call Jordan the god of basketball, shit like that. Like when Jesus made the dead rise, I guess that's why people back then was like, now he *gotta* be God!

Yeah, people funny like that.

Yeah, but Shameek, he think he God, too. Not, like, on no ego-trippin' shit or nothin', and he say it ain't no religion or whatever; he say it's his culture. So I be fuckin' wit' him. I be like, yo, when's it gonna rain? Or, take me to Spain for the weekend. He say, "Naw, not like that, god of the higher self, god of the mind." I say, "Yeah, god in your *own* mind..." He tell me the black man always been God, but I say, naw, we just ain't always been *niggas*! 'Cause yo, when you go through what we been through, stepped on like we dirt, you can go from one extreme to the other real easy—you know, from niggas to gods. Matter of fact, that's a book... But yeah, he believe that shit, but I'm like, what if God for real—you know, *God*-God—what if God step to him like, "You been frontin' like you Me, using My name; put up your mitts, shoot this, fair one." I asked him what you gonna do then, cause I know your arms too short to box wit' God. I mean, for real, if a cat was runnin' around doin' shit, sayin' he me, when I catch 'im I'ma beat that muhfucka ass!

Damn...slow down, it ain't goin' nowhere, yo! You eatin' like my man Cardboard when I be bringin' him shit to eat.

Who Cardboard?

Cardboard, he my man and he homeless, so since I choose not to have a home, sometimes I go down in the subway and chill wit' 'im. Bring him somethin', smoke a blunt wit' him or whatever and just kick it. He school me to a lot of shit. He a old cat, but the dirty clothes and shit make him look a lot older than he is. He probably fifty-five. People think he crazy 'cause he talk to himself all the time; matter of fact, that's how I met him. I was waitin' on the train and he was sittin' on the floor, talkin' shit 'bout, "You sure is pretty today. I like your hair." So I'm looking around, cause ain't nobody down there but me and him, to my knowledge, so I'm wonderin', what the fuck? Yo, I *know* this cat ain't talkin' to me, but I chill, nix it off. Then he say, "Come give me some sugar. Don't be shy, ain't nobody around." Yo, I flipped!

"Yo, motherfucka, you got your people mixed up! Fuck ya mean, some sugar?!"

I'm heated! Ready to hook off, the whole nine, 'til he look at me and I see surprise in his eyes. Like he ain't even know I been standin' there.

"Who you?"

I say, "Naw, who you talkin' to?"

He say, "My wife."

I look around. I told you we the only ones down there, to my knowledge, so I think, oh hell, here *he* go... But I play along. "Where she at?" He look at me like I'm the blindest motherfucka in the world and say, "Right there," and point over by the trashcan. He tell me, "She cookin' my favorite. Red beans and rice...and corn bread."

I'm tryin' not to laugh, 'cause the look on his face tell me he dead-ass lickin' his chops and all, but I'm high, bored, train ain't come yet, so I say, "Can I have some?"

"Sure! Baby, bring another plate, we got company."

Never did make the train...or get no red beans and rice.

But as time went on, he told me how his wife died

209

and he didn't wanna live in they house no more, and they ain't have no kids...nowhere to go... See, he know she dead, but he say she come see him, keep him company. Now, I don't believe in no ghosts or nothin', but who am I to say it ain't there just 'cause I can't see it? Maybe she do, maybe she don't—long as he believe it is all it come down to... Hold up...

Tito! Yo, Tito. It's me, sun, what up baby? When you gonna hook me up wit' the outfit, yo?

Yo, the cat across the street at the vendor's booth, that's my man Tito. He be designin' clothes except he ain't blow up yet. Mad cats be rockin' his gear, though. He used to hustle for Sammi; matter of fact, he was there the night Sammi got wet up—shot, that means shot. Yeah, I think he got hit in the exchange himself. After that, he put all his loot into clothes. I guess one man's mistake can be another man's lesson, you agree? Yeah, me too...

Where we goin'?

What I tell you about the questions, huh? Damn, you i-ight, you'll be home sooner than you think...

What time is it anyway?

Two o'clock? Yeah, I guess she home by now—I'm talkin' 'bout my girl Ko-Ko. She go to this art school 'cause she can draw real good. She be doin' graffiti, too. Put her name on everything, even me. See this tattoo? She did it, but the shit got infected and shit. Fuck it. I don't mind 'cause she my heart. I guess I love her. I just ain't never told her 'cause... I don't know... She know, though, even though I know she gonna flip when she see me, 'cause I ain't come through in a week. I be leavin' her little messages where I know she'll be 'cause she ain't got no phone. So I leave 'em at the store, the laundromat, at her school, and she be answerin'. Last note I got said, "I'ma beat yo' ass!" So when we get to the door stand to the side, 'cause bystanders get it, too...

{Mental Note: Her building sat on top of a store, or what is called a bodega. Sort of a corner-market-slash-

supermarket-slash-deli, all crammed into a candy store. It stands out because it is always accentuated by a yellow and red awning that borders the store. We entered through a side door and walked up the steps, to the floor directly above the store. He knocked... The door opened, and a beautiful Hispanic woman in a housecoat stood in the doorway. She smiled as we entered and he kissed her on the cheek. He addressed her in Spanish but soon reverted back to English.

He called his girlfriend's name, and out of the back she came. Her face said she was twelve, her eyes said she was twenty-eight, but she was actually twenty-one. And her eyes came into the room like a hawk looking for a target, full of anger, at the voice of her summoner; that is, until she saw me.

"Who you? You a cop? What you want wit' him? He was wit' me last night and the night before!" she fired off, like a well-rehearsed line she never needed to practice but could perform at any time. As he explained to her the circumstances of my presence, I couldn't help but think of an abused child who, after growing so accustomed to a raised hand bringing pain, my presence—a white man in this environment, uninvited—triggered her defense mechanism in reaction to other white men before me.

"He was lost," he began, "got off on the wrong stop and I told him I'd show him the way after I came to see my boo."

He reached for her but she slapped his hand away in order to relieve her mind of a week's worth of pressure, although I could tell she didn't want to.

"Oh, so you out playin' Good Samaritan while I'm worried to death about you?" she questioned.

"You worried now?" was his response.

"No, now I'm just mad as hell!"

"Hey, hey," her mother cautioned from the kitchen. She had been going about her cooking as if this was an everyday occurrence. Well, an every-week occurrence or whatever the case my be.

"You ain't even gonna braid my hair?" he asked, as

she turned to go back to her room and he followed.

"Braid your hair? Nigga, please," she said.

"Come on, yo, after I take a shower..." His voice was drowned out by the music and the shutting of the door behind them.

I sat there, on the couch, half-listening to a Spanish soap opera on the TV in the corner, as Ko-Ko's mother continued to busy herself in the kitchen.

Beautiful woman. Jovial. Healthy, but not fat or even heavy-set. The only signs of age were in the corner of her eyes and her mouth, and a wisp of gray hair that she pushed behind her ear as she asked me if I wanted anything to drink. I thanked her. She returned with a funny-colored blue fruit drink, and had she not been so hospitable, so polite, I would have hesitated to drink it. Not that I mistrusted her, but I was like an oddity to her. I could tell, ever so subtly, that, although I was partially welcomed, I was mainly tolerated. She fed me, like a child fed the no-armed circus freak a banana. Not to feed him, but just to watch him peel it with his feet.

She went back to her housework and began vacuuming, stopping only to bang on the door he and Ko-Ko had entered, to question why she heard no talking. The answer was too muffled to make out, and too low for them to be positioned vertically when it was given.

I smiled.

Young love. I thought back to my own youth and various infatuations and crushes. The little notes he said he left her, seemingly all over town, reminded me of the notes I left my wife sometimes on the refrigerator or in the bathroom or on the bedroom mirror and I thought, is the whole city his "house"? Was the store his kitchen, the school his den, the laundromat his bathroom? And although all men, I suppose, play the nonchalant game to hide their feelings—leaving calls unreturned, dates unfulfilled—did all women have to worry that their beau might be dead? Did my prom date, when I was an hour late because my car broke down, have visions of me lying in a pool of blood in the street, or evading the *law, like this woman instinctively did? Pat Benatar sang a song called "Love is a Battlefield," but here, I thought, love in a battlefield...*

Ko-Ko's mother continued to vacuum and I watched the lines jump up and down on the screen of the TV, like TV's do when a vacuum is on. I looked around the room and came to the conclusion they were Catholic because of the alter-like setup of candles, the picture of Mary and the baby Jesus and other religious reminders. Directly across from me on the wall was an abstract painting, a collage of contrasting colors that reminded me of works I'd seen in Soho and the creative juices of Manhattan, and I wondered where it had been purchased. On further inspection, I saw Ko-Ko's autograph and I remembered that she attended art school. It was definitely not going to waste because the picture was exquisite. Tastefully understated, but then again, all good art is. Arrogance doesn't canvas well.

I looked at the photos on the coffee table in front of me. One of a small girl whom I assumed was Ko-Ko, and next to it a black and white photo of a woman identical to Ko-Ko—her mother, I presumed, at Ko-Ko's age. The last picture was one of him and Ko-Ko with a mural of a sunset as a backdrop. She smiled, enveloped in his arms, and he was looking not at the camera, but at her. I thought, yes, he loves her. Then I thought of my own wife. I should ask...then I recalled they had no phone. I sighed, looked at my watch. Quarter to three. I remember him saying something about a shower, braiding his hair, and what I thought they were doing now, making up for seven days.

I settled back on the couch.

I noticed a Time magazine, for which I had written several times, so I picked it up to see if this was one of the issues. As I picked up the magazine, I noticed an artist pad underneath with a collage of shapes and colors, not unlike the picture on the wall. I put the magazine down and picked up the pad to discover these were not just shapes and colors, they were words. I remembered he said that she did graffiti. The words and colors blended beautifully together and the whole pad was full of this exaggerated word play. I started to recognize schemes and motifs. Some had Oriental leanings, down to the Chinese-style background—ninjas and letters—shaped like Chinese letters but in English or Spanish. Some were easier to decipher than others because of the easily discernible blocked letters, while some had this incredibly complex three-dimensional perspective. Most of the illustrations had photographs taped to the page, and the picture in the photograph was the same as the illustrations. These illustrations had been brought to life, using the city as a canvas; I noticed the murals were on the side of trains, buses and buildings.

Now, I have seen plenty of graffiti in the past, mostly vandalism, mainly sayings and figures. I had also done a study of gang graffiti and the way these markings were used to demarcate territory, but now, I started to see symmetry where before I had only seen scribbles. Art, where before I saw only an eyesore. A statement, where before I only saw an excuse.

I gazed and gazed, and over time got better at reading the different illustrations, and my favorite, after much deliberation between several, was one where the words were catty-cornered and angled towards a mirror. The words reflected backwards from the phrase, and it read: Life is a mirror... Reflect.

I looked at my watch. Three thirty-nine.

I dozed.

I awoke to him emerging out of the back, hair neatly corn-rowed, in a green sweat suit with Ko-Ko in close tow.

"Gimme my candy, boy! Stop playin' so much!" she said, sounding playfully aggravated. He had his hands to his ears, like a little child does, saying, "La-la-la, I can't hear Ko-Ko! I can't hear Ko-Ko!"

She hit him. "Stop doin' that! I hate it when you do that!"

"Then stop bothering me about my Jolly Rancher," he said.

"It's my *Jolly Rancher*," she retorted.

"So why is it in my sweat suit?" he asked.

"'Cause I had it on."

"What you doin' wit' it on?" he wanted to know.

"'Cause you was gone for a week," she shot back, as if to say, what else did you leave me?

He responded, "Then it been in my pocket for a week."

"Mama!" was her response.

"Boy, give her a piece so she can shut up," came the voice of Ko-Ko's mother.

They argue like brother and sister would if they weren't brother and sister, but man and wife.

He broke the green stick of candy in half.

"You only want it 'cause I got it," he said.

"So?" was her simple reply as she slipped the candy in her mouth.

He opened the door and I guess we were leaving.

"I love you," her voice seemed to sing.

When we got outside and were walking around the corner, she appeared in the window.

"Yeah," he said, "love this," and he casually gave her the middle finger.

"That's why I beat you for your can—" she never finished her sentence, as the candy tumbled out of her mouth and hit the ground a few feet from where we were walking. He turned back, laughing, then ran over to the candy, pointed up at her then down at the candy, all the while doing a silly little dance around it. She laughed. I chuckled.

"Now! Now who beat, huh? Now who beat?" he said as he picked up the candy, flicked his tongue at her, and put it in his mouth.

"Ew, you nasty! I ain't never kissin' you no more," she said laughingly.

"Just be ready when I get back or I'm goin' to the movies by myself," he said as we walked away.

"I love yooouuu!" Her voice filled the air as the sun made its westward descent before us.

He spoke...}

215

Yeah, that's my boo. She hold me down.

She pretty too, huh? Yeah, I saw you checkin' her out, and the way you was lookin' at her mom. She pretty too, for an old lady. Well, not old, I'm glad she ain't hear that. Just, you know, motherly. She like my second mother, well, my only mother 'cause I ain't seen my mother since I was gettin' money wit' my man and them. After I got kicked out for the last time, the cat she was wit' got a job or somethin' in Virginia and her and my sister moved down there. Yo, they ain't tell me shit! I just came by one day, you know, to check on 'em, hit 'em off wit' some loot, and they was gone.

Nosy-ass Miss Johnson next door had to tell me. Fuck it. I guess they still down there, I don't know. But yeah, Ma back there, she like my moms. I told her I'ma marry her daughter and she say, "Then y'all can stop fornicatin' under my roof." I say, "Yeah, but that don't mean we gonna stop fuckin'." Well, I don't say that to her 'cause she don't like people to cuss, but I be thinkin' that.

But yo, I got one more thing to show you. It's in this park right here. See all these cats playin' ball? These your next Jordans, Iversons, Bryants...the black top. This the future. See my man wit' the red and white Jordans on? Naw, the Puerto Rican cat...right there, just slammed the ball. That's Ko-Ko's cousin Mikey. He seventeen, nicest cat out there, and it's some ghetto superstars out there. I stay on top of 'im 'cause motherfuckas out here is trife and I know he be seein' that shit. I know he want the good life, everybody do, but I be tellin' him, just keep doin' yo' thing 'cause you gonna be rich. Then you can have the Rolex, the Lex Coupe, the ice—shit, you could ice your whole mansion out, nice as you is! Then you can get your mom and your aunt and me and Ko-Ko outta here 'cause I told him I'm marryin' Ko-Ko, so he gotta take me, too! But I be on 'im though. Like, one time I was comin' through the park and I seen him and some cat skippin' school, smokin' weed. So I roll up on 'em. "The fuck you doin'? Why you ain't at school? You smoke weed now, huh? So you wanna get high,

216

huh? I-ight, let's get blunted."

So I fire up my blunt. I smoke the blunt wit' 'im and his man and after a while I start fuckin' wit' him. I be like, "Yo, you ain't hear me?" But I don't be sayin' nothin'. He was like, naw. Then I be movin' my mouth like I'm talkin', makin' my voice go in and out like every other word. I could tell by the look on his face he fucked up, so I'm tryin' to make the nigga think he crazy.

So next day, I see him, I'm like, "Yo, let's get blunted." He like, "Hell naw! That shit had me buggin'!"

He ain't smoked weed since. Wish I had a motherfucka like me when I was his age...

Fuck it...

Yeah, that there the future, just gotta stay away from them crab niggas sittin' over there on that bench. Two-bit ass drug dealers, but really they cowards wit' guns and a scared nigga'll kill you quick. Fo' real. They ain't no real hustlers. Now don't get me wrong, ever since I had my awakening wit' the pregnant lady, I hate drug dealin', but I understand why some cats do it. But it's a difference between hustlers like Grand Daddy and them niggas there. A certain code that their kind can't comprehend.

Crab-ass niggas.

You ever seen a crab in a bucket? One try to get out, the other ones try and pull it back down. That's them, the last crab in the ghetto bucket, so sometimes outta spite, I get the heater and jook 'em. That means stick up. Just to let 'em know, fuck you. Then I give they jewels and money away, flush the drugs, unless of course it's weed...

I ain't no Robin Hood, just one step up in the ghetto food chain. They suck people blood and I drink theirs.

Let's bounce.

{Mental Note: It was dark now. The street lamps brought much-needed light to the shadows, but before we left, I took another look at Mikey on the basketball court. Poetry in motion. He called him the future, and if he was, then the future looked flawless.

*But then I turned to the park bench where he'd
pointed out the crabs. I saw them as spiders—spiders with
deceitfully silken webs, spun around the park bench with the
enticements of money, power and respect. Just waiting for
young men like Mikey who resembled them but weren't like
them, but they stayed close, hoping to catch him in the web. I
wondered how many of the crabs had been like Mikey, with
some glimpse of a future, a better life, until the lure of instant
gratification ensnared them.*

*We turned the corner, leaving the park. He stopped on
the corner to light a cigarette, the match illuminating his face.
He threw the match. Spoke.}*

Yo, I told Ko-Ko I'd take her to the movies and shit,
just hang out, so I gotta go see a cat about some ends he
owe me.

But before I go, I hope you understood what you saw,
what I said, before I tell you what I got to say...

*{Mental Note: He lit the cigarette and blew the smoke
straight up in the air, and I thought, finally, what was all this
for? What was it about?*

*He began, "What I wanted to say is this—" and as if
on cue...*

It happened.

*Gunshots shattered the night like glass. He turned, I
turned—just in time to see a dark-colored car shooting onto
the basketball court we had just left. The crabs returned fire,
people scattered everywhere, screaming, and he ran to the
basketball court with me close behind.*

*Some of the ball players were huddled on the court.
One was on the ground. I saw the sneakers...red and white
Jordans.*

He screamed, "Mikey!"

*It was Mikey, bleeding on the court. Mikey. Ko-Ko's
cousin. The future.*

Dying?

Dead?

He pushed and shoved until he had cleared a path to Mikey. He kneeled beside Mikey.

"Mikey! Mikey! Damn, Mikey, no..." His voice trailed off in anguish.

Someone bent to touch Mikey.

"Don't touch him! Don't fuckin' touch him! Get the fuck outta here, call an ambulance!"

Someone informed him they had been called. In the distance I heard the singsong voice from earlier, this time devoid of its melody. Ko-Ko.

"Where my cousin? Where he at?" You could detect the tears in her voice even as she crossed the street. Where he had been dazed, whispering inaudibly to Mikey, the voice brought him back.

"She can't see him like this." He darted from the crowd to meet her as she reached the entrance to the park.

"No! Where Mikey?! I wanna see him, get off me!" she hollered, tears streaming her bronze face, and she collapsed in his arms.

"Why?" she asked over and over. The same why I had been asking myself.

"I seen 'em, boo. I seen them motherfuckas. I know who the fuck they is," he said.

She looked up into his eyes. Whatever was spoken was wordless, not like the wordless stories from the bus, to me...this was total silence.

In the background, I could hear Ko-Ko's mother calling.

"Yo, take Mommy upstairs. Don't let her come over here. I'll meet you when you come out." Ko-Ko was off. He turned to me.

"Let's go. Your car's around the corner." The look in his eyes. I understand what it was he told Ko-Ko and what he meant to do now. I stuttered, "I'm not...I-I don't have anything to do—" that's all I got out before I saw a glint of steel and felt its coldness to my jaw.

"Either ride for Mikey or die wit' Mikey! Ain't no other option! I'd just as soon leave you leakin' and do it myself!

Either way, it's gettin' done."

So just as this had started, I was again forced into a situation that I had not chosen.

We half walked, half jogged around the corner, him watching behind me and, to my surprise, my car sat under a flickering street light. We got in.

Key in the ignition?

I started the car and turned it around.

"Pull in front of Ko buildin'," he said, gun in his lap, like a bulldog licking its chops at me. I saw the patrol car as we passed the park. I glanced at it and, as if reading my mind, he repeated an earlier statement. "With or without you, it's gettin' done," but this time a whole lot calmer, tinted with an edge of macabre.

We pulled in front of the building. Ko-Ko was already waiting...with an automatic Mac-11.

"Pop the trunk! How you pop the trunk?" he asked. I pointed to the glove compartment. The trunk popped.

"Ko, get in the trunk. You know what we gotta do," he said.

She nodded in agreement and got in the trunk, Mac-11 and all, and pulled the trunk down, closed but not locked.

"Drive," was the command from my captor.

I drove.}

Make a right. What I tell you? Huh? What I tell you?

Ain't nobody safe! Nobody! You could be a church boy, a schoolboy, whatever, but if you here, you ain't safe! It's like, like, fuckin' rain. Bullets of rain. If you out there you gettin' wet. No matter what you do. You could wear a raincoat, boots, umbrella, and even you get out the rain, you can still tell where you been by the tracks. I'm sick of this shit.

Make a left. A left, yo! Fuck, you deaf?!

Damn, yo, why Mikey? First my man, now Mikey, who next? You? Me? Ko-Ko? Fuck it now.

Whatever, whatever. What do it matter now?

Nothing matters.

{Mental Note: This is crazy!

I have a home, a wife, a daughter, a son, a career, most importantly, a future! A life! Why am I now driving to avenge the death of a life I knew nothing about? Cared nothing for except out of human compassion? The threat of death?

Death?

What was worse, a pending doom or doom itself? Should I say, kill me? I refuse to be shackled to your fate unwillingly. Do what you must. I know he would kill me. Not because I wouldn't comply, but because I had been there. I had seen them take a life that didn't belong to them, didn't belong to the streets, so therefore the streets had no right to take it. So if I refused, I would be refusing to do justice by his criteria, just like refusing jury duty would have its consequences in another court of law. No. I could not refuse and die. Maybe we wouldn't find them. Maybe he would calm down and think of Ko-Ko, his love, who had a future in art. Convince her to let it go. I began to open my mouth, plead my case, plead her case, make him see reason, but just as I did—}

This the block. Make a right. I-ight, I'ma duck down in the seat. Go past the corner and it's the yellow house. Yeah, I see 'em. I see 'em!

Pull in front, tell 'em you lookin' for Main Street. Be cool...if you do this right you won't have nothin' to worry about but the nightmares as long as you *don't panic*. That's all.

Don't panic.

{Mental Note: Whatever hopes I had of not finding them were gone as I neared the yellow house. There were five or six standing on the porch. I slowed as I neared them, one last visage of hope. The hope that they would sense something in our approach and would run, go inside, anything, but as I neared, all eyes turned to me. I stopped in the middle of the street, lowered my passenger window and

221

hollered to the crowd through it, over his lowered head.

I heard myself stutter. "H-how do you get to Main Street?"

One of them replied, "What? Main Street? Fuck we look like, traffic cops?" They laughed.

He said, "Tell 'em you late for a date."

"I'm late for a date," I mimicked.

"Tell 'em you'll pay 'em."

"I'll pay you."

That got their attention.

"Damn, you wanna know that bad, I'll give you a tour of the city," the taller young man said as he approached the passenger window. I felt myself suppressing the urge to yell, "Go back!" But I knew it was him or me at this point, or him and me because he wouldn't escape. Not now. Not being this close, and I'd never be forgiven...in this life. The young man leaned on the lowered window frame.

"Now how can I help?" was all the young man could manage before he grabbed him by the collar and said, "Help yourself," and blew the man's head all over the roof of my car. The other men turned around, startled, taken by surprise, as Ko-Ko sat up in the trunk and screamed, "All you gotta die! Just die!" And let off a barrage of bullets that cut down three of the remaining six. He fired out of the window, but by now the remaining three had taken cover, only one being slower than the rest, and got cut down. "Go! Go!" he screamed at me. The two remaining were firing back and as Ko-Ko tried to close the trunk, I heard her scream and gunshots rang out. "Ko-Ko!" He screamed, and then, "Stop the car!"

Before I stopped, he was out, firing, the men firing back. He grabbed Ko-Ko out of the trunk and dragged her into the car...

Bleeding profusely yet smiling with a soft radiance she said, "We got 'em, Mikey. We got 'em, didn't we baby?"

Those were her last words.

I skidded away as a gunshot shattered my back window, but not seeing the stop sign, I was sideswiped by an oncoming car. We were smashed between the car that hit us and a parked car, sandwiched. I looked at him cradling Ko-Ko, crying, totally oblivious to our situation. I heard the sirens.

"We've got to get out!" I yelled, while frantically trying to open the door. I glanced in my rearview mirror. The two men were coming. Cops coming one way, killers the other way, who would reach us first? What was my choice? Death? Prison? What would happen to my wife? My kids? And if I could get away, where would I go? They would identify my car. Would the cops catch me? The killers? My head spun and I went into vertigo, I felt...

Trapped...

I heard a resounding scream of "Noooooo!"

I realized it was me as it echoed throughout the car, throughout my entire body, and I heard him...as if he had come right up to my ear, I heard it above the scream or somewhere within the scream.

I heard him say, "So now you know."

I passed out.

I awoke with a start to a tapping sound on my window.

It was a policeman, tapping his flashlight on my window. I quickly glanced to my right.

He was gone.

Ko-Ko was gone.

They must've run. But Ko-Ko, she was dead.

Wasn't she?

I looked at my ceiling. No blood. The policeman tapped the window a little harder. I let it down.

"Sir, are you okay? We got a call about a man in a blue Lexus sitting at this light, asleep," he informed me.

Asleep? At a light?

I glanced at my clock: 4:10. Did I...

The officer interrupted my thoughts. "Sir, are you okay? Have you been drinking? Do you mind stepping out of the car?"

I got out slowly and stood on unsure legs and wobbled a little, a sure sign of intoxication.

"Sir, let me see your license and registration." I started to get back in to get it. "No, we'll get it. Tony, get that, would ya? Glove compartment, right?" I nodded as his partner went around the car and opened my passenger door.

It was unlocked.

"Sir, you mind walking this yellow line?" the officer asked me.

"S-sure, I don't mind," I heard myself say. I was still dazed but walked the yellow brick road of sobriety successfully. He still wasn't satisfied.

"Extend your arms, close your eyes, and touch your nose," I felt like I was playing Simon Says. I started to tell him, you forgot to say Simon. I obliged him. I then showed him my license.

"Next time you wanna sleep, how 'bout you do it somewhere besides the middle of the street? Besides, it's the middle of the night, anything could happen. Cops can't be everywhere," was his last remark as he and his partner got back in their squad car and said something about donuts.

I leaned against the door for support, support being an understatement.

Asleep? Could I have dreamt this?

No. It was too vivid, but dreams are often just that, vivid. My thoughts turned to Dickens and the Ghost of Christmas Past.

Had I been...scrooged?

"No, this was something more," I spoke aloud. To myself. But what did it mean? I raised my head and surveyed the desolate streets. I slowly exhaled and got back in the car and pulled off, but it seemed a distant ideal.

As I drove I tried to think about everything I had seen, or at least experienced. Mikey, the picture at Ko-Ko's house, the people on the bus, the baby pacifier, the funeral.

I had to know.

I looked around for a newspaper stand and spotted one a block away. I pulled over to it, in mounting anticipation, and searched my pockets for a quarter. I inserted the quarter and took out the paper. I checked the local news.

Nothing.

I checked the obituaries.

Still nothing.

I thought, maybe the death of just another inner city youth wasn't newsworthy. Frustrated, I put the paper back, mangled, into the stand and closed the door of the machine, my frustration feeding my anticipation and vice versa.

Then it hit me.

His story on the rooftop! He spoke endlessly of friends and places, but he never mentioned any streets or addresses, except one. Jewel's apartment!

Apartment 151!

That's it! That had to be it, because it was all I had to go on. So just like a detective, I went off my gut instinct and climbed back into my car.

I headed for the inner city.

As I neared the inner city, I thought of turning back. This is crazy, I thought, driving into the ghetto in the middle of the night, going to the projects all because of a crazy dream! But it wasn't a dream, I kept telling myself, there's something here I need to know. Why else would he have given me the address? I had to know if he really existed, and if so, how the hell he had contacted me. But he said I called him. Questions raced through my mind as I went to project after project, trying to find the one in my...

Here it is!

I'll be damned, this is it! There, right there, is the abandoned building he called the top spot. I parked my car. I saw signs of life and remembered him saying, "Somebody always in the projects..."

Here it was, almost five in the morning, and there they were. I tried to look like a cop. As I got out, I adjusted an imaginary gun at my waistline.

I walked.

Five buildings. Where was 151?

"How you doin', officer?" a homeless woman asked. *My charade had been successful.*

"Uh, fine. Could you tell me where apartment 151 is?" I asked in my best policeman tone.

"Them the hundred buildings right there," she replied. I nodded my appreciation. As I walked, I heard her say, "Never seen a cop drive no Lexus before. Must be doin' all right," and then she laughed.

I entered the building. 151 was on the fifth floor and the elevator didn't work. I found the stairs. Dark. Lights busted out and the overwhelming stench of urine filled the air. I wished my imaginary gun was real. I ascended the steps, listening, hearing only the pound of my own heartbeat and the scuffle of my shoes against he concrete. I heard a scurry and saw a fuzzy shape scramble across the floor. I hoped it was a cat, because if a rat was that big...

I got to the fifth floor and walked down the hall. Three doors down was 151. I paused.

What would I say? "Sorry to bother you, but I dreamed of this apartment. Does he *live here? No, no name, just* he.*" Maybe I would pretend to be a cop.*

I knocked on the door.

I knocked again... This is crazy.

They're asleep. Maybe I should just turn—

The door opened and I froze. The man in the door was the man in the casket at the funeral!

I fell back a step, mouth agape, as he rubbed the sleep from his eyes.

"Yeah."

I couldn't speak.

"Yeah?" he repeated more firmly. "What you want? You a cop or somethin'?"

Then I saw her. Jewel, standing behind him and I thought, joined at the hip. "I-I...it's you," was all I could get out.

"What you mean, it's you? You got a warrant or somethin'?" he asked, irritated.

226

"Yes-I mean, no-I mean, I'm looking for your friend," I said.

"My friend? What fuckin' friend? Jewel, go get my shoes." Jewel departed but I noticed he was already wearing shoes, so I tried to speak quickly because I could guess what "shoes" was a code word for.

"No, you don't understand. I'm talking about your friend, your best friend. You guys grew up together, fought over a girl named Val, Jewel's sister, just to play Atari, went to the top spot..." I tried everything I knew before Jewel could return with his "shoes."

"Yo, who told you that shit? About Val and the top spot?" he asked as Jewel returned, but she had no shoes. I wondered what she had.

"Your friend. He told me," I said.

"My friend? When? When did he tell you?" he asked as his eyes became cloudy.

"Who, Justice? Who he talkin' 'bout?" Jewel questioned.

"Yo, just chill. Go check on Eternity," he told her. She walked away. "I asked you a question," he demanded, turning his attention back to me.

"I-I don't know," I told him. I didn't. I couldn't say last night because I had spent a whole day with him, and that would make last night today. "I don't know," I repeated more to myself than to him. I guess he noticed my sincerity through the confused perplexity, and he softened up a little.

"Well, he couldn't have told you in the last three days... He died on Friday," he spoke as a single tear fell.

"D-died?"

Died? I couldn't... He—Justice—continued, "Friday. He...he jumped off the building. He—" his tears broke off his words.

"He jumped? No, he said you, but I—" I was totally confused.

"The wake was tonight. Jewel! Bring the wake program." Jewel came to the door, carrying Eternity, the same little girl he had held at the wake. His wake?

227

She handed him a piece of paper, and he handed it to me. I looked at the program, and on the cover was his face and his name. It read:

Kwame Jamal

1972-2000

"Kwame?" It was the first time I had heard his name.

"Yeah, everybody called him Truth," Justice told me.

I didn't know what else to say so I just stared at the program.

"How did you know him? You wanna come in?" His voice turned friendly, and I guessed a friend of Kwame/Truth was a friend of his.

"No-no, it late. I-I shouldn't have bothered you. Can I keep this?" I was referring to the program. He nodded yes.

"Thank you. I'm sorry for your loss," was all I could say.

I turned and walked away...

CHAPTER FOUR

{Mental Note: As I sat watching the sun rise over the projects, my face a distorted rogue of perplexity, I remembered a book I had read entitled Black Like Me. *It was about a white man who had chemically tinted his complexion to appear black in order to experience the Deep South of old. I saw it in a dime store drugstore as a senior in high school. I had wondered why a successful white man with all the privileges America had to offer would voluntarily become the outcast, the downtrodden, the utterly disenfranchised that the blacks were and, in many ways, still are. Then time answered my question, or times to be more exact. My college years, my Woodstock years, my Hendrix years—and the period shaped me and opened up a whole new horizon I wanted to know. But want to know like one wants to know how it feels to get shot or how it feels to be beheaded or any other pain you cringe at watching, but secretly wonder about that feeling. Yet I was not as bold as the author of* Black Like Me *and preferred to stay out of the game and keep scores and statistics.*

Analyze.

Criticize. Criticize the coaches, the teams, the fans, and in the end feel like I know. I chose to become a sociologist and attempted to quantify the visceral, to observe empirically the emotional while remaining detached. I wrote books on the conditions in black America based on demographics, statistics, controlled groups and I had prejudged a life I didn't understand, arbitrarily critiqued, pain I had never felt.

Now here I was, dawn in the ghetto, sitting, watching, listening. Wondering, who was Kwame Jamal? Why did he come to me, if he came to me? But he had to, Justice's eyes confirmed it when I spoke of incidents intimate to their childhood. How else could I have known?

Yes, whatever happened was real. All the names—Grand Daddy, Jewel, Val, Bang...Ko-Ko. My thoughts went to her. What happened to her. Did she really die in a hail of bullets? Did Mikey?

I had to know.

I started my car and glanced up to where the sun seemed to be touching the top spot, and, for a second, the time it takes to blink, I saw a figure on the roof, but just like that...it was gone.

I drove off.

I must've driven over an hour, searching corner store after corner store, park after park, each one looking like the last, never getting my true bearings and ending up wondering if I was going in circles.

In more ways than one.

Then I remember this story had to end where it began, and I quickly u-turned, retracing my steps. My destination became again his neighborhood, not the top spot—no that was for the living...I headed for memories, for memorials in remembrance of the dead. I found the brick wall he had shown me, and then I saw her.

Tears lined her cheeks and filled the gas mask she was wearing to protect herself from the toxic fumes of spray paint. She was finishing the mural, the memorial that said, yes, he did exist. Yes, he came and yes, he was loved.

It was simple.

Not abstract in style and lettering, but form. Solidly blocked. Still, the letters had a cryptic appeal, easy to discern but never truly decipher. It said, "Siempre Amor," and then his and her name, Kwame and Ko-Ko, interlocked one on top of the other. The former then the latter and there was a picture. The picture from the coffee table, of him holding her and she smiling at the camera.

He loved her.

She loves him.

Her man.

And even though he had left of his own free will, almost like walking out on her, she still understood. Or, if not understood, forgave, and it all made—I cringe to use the word—sense.

He had found his niche. To be remembered as he was then and not now. Because by anyone's standards of success, he was a failure. Anyone, that is, who didn't know him, and although I didn't know him, I knew enough to know that he found in death what he held dear in life.

So as I looked at this testimony, I thought it fitting. A simple brick wall, as hard and cold as the streets that spawned his memorial. A memorial to a martyr? To a soldier in this ongoing war, so even though his death was senseless, still it was sublime. He had reached beyond the obscurity, the invisibility to be heard. Heard by a man who could give voice to his pain... But as I thought...

No.

No, that wasn't his way. The way I had come to know him, the free floater, the ghetto philosopher. No, he wasn't that noble minded, that revolutionary.

No.

His was a quiet revolution, one that happens everyday, like the revolution of the earth around the sun, the moon about the earth.

Yes, subtly yet sharply, I remembered his last words to me.

"Now you know," and I smiled. My friend had come for one simple reason, because I called him. And indeed, I did...

...and his name was Truth...

COMING SOON:

METHOD
By Teri Woods

TRIANGLE OF SINS
By Nurit Folks

DUTCH
By Kwame Teague

Teri Woods Publishing
an Entertainment Investment Group
ORDER FORM

TERI WOODS PUBLISHING
P.O. BOX 20069
NEW YORK, NY 10001
(212) 252-8445
www.teriwoods.com

Sam/Glory	$14.95
Shipping/Handling (Via U.S. Priority Mail)	$ 3.50
TOTAL	$18.45

PURCHASER INFORMATION

Name: _____

Reg. #: _____
(Applies if incarcerated)

Address: _____

_____

City: _____ State: ____

Zip Code:

TOTAL NUMBER OF BOOKS:

For orders being shipped directly to prisons, TWP deducts 25% of the sale price of the book. Costs are as follows:

Sam/Glory:	$11.21
Shipping and Handling	$ 3.50
TOTAL :	$14.71